"Time to spar," the teacher called out.

They picked up their gear and moved to an open spot on the mat.

Molly held the padded kick shield in front of her body. "Put up or shut up," she said with a glint in her eye.

The corners of her mouth turned up in a wicked smile. The first few he took easy, since he didn't want to send her flying across the mat.

After a minute, Molly lowered the pad. "Seriously? Don't hold back. Show me what you've got."

No matter how much he wanted to spare Molly's body, his male ego rose to the challenge. His next combination should have landed her on her rear, but she held her ground. With every blow, a smile grew on her pretty face. He couldn't help but stare, so he wasn't paying attention when she swept her foot underneath him and sent him sprawling onto the mat.

"You're daydreaming." Molly cocked her head and stared down.

"You don't fight fair." His lungs were caught in a battle between breathing and laughing.

"Of course not." She reached to take his hand and pulled him back onto his feet. "I grew up with five older brothers. That is the definition of not fair."

After All

by

Laurie Winter

Warriors of the Heart Series, Book 3

After All

Cover Art by *Tina Lynn Stout*

The Wild Rose Press, Inc.
PO Box 708
Adams Basin, NY 14410-0708
Visit us at www.thewildrosepress.com

Publishing History
First Sweetheart Rose Edition, 2018
Print ISBN 978-1-5092-2041-0
Digital ISBN 978-1-5092-2042-7

Warriors of the Heart Series, Book 3
Published in the United States of America

Dedications

To my supreme editor, Leanne Morgena,
whose professionalism and dedication to the craft
of writing have been invaluable.
Yours is the voice I hear inside my head
every time I write!

~*~

And to my mother, storyteller extraordinaire.
Thank you for instilling a love of reading
in your children, your grandchildren, and your students.

Chapter One

As the radio in her squad crackled to life, a shot of adrenaline jolted Molly Hernandez out of her musings. Leaning over, she turned up the volume. Whatever the call, she hoped it would be important enough to get her out of that morning's obligations.

"90220 to 175 Tipilu Road, Red foreign-made sedan, damage to driver's side door," a curt voice from dispatch sounded.

Not her code and not her call. She exhaled a long breath, expelling her disappointment. Another officer would handle the problem. Too bad, because today she wanted to burn out of the parking lot with tires smoking. Instead, she sat in her squad, staring up at a two-story, red brick building. Sure, the place seemed harmless enough. Liberty Ridge Middle School was nothing special. Inside though, down a long corridor on the second story, sat the classroom of Mr. Drew Atwater.

Time to pull up your big girl pants and do your job. She exited her car into the Texas heat, and her blue polyester uniform instantly stuck to her skin. Molly cursed the sun, which wouldn't concede summer was over. With quick steps, she hustled to the middle school's front door.

"Good morning, Officer Hernandez." Mrs. Appleman greeted from the seat behind the front desk.

Mrs. Appleman held the title of receptionist since Molly had been a student. She'd always reminded Molly of an apple—short and round, with a head of bright red hair. "Good morning. I have a presentation today." Molly caught Mrs. Appleman's gaze dart down to the Glock resting in the holster on her hip, along with the taser gun and the rest of her kit. She carried about twenty pounds of equipment on her duty belt. In her opinion, the kids benefited from becoming comfortable around a uniformed cop.

"That's good." Mrs. Appleman angled forward in her chair. "Students these days have no respect for authority. I'm so happy the police department finally assigned a School Resource Officer. About time, if you ask me."

"I'll pass that along to the Police Chief." Molly forced a smile. Today was her fifth presentation in the past two weeks, to a homeroom of middle schoolers— the one she dreaded most. Not that she'd let her feelings get in the way of doing her job.

"You'll be in Mr. Atwater's homeroom today?" Mrs. Appleman asked.

Inwardly, Molly groaned. She didn't miss the dreamy smile on the receptionist's plump face. "Yes. I should be heading up there. Nice to see you again." She took one step, and then another, up the stairs and down the hall. Before she knew it, she stood at the closed door of room 215. A deep voice sounded from the other side, telling students to take their seats. In her ears, the other voices were muffled by the sound of her own pounding heart. With each beat, the deep vibration hammered her rib cage.

Before knocking, she rolled back her shoulders and

straightened her spine. Through the small window, she saw Mr. Atwater smile as he approached the door. How did he manage to make her all rubber kneed with a single upward tilt of the lips? The door swung open, and there he stood, as handsome as she remembered.

"Hi," he said in an upbeat tone. Drew stepped aside to let her into the classroom. "I was just telling the class to get settled. We're excited you're here."

Excited. The polar opposite of her own emotions. "Where would you like me to set up?" Molly scanned the room, full of gangly teens. Then, her gaze came back to rest on their teacher. She pulled together a quick mental profile—Drew Atwater, six feet tall, approximately two hundred pounds, muscular build, black hair buzzed short, the most beautiful brown eyes...never married, half-African-American, half-Caucasian, and one hundred percent hunk.

Drew had never been accused of doing anything that would warrant a police profile. Even so, Molly could give a full and complete description, if needed.

"You can use the podium." He removed his own papers from the wooden stand.

"Thanks." She set down her folder. In front of her were twenty seventh-graders, most acted bored and uninterested, with drooping heads and slouching posture. A few girls had a love-struck, puppy-dog look in their eyes. Could she manage the next thirty minutes while avoiding that same expression?

Drew taught science at the middle school, so his room was full of glass beakers and jars. A plastic skeleton wearing party beads hung tucked in the back corner. Along the side wall were tanks of various sizes. Inside one, a moss-colored turtle swam lazily through clear water. Drew had only taught here for three weeks, but he'd made his classroom a fun place to learn.

Sitting behind tall counters, the students stared back.

She hooked her thumb in her duty belt and focused on her presentation. The familiar gesture removed any lingering anxiety. "My name is Molly Hernandez. Part of my duties as a Liberty Ridge police officer is working with the schools. I'm a liaison, between you students and the department. Today, I'll talk about some of the dangers you may face during your teen years. I also want to build a relationship with you, so if you do ever need the police, you'll feel comfortable asking for help."

Liberty Ridge was a small, close-knit town. Most of the kids who lived here already trusted the police. They were the good guys—the ones that kept them safe. Some, for whatever reason, considered the police their enemy. Part of her training as an SRO was breaking down those barriers.

"You may find yourself in an uncomfortable situation and not know what to do," Molly continued. "Someone offers you drugs or alcohol. Or let's say you witness another person being abused. If you've created an action plan, you're more likely to have a positive outcome." She glanced around the room. Half of the kids seemed spaced out, especially the ones sitting in the back. Frustration simmered inside her, heating her body until she felt sweat trickle down the back of her neck. Connecting with young people wasn't something that came naturally, which had been proven during the last few minutes. She'd take wrestling a grown man to the ground and slapping on handcuffs over speaking to a classroom of kids any day. The touchy-feely stuff made her squirm. Regardless, she'd do a good job in her new role, for however long it lasted. And maybe a few girls would decide that being a police officer wasn't just for boys. "I have several handouts," Molly said. "I need a volunteer to pass them out."

The hand shot up of a little blonde girl, and Molly nodded. During the trip up to the front of the room, the girl's gaze never left Mr. Atwater. *Poor thing. Must be hard having a teacher so good looking.* Did these girls learn anything in class, besides how broad his chest looked underneath that green polo shirt?

While the girl passed out the handouts, several boys started goofing off.

Disruptive behavior will not be allowed. "Let's do a bit of role-playing. You in the blue shirt." She pointed to the ringleader. "Come here and stand by me."

He smiled, showing off a row of gleaming braces, and swaggered to the front of the room.

The kid was probably six inches taller, but the height difference wasn't a problem. "Let's say I've just offered you a bag of weed for free, no strings. What would you do?" Should be an easy question.

"I don't know. Smoke it?" Shrugging, he laughed and combed his fingers through his shaggy brown hair.

A few brave souls joined in.

Good grief, this kid was only thirteen years old. Not exactly the reply she'd expected, but she'd roll with it. "Okay. You smoke a joint at school but get caught."

"I'm a minor. You can't arrest me, plus it's just dope." He rocked back on his heels and avoided looking at both Molly and his teacher.

The kid at least had the decency to act nervous.

"See these handcuffs?" She pulled them out of the case on her belt and lifted them to dangle off her index finger. "I put these on you right here in school. Right in front of your classmates. Then, your parents talk to the police, the school, and a very expensive lawyer. After that, you go in front of a judge and hope he or she is having a good day." Molly rested an elbow on the podium. "Sure, you probably won't end up in jail, but you will get some type of probation and community service. Plus, the school will hand out either a suspension or an expulsion. The disciplinary action will be part of your school file, which becomes attached to your college applications." After glancing around the room and seeing shocked expressions, she jerked her head. "You can go sit again."

The smug smile on the boy's face had disappeared. As he shuffled to his chair, he kept his gaze fixed on his scuffed-up skater shoes.

"My point is this…you may think having a little weed is harmless. Or doing drugs makes you look cool." She leveled her gaze at the students. "But if you get caught, you won't feel very cool. Keep that in mind when you're offered drugs. And yes, I said *when*…not *if.*"

Now, she had their attention. She'd been tough on that kid, maybe too tough. Better now than later, when she was called back into the school for a drug bust. "My purpose wasn't just to scare you or make you uncomfortable." She softened her expression with a smile, in an attempt to appear like an ally, not the enemy. "Your actions have consequences."

She peered at Drew, who sat on the corner of his desk, foot swinging back and forth. He gave her an encouraging smile. She thought back to the first time she'd seen him—the new guy in town. When he'd come over to introduce himself, her heart had stopped for several beats.

Drew Atwater—former soldier, just out of the Army—ready to settle down in Liberty Ridge. Molly, on the other hand, had just completed her application for the Drug Enforcement Administration, which meant she'd move soon. Drew wanted to start a family. Molly's ability to have children had been taken away two years ago. She knew her physical attraction would never lead anywhere.

Summoning her professional willpower, she turned her attention back to the students. She needed to finish her presentation and get away from Drew. He was a persistent reminder of what she couldn't have.

****

What a great start to the day. Drew's normally rowdy homeroom now sat in rapt attention. Molly had a way about her that didn't leave room for antics, even if she was so short she could barely see over the podium. A tight bun pulled back her glossy brunette hair. And the way she looked in that police uniform—wow.

"Mr. Atwater?" Molly's voice sounded. "Earth to Mr. Atwater."

Laughter brought his attention back to where it should be—the students in his classroom. "Sorry." He smiled, hoping no one noticed how distracted he'd been by Molly. "What did you say?"

"I asked if you had anything to add. I'm done with my presentation and answered the students' questions." Molly arched a dark eyebrow.

"I have nothing to add except to thank Officer

Hernandez for coming today." Smiling, he stood from his perch on the corner of his desk.

With that, the bell rang, and the classroom filled with noise. Kids gathered their books and papers while making their way to the door. A few approached Molly and thanked her.

Once all the students left the classroom, he came to stand by Molly. The top of her head was at the same level as his chest. "You did a really great job."

Molly's gaze stayed glued to the papers she gathered. "You have a nice group. I hope they all stay on the right path."

Sam Sheehan came to mind. Drew knew the kid had a tough home life. Always sitting in the back, Sam rarely spoke during homeroom. His school records said he'd been suspended twice and almost expelled. If Molly managed to make a connection with Sam, that would be a win.

Molly grabbed her folder off the podium and lifted her head to meet his gaze.

The air in his lungs warmed and expanded, like his chest was a hot air balloon. Even though she was a foot shorter, her large eyes closed that distance. Behind their polished surface lay a stone wall, which guarded any display of emotion. She lowered her eyelids very slightly.

Molly turned to leave.

His brain refused to communicate with his mouth. Thankfully, his body jumped into action, and he followed her to the classroom doorway. "Will I see you at Heath and Grace's tonight?"

Clutching the folder against her body like a paper shield, she straightened her shoulders. "No. I can't."

Her lips parted in the smallest of smiles. "My parents want to take me out for dinner. They complain about how I'm always too busy, and they never see me. I live five miles away, and I see them all the time. My *mamá* has a special talent for guilt trips."

He laughed. "Well, have fun with your parents. Too bad you can't make it. But I'm sure we'll see a lot of each other, in school and around town." That's exactly what he counted on.

"Sure...maybe. See you around." She strode down the crowded hall, weaving around kids like an expert barrel rider.

He watched her disappear around the corner, and the hallway dimmed without her presence. Stepping back into his classroom, he barely noticed the kids for his next class coming in and taking their seats. His head was too full of Molly.

He'd met her last month and had been instantly attracted. When he'd asked her out the first time, she'd turned him down cold. He'd just wanted to take her out for dinner, nothing serious. For his next attempt, he'd tried the double date approach with their mutual friends, Heath and Grace Carter. Another rejection. Molly had no interest in dating him. Why? He had no flippin' idea.

As far as he knew, she wasn't seeing anyone. When they'd spent time together, she seemed to have fun. They both enjoyed working out and watching sports. He'd even discovered she was a soccer fan, like him. But Molly only wanted to stay casual friends. Drew didn't need any more friends. What he needed was a wife.

Shouts from the back of the room refocused his

attention to his class. A room full of students stared back with wide, blinking eyes. He took a seat on the stool behind his podium and began a lesson about the life cycle of amphibians.

The rest of Drew's day flew by. The final bell rang, and he went to change clothes for soccer practice. An hour of running around the soccer field left him hot and hungry. He stopped at home for a quick shower before heading over to Heath's house. Heath and his new wife were hosting a small party. A not-so-subtle way of introducing him to some of the women in town. Drew was okay with that. Whatever was needed to get the job done.

Since leaving the Army, he'd wanted nothing more than to finally start the second half of his life. He was ready to put down roots in his new hometown of Liberty Ridge, Texas, find that perfect girl, and start a family. Marriage and children had been put on hold while he'd served. Never wanting to bring a family into his crazy, unpredictable military life. He'd seen too many soldiers leave behind a widow and fatherless children.

Now, that life was all behind him. He was ready to change his single status. If only Molly Hernandez would show interest, he might not need a whole year like he'd originally planned.

Drew pulled onto the driveway of True Horizon Ranch. Coming to Heath's house always produced a twinge of envy. Heath was a happy newlywed and totally crazy about his wife, Grace. Together, they ran a Texas Longhorn cattle ranch—a perfect life.

As he approached the deck at the back of the house, he heard music and the mixture of happy voices.

Heath stepped over to greet him. "Hey, man." He reached out and shook Drew's hand. "Happy Friday."

"You're telling me. Dealing with kids all week has left me with a strong desire for a beer."

"Well, I can help with that. Come step into my office." Heath led Drew up onto the deck and over to a red cooler. He lifted the squeaky lid and pulled out a beer bottle dripping with melted ice.

"Thanks," Drew said. "I've survived my first three weeks as a teacher. Cheers to that."

Heath lifted his bottle, clinking it against Drew's. "Cheers, man. You happy with your decision to move down here and teach?"

After taking a long drink of cold beer, he sighed. "So far. Liberty Ridge is a nice town. The people are friendly."

"How about the ladies? Anyone at the top of your list?" Heath wiggled his bushy brows.

Drew grinned and took another drink. His friend knew about Drew's compulsion to over-plan and create lists. "The town definitely has its share of eligible women. It will take time, you know, to find 'the one.' " Molly's pretty face immediately flashed in his mind.

"Grace invited a few of her friends." He pointed at a couple of blondes sitting to their left. "Let me give you some advice. Take your time and don't do anything dumb. You can't rush these things. Love can't be micromanaged."

Rushing, that's exactly how he felt. A heart-thumping, chest-squeezing race to disarm the bomb before the clock runs down. He'd waited ten years and wouldn't wait any longer. Sure, he'd had a few dates during his time in the service, but no one who'd he'd been serious about. Now, he would date as much as possible. He'd given himself a year to find a wife, and then start a family. Drew glanced at Grace's friends and felt not even a small hit of attraction. No surprise, since none were as pretty as Molly.

They caught his gaze, and both sent an inviting smile.

Heath cleared his throat. "I heard Molly was in your classroom today."

Drew played it cool, like he hadn't just been fantasizing about her. "She's good with the kids. The department picked the right person for the SRO."

"Too bad she won't go out with you." Heath's bushy beard didn't hide his smirk, and he shook his head. "But don't worry, she didn't like me very much either, at first. My falling in love with her best friend didn't exactly help. A few threats of bodily injury may have been involved, but I digress. I was in the Army for a long time, and few people frighten me as much as Molly. You better be careful if you plan on asking her out again."

The image of little Molly intimidating Heath, a man inked with military tattoos, made him laugh. "I'll keep that in mind."

Grace approached, wearing a warm smile. "Hi, Drew. Have you met Lauren and Christina, yet?" She pointed to her friends. "I've told them all about you. Only the good stuff, of course. They can't wait to meet you."

With one last swig, Drew drained the last of his beer. Maybe Molly would change her plans and show up. A guy could always hope. He'd go over and talk with the two pretty ladies, who'd want to hear all about his time in the Army, but only the sexy, exciting parts. He'd gone through this dance dozens of times before and knew enough to leave out the stories of death, blood, and destruction.

Once he spent some time with them, he might feel a spark of chemistry. Somehow, he doubted he'd feel anything remotely like attraction. For some reason, he was fixated on the one woman in Liberty Ridge who wanted nothing to do with him.

Chapter Two

Early morning was always Molly's favorite time of day. She loved the sounds of birds, who like her, took the sunrise as a cue to start their day. Otherwise, the world was silent. She sat on her small, backyard patio and savored each sip of coffee. The temperature was a perfect sixty degrees. A light breeze tickled her arm, making her skin as bumpy as a freshly plucked goose.

A pair of mourning doves, she liked to think of them as *her* doves, wobbled around her yard in search of food. They foraged the grass for the sunflower seeds Molly tossed down earlier. This past spring, she discovered their nest up in a mesquite tree. Now, at the end of September, their breeding season was almost over. The pair might have one more brood of eggs to lay and care for before taking off for the winter. Maybe they would find each other next spring and start the cycle again.

The cooing sound of the doves helped Molly clear her mind. The birds had a simple life—food, shelter, a loyal mate, and young to care for. But she wanted more than to just exist. She had big dreams.

Last Friday, she'd gotten the call to come down to Houston for her final acceptance interview with the Drug Enforcement Administration. Surprisingly, the idea of being questioned by a panel of Special Agents and government officials didn't scare her. She actually anticipated the challenge. Every step put her closer to her goal of becoming a DEA Special Agent.

Molly watched the doves for a few minutes longer then noticed her empty coffee cup. Time to get moving. Sundays weren't meant for being lazy. She stood and stretched her legs, causing the doves to fly to a tree at the back of her yard. Kickboxing class didn't start for another two hours. Plenty of time to squeeze in a quick run.

Unfortunately, her six-mile run didn't take the edge off her frustration. Mainly, because she'd spent the whole time unintentionally fantasizing about Drew. She imagined what would happen if she agreed to go out with him. Over time, would that spark of attraction cool off or heat up? If she kept obsessing, she'd drive herself crazy. She needed to forget all about Drew. Totally wipe him from her brain. No more imagining his eyes, or his smile, or how good he must look with his shirt off.

A month ago, Heath had introduced her to Drew. Leave it to Heath to mess with her head. At the time, she really liked Drew and hoped he would ask her out. But that was before she overheard him tell someone else he was on a one-man mission to find a wife and start a family. Molly knew right then and there that she needed to get over her attraction to Drew. Not only did her goals not align with his, they were so far apart they could be from different planets. Mars and Venus—no, more like Mercury and Pluto.

Grabbing her duffle bag, she headed off to kickboxing class. Her gym was located in an old warehouse building. The gym's owners had taken the town eyesore and turned it into a top-notch fitness center. She loved kickboxing with a passion. What better way to burn off steam than punch and kick things for hours?

Her regular partner, Greg, stood off to the side.

"You ready?" She tossed her duffle bag on the ground.

"You bet." He hopped around, throwing punches in the air. "*Ohhh.*" He howled and grabbed his lower back. Greg dropped down to his knees.

"What did you do?" she asked. Greg, in his mid-forties, exuded the energy of a man half his age. But he was getting up there, and obviously not as limber as he used to be.

"I think I pulled something. Let me lie down for a minute. Maybe my back will stop spasming." He hunched over like an old man and shuffled toward the corner of the room.

Class didn't begin for another ten minutes, so Molly started her stretching routine.

People entered the building in small waves.

Two women came in wearing clothes so tight, it was a miracle they could breathe. She didn't remember seeing them at the gym before. The women looked like store mannequins dressed in fashionable workout gear. Strike a pose, pretend you're stretching, see if anyone notices how great your butt looks in those spandex pants. Molly smiled at the thought of them keeping up with the high-intensity kickboxing class. Give them ten minutes, and they'd be limping out the front door.

Killing time, she taped her hand then slid on her gloves. She headed over to the punching bag to warm up. As she drove her fists into its hard surface, the bag swung back and forth. A slow burn flowed through her muscles. After one last kick and punch combo, she grabbed the bag to steady it.

"What did that thing ever do to you?"

From behind her, she heard a familiar voice. Molly punched the bag one more time before calmly turning to face Drew. He stood before her with a sexy smile. How would she forget about him when he kept popping up everywhere? Even the gym wasn't safe. At this rate, she'd never break herself of her Drew Atwater habit.

****

When Drew walked into the gym, his gaze went directly to Molly. She mercilessly kicked the stuffing out of a poor punching bag. The girl could throw a punch. Heath was smart to be scared.

He went over to stand behind her and took a minute to admire what he saw. Molly was probably one hundred pounds sopping wet, but her small frame was a combination of strength and perfect curves. His gaze meandered down her legs. The tan skin of her calves moved smoothly over the arch of muscle. Then he finally got up the nerve to talk to her.

She swung around to face him.

The fiery expression in her eyes forced him to retreat a step.

"What?" Her gloved hands rested on her hips.

"Um…I just said I felt sorry for that bag. You hit hard for a pixie."

Molly's expression softened only a fraction. "Pixie, huh? You spend an hour with me in here, and then tell me who's the pixie."

Flutters erupted in his gut, either from nerves or more likely, a punch of attraction. Probably a bit of both. "This is my first class, so go easy."

"Don't tell me." She pointed to the teacher. "Tell him. And your partner." Slipping off her gloves, she squirted water into her mouth.

"I hoped you'd be my partner." More like prayed. She smelled so good—a blend of sweat and flowers. A weird but intoxicating combination. He pointed to the tall, blonde woman in tight workout clothes. "You'd do me a huge favor. I went out with her last weekend, and I think she's here because of me. I'm afraid she wants to partner up."

Molly peered over her shoulder. "You sure think highly of yourself."

"Really, I don't. Please." He was ready to beg. "I'd owe you one."

"Let me check on Greg." Molly walked over to a middle-aged man lying down on the floor at the edge of the mat. After talking with him for several seconds, she strolled back over with a frown. "Okay. We can be partners, but just for today. And I'm not going easy on you."

"Great. I'll try to keep up." *Yes!* His plan had worked.

She didn't look happy, but she had agreed to be his sparring partner. When he'd signed up for this class, he knew Molly was a regular. Back then, he'd hoped the time together would help him get to know her better. Now, he just wanted to survive.

The kickboxing class started out innocently enough. A few burpees and sit-ups, and then each participant took turns on the bag. One would hold while the other performed kick-punch combos. After thirty minutes, Drew was winded and dripping with sweat. Molly, on the other hand, looked like she was getting warmed up.

"Time to spar," the teacher called out.

They picked up their gear and moved to an open spot on the mat.

Molly held the padded kick shield in front of her body. "Put up or shut up," she said with a glint in her eyes.

The corners of her mouth turned up in a wicked smile. The first few he took easy, since he didn't want to send her flying across the mat.

After a minute, Molly lowered the pad. "Seriously? Don't hold back. Show me what you've got."

No matter how much he wanted to spare Molly's body, his male ego rose to the challenge. His next combination should have landed her on her rear, but she held her ground. With every blow, a smile grew on her pretty face. He couldn't help but stare, so he wasn't paying attention when she swept her foot underneath him and sent him sprawling onto the mat.

"You're daydreaming." Molly cocked her head and stared down.

"You don't fight fair." His lungs were caught in a battle between breathing and laughing.

"Of course not." She reached to take his hand and pulled him back onto his feet. "I grew up with five older brothers. That is the definition of not fair."

"Wow. Five brothers."

"Yeah, wow. It's a miracle I survived."

"I think you could have survived ten brothers," he said. "No wonder you decided to go into law enforcement, and why you don't take crap from anyone."

Molly tossed him the kick shield and slipped on her

gloves. "Some people thought my brothers spoiled me." Her foot connected with the pad. "Just the opposite. They pushed me to keep up. I hated being left behind."

A pink boxing glove pounded the pad in his hands. Drew planted his feet and tried to hold firm. "You ever spar for real?"

"I have, but it's been awhile. You don't have as much fun when you're punched in the face at full force. I teach a women's self-defense class at the community center." She executed another kick-punch combo.

The action forced him to slide slightly. He hoped she didn't notice. Of course she did, and a spark of amusement lit her brown eyes. "My my, Molly." Heat spread across his face and down his body. "Aren't you full of surprises?"

****

Class was over too soon. Molly cleaned up the equipment and headed toward her duffle bag, with Drew at her side. When Drew pulled off his soaked shirt, revealing a chiseled chest and abs, her already pounding heart shifted into overdrive. She tried not to drool as he wiped down his bare chest with a towel.

"Why don't you have any tattoos?" she asked after taking stock of his body. "Every guy I know who's been in the military has tattoos. Take Heath, for example."

He cocked an eyebrow and smirked. "Heath went a little crazy with the ink. How do you know I don't have any tattoos? They could be hidden."

Her face flushed warm. "So, where are they?" Now, she imagined all the secret places his skin could be marked.

He ran his hands up his chest and winked. "No. I

don't have any. To mar this skin would be a sin."

He did have beautiful skin—light golden brown and seemingly as smooth as fine whiskey. Why mess with perfection? Bet his skin would feel wonderful under her palm. *Stop wondering because you'll never know.* Then she noticed two scars. The first, on his shoulder, was the size of a quarter. The other was a long line running down his side. "What's the story behind your scars?"

His smile faded as he pointed to the one on his shoulder. "This is courtesy of the Taliban via a 39mm bullet. Lucky for me, their aim was off that day. The long one I got during a Special Forces training exercise." He took a clean shirt out of his bag and slipped it on.

"I'm glad you made it back safe." She picked up her bag and headed for the door. The thought of Drew being shot at, nearly dying in a foreign country, left her rattled.

Drew fell in step next to her. "What's your agenda for the rest of the day? You want to go grab something to eat? I don't know about you, but I'm famished." Drops of sweat fell off his face, dotting his clean shirt.

Her mind struggled with a reason to turn him down. "I don't usually have a daily agenda...and I don't have time right now."

He placed his body in front of her.

Molly stopped in her tracks.

"I know I'm being pushy. I'm new in Liberty Ridge, and I could use a friend who's not named Heath. The man's like a brother, but I've spent years living with the dude and I'm kinda getting sick of his scruffy face."

That is funny. Molly didn't know if she could be friends with Drew. Whenever she was with him, all she wanted to do was kiss him. If her life had turned out differently, she could give into that craving. "Sorry. I forget sometimes that you didn't grow up here and don't already know everybody and their mother. I honestly have to meet Grace at the police station at noon, which means I need to get home and shower."

"Can I at least walk you home?"

He sure was persistent. Inside her chest, her heart did a little dance. "Sure." She relented. "I live five blocks away across the Hickory River Bridge."

"Perfect." He grinned. "My house is down that way, too. I bought the old Miller house on Elm Road."

That house was huge. A two-story colonial with a large yard and enough bedrooms to house a baseball team. "I went to school with April Miller," she said. "That's a big house for a single guy."

"At first, I had some doubts about buying a house that big. Hopefully someday, I can fill all that space." Drew glanced over at her.

Her stomach dropped. Keeping her face impassive, she blocked out the image of him happily married and surrounded by children. "Good luck with that." When she stepped onto the old, wooden bridge that crossed the Hickory River, she went over to the side rail and gazed at the water below. She and Grace used to come here all the time as girls. They would sit with their legs dangling off the side and talk for hours—about whom they would marry, and how many kids they'd have. Grace knew all her secrets. She was the one who held her hand in the hospital when all her girlhood hopes and dreams disappeared after a radical hysterectomy.

Her body had betrayed her but hadn't beaten her. A fire had been lit that day in the hospital. She'd decided to take the second chance she'd been given and pursue a new dream. Before, a career as a Federal Drug Enforcement Special Agent had seemed like a wish made on a shooting star. Now, she was closer than ever to achieving that goal. Leaving for Quantico and Special Agent training might be only months away.

Chapter Three

While watching a range of emotions flicker across Molly's face, Drew wondered what he'd said to upset her. After all the time he'd spent figuring out what made her tick, he should earn a degree in Molly Hernandez. She still wore her workout clothes, and Drew's chest constricted at the sight of her. His mind searched for something to talk about, other than how much he wanted to touch the bare skin of her arm and steal a kiss. "Did you know I'm from Detroit?" Best lead their conversation to safe territory.

She shook her head. "You never told me where you grew up."

"My dad's a cop, and my mom works in finance at a bank." Drew had spent most of his adult life living away from home—first in the Army, and now here in Texas. The decision to move to central Texas hadn't been easy. He did miss his family, especially his sister, whom he worried about every day.

Molly leaned against one of the bridge's wooden beams. "Your dad's a Detroit cop. That's a tough gig."

"My folks still live in Detroit. They raised my sister and me there, because they wanted us to be a positive influence for the city and help bring about change. A good idea in theory. A lot of families had moved out over the years because of the crime. People don't feel safe when you could get robbed on your way to the grocery store."

"How did your parents feel about living in the city with two kids?"

Drew watched the churning, brown water of the river. Over at the park by the river bank, children played on colorful playground equipment. He tightened his grip on the wood railing. "They refused to be chased out by thugs. My sister and I went to Detroit public schools. We had a tough time."

Molly turned her body to face him and met his gaze.

She appeared interested in what he was saying. *Finally, I'm doing something right. Keep going.* "My dad is a huge guy. When he's in uniform, he looks very intimidating. But my mom, she's a tiny thing, like you. Growing up, if I ever misbehaved, Mom was the one who scared me more."

"I'm glad to hear that." She straightened her posture and smirked. "I find my gender and size can work as an advantage on the job. When I'm playing the 'good cop,' my height makes me unintimidating. People trust me. Then when I'm dealing with someone who's being uncooperative, they underestimate me. Big mistake."

"Ha, you can say that again. After that kickboxing class, I'd say you are surprisingly strong for a pixie."

"There you go again...calling me a pixie." She folded her arms across her chest and frowned. "Why?"

Couldn't she tell he used pixie as a term of endearment? "I don't know." He shrugged. "Don't be offended. You're the toughest pixie I know."

"How many do you know?"

She actually gave him a full-blown smile, knocking

the breath out of his chest.

"Come on." She gestured toward the other end of the bridge. "I need to get home."

He walked by her side until they reached Molly's townhouse. "Why did you become a police officer?" They'd be at her front door in a matter of minutes, and he had a million more questions. With every step, he was running out of time.

"I like helping people. After I earned my Criminal Justice degree and went to the Police Academy, Liberty Ridge P.D. hired me. I figured my hometown police department was a good place to start."

Start? Why wouldn't she want to finish her career here, too? "Aren't you happy here?"

"A town of this small size doesn't have a lot of opportunities for advancement. I applied to the Drug Enforcement Administration last spring. I'm finishing all the requirements to get into the Training Academy. Being a DEA Special Agent is very dangerous, so I'm committed to staying single and unattached." She stared straight ahead. "That's why I won't go out with you. Right now, I can't afford to date."

Molly's refusal to date stuck a pin in Drew's balloon. "My dad rose up the ranks in the police department, even with a family. Law enforcement can be dangerous, but he didn't let that stop him from building a life with my mom."

"Your dad made the choice that was right for him, but I don't want that responsibility," Molly said.

Her tone sounded bitter. Is that what she thought of a husband and children—an unwanted responsibility? Molly was a young, vibrant woman who could grab the world by the collar and take anything she wanted. If she wanted a career and a family, she could have it. He'd seen that very thing with women in the military. Many females in the Army were soldiers, wives, and mothers. Juggling all the demands of the job with a family was a challenge for sure, but it could be done.

Molly crossed her arms over her body and raised her chin.

Great. Just when he thought he made some progress. "I have no doubt you'll succeed at anything you set your mind to." What else could he say?

She ascended the stairs to her townhouse. "Will I see you again in class?"

"Only if you're my partner." He suppressed the flirty grin that instinctively pulled at his lips. "I promise, next time I'll bring my game."

"You'd better. I hate thinking you held back because I'm a woman."

"Never." He raised his hands, palms out. "I've gotten out of shape over the last year. I hope you can help me rectify that."

Her gaze lingered on his body. "You don't look out of shape."

A jolt of pleasure shot through him. So, he hadn't imagined her attraction. The feeling was mutual. While he walked to his car, which was parked back at the gym, an idea poked at his brain. A way to help the kids of Liberty Ridge. And with any luck, a way for him to spend more time with Molly.

****

Thursday afternoon, Molly sat behind her desk at the police station. Paperwork—always piles of paperwork. Every little thing she did as a School Resource Officer needed documentation, since the position was new to the department. The Police Chief wanted reports on what she was teaching, what classrooms she'd talked to, and calls from the schools to deal with troublesome students. He wanted measureable results.

She'd signed off on a report when the Police Chief called her name from his office. Molly pushed back her chair to stand. Wonder what he wanted?

For the most part, Chief Jones was good at his job. He knew how to get things done and had a natural propensity for politics. But she rarely saw him away from his desk, which made her wonder if the stocky man and the piece of furniture had slowly become one.

"Molly, honey. Take a seat," Chief Jones said when she entered the office.

She hated how he used terms like sweetie and honey in conjunction with her first name when addressing her. Like she was a little girl, not a professional officer of the law. "What can I do for you, sir?" Hopefully, no more reports. Her poor fingers couldn't take anymore.

"I just got off the phone with Judge Hurley. He oversees the juvenile court."

"I'm familiar with Judge Hurley. I talked to him before I started as the SRO."

Chief Jones rubbed his hands together. "That's good to hear. The judge had nice things to say about you." The Chief picked up several thick folders off his desk. "He's starting an outreach program for some of the underage offenders he's seen recently come through his court."

Molly took the folder the Chief held out. A name marked each folder. This wasn't good. "Did he ask for the SRO's help?"

"Not exactly. The leaders of this new program will be volunteers, one lay person and one police officer. The purpose is to lead these kids in the right direction and be a positive influence in their lives, so hopefully they'll stay out of the legal system."

"Randy Grange would be perfect." Molly didn't want the chief to consider her as said police volunteer. "He has two teenage sons."

"You'd be perfect, Molly. Take those folders and look them over. Start coming up with activities to do with the teens—service projects and outdoor adventure stuff."

"I'm really not the best suited for this." A combination of irritation and panic left her feeling ill. Did the Chief not understand the meaning of the word *volunteer*?

Chief Jones waved off her concern like a pesky fly. "Nonsense. You work in our schools."

She stared at the folders on her lap. Molly already had enough to do between her regular patrol duties and her role as SRO. Did the Chief really have that much faith in her abilities, or did he just see someone who didn't have a life outside of her job?

"Don't worry." The Chief raised his wiry eyebrows. "You won't be doing this alone. The person who suggested this program will help you run it. He's a teacher at the middle school."

Perfect. And she thought this situation couldn't get any worse. Pressure built behind her eyes, and she rubbed at her temples to soothe her growing headache. "Let me guess...Drew Atwater." Unbelievably, Chief Jones winked.

"Good guess. Now spend some time reading about the kids in the program. A few of them you may already be familiar with. They all have some community service hours to work off. Their participation with the program will go toward fulfilling their obligation."

Standing, she made an effort not to sprint out of the office. "Will do, Chief," she said before returning to her desk. She thumbed through the folders. The Chief was right. Some of these kids she knew. Some of them she'd arrested.

This was all Drew's doing, leaving her with a strong urge to either kick him or hug him, or both. His heart was in the right place, because he was the type of guy who wanted to make a difference. And she had to give him the benefit of the doubt. He had no idea she'd be tapped as the police volunteer.

Or had he?

The last time she'd seen him, when he'd walked her home after kickboxing class, she'd made it crystal clear she was a career-minded woman. Drew had sniffed around the wrong shrub if he thought she'd be the future Mrs. Atwater. She'd been blunt. Some would say rude. But he had to stop asking her out.

Now, she'd see him while they worked together on this new program. Could she avoid falling any harder? The ties holding her to Liberty Ridge were growing tighter. With each tug, the urge to leave increased.

For the rest of the afternoon, she worked at her desk until she noticed the time. The day shift was long gone. She should head home, get some dinner, and curl up on the sofa to watch TV. The thought of her empty house made her reluctant to leave. Her life pin-balled between work, the gym, and her quiet townhouse.

After logging off her computer, she placed the juveniles' folders in a locked drawer, and then went to the locker room to change out of her uniform. Now back in her street clothes, she made her way out of the station. "Bye, Mike," she said to one of the night-shift officers.

Molly walked almost everywhere in town, and most days she walked to the station and back. The night air felt refreshing after being cooped up indoors. With each step, the tension in her neck and shoulders loosened.

As she walked down Main Street, she passed the Desert Rose Restaurant and peeked inside through the front window. The sight of Drew sitting across the table from an attractive woman punched her gut. There he was, looking so good it should be criminal, wining and dining his lucky date.

Her appetite instantly soured. She was jealous and not too proud to admit it. If the woman was in the process of winning Drew's heart, well—Molly didn't want to go there. Every single woman within a thirty-mile radius knew about Drew and his plan to find a wife. He was handsome, former military, and an all-around good guy. What was there for a girl not to like?

Drew would have no trouble finding someone ready, willing, and able to take that walk down the aisle. Unfortunately, the woman wouldn't be her.

Molly's legs shook. She put down her head and continued past the restaurant heading home. The scene of Drew and his date kept replaying in her mind, like the end of a movie reel.

He'd asked Molly out, more than once. She'd been the one who'd turned him down. She was the one who'd pushed him away. Sadly, that fact didn't dull the pain in her heart.

$$****$$

Drew's evening was not going well. He couldn't blame Allison, his date, or the atmosphere in the restaurant. The food tasted good, and Allison was pleasant company. He knew exactly why he approached this date with half a heart.

Heath had set up Drew with Allison, which at the time seemed like a good idea. Drew found her cute and funny. They both loved comedy movies and country music. Over dinner, Allison tried hard to keep his attention. But if she'd jumped up on the table and started Irish dancing, she still wouldn't hold Drew's interest. He couldn't stop focusing on her flaws—her laugh was too high pitched, she slurped when she drank her wine, and the nervous twirling of her hair.

Just before he met Allison at the restaurant, he got a call from Judge Hurley, telling him Molly would be the police volunteer for the juvenile program. He and Molly would make a great team. The news had sent his pulse racing.

"And so I said, excuse me…but that's not my dog." Allison laughed.

"What?" Drew hadn't realized she was talking. "U-uh," he stuttered. "You have a dog?" He was totally lost.

Allison scrunched her face and studied him. "Are you okay? You seem distracted."

"I'm sorry." His shoulders sagged. "I've had a long day. I'm working on a new project and that's been on my brain."

"Why don't we call it a night?" Her smile faltered.

She reached over and laid her hand on his arm. "We could try dinner again some other night."

He waited for a spark from her touch. Nothing. Dead as a blown fuse. Now if the hand had been Molly's on his arm, he would have gotten a 10,000 volt like touching a hot wire, smoking hot jolt. "Sure. I'd like that." He hated lying, but he'd never been good at letting down people.

Drew paid the check. With a polite kiss on the cheek, he escorted Allison to her car and watched her drive away. Another night of going home alone.

Chapter Four

Highway 95 was a straight, flat piece of asphalt that lay on the west side of Liberty Ridge. For years, the city's police ran regular patrols to catch speeders, who loved flying down the highway. Molly cringed every time she was assigned to patrol Highway 95, and today was no different. With the radar gun ready, she sat in her squad, tucked off on the shoulder.

Twenty minutes in, and she was already incredibly bored. Hardly more than a dozen cars had driven past. Her mind wandered to places she'd rather forget. Tomorrow would be the two-year anniversary of her diagnosis. She remembered the chemical smell of the doctor's office and the dread that ripped her apart while waiting. Even before he entered to read her test results, she knew something was not right.

"Ms. Hernandez," Dr. Yu said. "After analyzing the cultures collected from your biopsy, we discovered abnormal cells." He coughed and looked down at the lab report on his desk. "You have cervical cancer."

For Molly, the office spun. The word *cancer* reverberated through her body. Her lungs gasped for breath. How could she, at twenty-six years old, have cancer?

"I'm sorry, Molly, but the tests are conclusive. I will refer you to a specialist, Dr. Ellen McKinney, who'll oversee your treatment. She is the best in the region for treating this type of cancer. You'll be in excellent hands." Dr. Yu gave a stiff smile.

She shook his hand, hardly registering his cold touch on her already numb body. Walking out of the office and across the parking lot in a daze, she barely noticed the heat radiating from the blacktop. Somehow, she found her car. Once inside, she let one tear escape, and then another and another. After pulling herself back together, she drove to her parents' house and spent the day cuddled on the sofa, wrapped in *Mamá's* embrace.

Lost in the memory, Molly placed her hand on her abdomen. The scar lay hidden underneath the bulk of her uniform, but she knew it was there.

A car drove past, and she looked at her radar gun. Only two miles over the speed limit. Good. She didn't feel like handing out tickets today.

Trying to keep her mind busy, she grabbed the files of the juvenile offenders who joined the new program. She opened the first one—Mark Williams, age sixteen, property damage. Next was Laura Burke, age fifteen, caught with prescription drugs on school property. Sam Sheehan, age thirteen, possession of stolen property. These kids were so young and already in the system. Sorrow pressed against her heart.

The next file Molly studied was even more depressing. Whitney Milan, age seventeen, caught shoplifting four times in the past year and six months pregnant.

Molly read through every folder and recognized the trend of minimum parental involvement. Many of these kids had either a father or mother, or sometimes both, who had their own troubles with the law. Of all the case files, Whitney's was the most alarming. With a baby coming, she had a limited time to straighten out her life.

Drew's program was a good idea. These kids needed help. Just tossing them into juvie wasn't the best way to deal with their problems. But Molly knew she wasn't the best person for the job. If everything went as planned, she'd soon leave Liberty Ridge.

The radar gun's alarm jarred her, and her attention focused on a motorcycle rocketing down the road like a bat out of hell. "Heath," she hissed. After taking a few deep breaths to force her pulse back down to a normal rate, Molly activated the siren and flashing lights.

About one hundred feet down the road, Heath pulled off onto the shoulder.

Molly parked right behind him, ran his motorcycle plate in her computer, and then marched over to the motorcycle.

"Good day, Officer." Heath saluted and grinned. "You look especially lovely today."

"Save it." Her lips pinched into a tight line. She wouldn't fall for his charming act. "Do you know how fast you were going?"

His smile grew larger. "No, but I'm sure you'll tell me."

Typical Heath. When she'd first met him, she hadn't been a big fan of Heath Carter. He got into a bar fight and ended up in her jail, which only made him less desirable, in her opinion. Then, he started becoming close with Grace, and Molly hated the idea of her best friend being dragged down by a scruffy drifter. Back then, Heath had been slightly feral—tattoos, long hair, and a beard so thick it could've nested a family of sparrows.

He also suffered from severe PTSD. Grace saw

something in him no one else had. She helped change his life for the better. But even after marriage, Heath had retained a bit of a wild side.

"You were going seventy-five in a fifty-five miles per hour zone." Molly set her hands on her hips.

"At least I'm wearing a helmet." Heath tapped the hard piece of plastic on his head. "Gotta protect my valuable brain."

A helmet was definitely an improvement, although, she questioned the value of his brain. "I'll give you a gold star for the helmet, but you were still speeding."

Heath laughed. Behind the rough-and-tough exterior, Heath was good natured and fun to be around, though Molly would never admit that out loud.

"Come on. I was just having some fun. Please don't write me a ticket. Grace will string me up by my toenails."

Did he really think his pleading would work? "I would like to see that." Her face stayed expressionless, not giving away the pleasure she received from watching him squirm.

"I'll slow down. I promise." His hand criss-crossed over his heart.

"Okay, I'll let you off with a warning." She narrowed her gaze. "But if I catch you again—"

"I know...show me no mercy." He hit the ignition.

The rumble of his Harley filled the air, permeating into Molly's chest. Heading back to her squad, she heard him call out her name.

"I heard you and Drew will spend a lot of time together. He sounded excited about the prospect. What's the deal, Molly...why won't you go out with the poor guy?"

She didn't miss a step. "None of your business. Now go before I change my mind about giving you a ticket."

His laughter sounded over the motorcycle engine, and he drove away.

Good grief. That man seriously riled her nerves. Only after she got back into her car did she finally allow herself to laugh, too.

****

Everything was finally coming together. The funding for the Second Step program had received approval. Judge Hurley, the Police Department, and most importantly, Molly, were committed.

Drew looked at the clock. The group of teens should be here any minute. Their first meeting was scheduled to start at three o'clock on the dot. Molly should be here already, but she'd wanted to stop at the grocery store for snacks.

He paced back and forth in the small meeting room at St. Matthew's Church. Looking out the large picture window, he waited for Molly's car to pull into the parking lot. Where was she? Had she decided not to come?

After meeting with Judge Hurley and signing the confidentiality agreement, he was anxious to make the program a success. The kids reminded him a lot of some of the ones he'd grown up with in Detroit. A few bad choices could ruin a young life. Back then, he couldn't do anything to help. Now, as an adult, he could. While he waited, Drew texted his sister.

—*How have you been feeling lately?*—

—*Better. My headaches have gone away. Thanks for checking on me, little bro*—

—Call if you start feeling weak and tired again. Don't hide that from me, or Mom and Dad.—

—Like I could hide anything from Mom. lol—

Smiling, Drew slipped his phone into the back pocket of his pants. He needed to plan for his family to come for a visit. Soon.

Molly burst through the open door with her arms full of grocery bags. "Sorry, I'm late."

He walked toward her to grab a bag.

She elbowed him out of the way.

In shorts and a purple v-neck shirt, she looked very pretty. Her dark, brunette hair was pulled up in a ponytail, showing off the soft curve of her neck. If he thought he was nervous before, seeing Molly only intensified the buzz.

"I brought chips, salsa, cookies, and a couple two liters of soda. Do you think that's enough?" Her eyes widened. The curly, short hairs around her temples were damp with perspiration.

"Sure. What you got is perfect. The program has ten kids, if everyone shows up. Thanks for thinking of food. Teens like to eat." *Stop babbling like an idiot.*

Her face relaxed slightly. "You'll lead the meeting, right?"

"Yes." He patted her shoulder, and then let his fingertip slide partway down her bare arm. Arousal hit him. "Don't worry. We got this."

She began setting up the food.

Thankfully, Molly seemed unaware of the heat burning inside his body. He wondered what he could do to break through her tough exterior. A jackhammer? Heath had once told him Molly did have a soft side, having seen it when she spent time with her close friends and family. Would she ever let her guard down with him? He liked a challenge as much as the next guy. And since he was a former Green Beret, maybe even more so. But he had some serious doubts he'd ever earn Molly's friendship, let alone her love.

The clock read 3:10 when the teens filtered in.

He should have stressed the importance of being on time. A small girl with stringy, brown hair entered the room and sat toward the back. She wore an oversized T-shirt and carried a worn canvas bag.

"Hi," Molly said as she approached.

The girl recoiled in her chair.

Molly took a step back. "I'm Molly Hernandez. Are you here for Second Step?"

"Yes." The young girl's gaze stayed focused on the floor.

Her voice was so quiet Drew had to strain to hear her.

"What's your name?" Molly asked.

"Whitney Milan."

"It's nice to meet you." She smiled and reached over to shake the girl's hand.

Drew noticed Molly's gaze flick down to the small bump hidden under the girl's shirt.

By twenty minutes past three, Drew decided the room was as full as it was going to get. Eight teens were there in all. Not bad. Only two missing. Drew started by introducing himself, and then introduced Molly, who stood in the back.

As he talked about the program's goals and expectations, he remained conscious of Molly. He was always aware of her, whenever she was close. His gaze returned to her, like a compass magnet to the North

Pole. "I'm looking for service project ideas or fun things to do as a group," Drew said to the blank-faced crowd. "Anybody?"

Silence.

Did any of these kids have a pulse?

After a long few minutes, a whisper sounded from the back. "How about a self-defense class?" Whitney's chin quivered.

"I teach a self-defense class." Molly nodded.

The group quickly spun in their chairs, like they'd forgotten she was back there.

"I'd be happy to do a special class." Molly stepped forward and uncrossed her arms. "Just remember that the methods will be strictly self-defense, no fighting. And, Whitney, you will probably have to wait, or at least take extra precautions."

Whitney's face flushed red, and she lowered her gaze to the ground.

"How about canoeing?" A boy with long, blond hair asked. "I've always wanted to go canoeing."

A low murmur filled the room. More kids joined in the conversation.

He glanced at Molly, who wore a beautiful smile. They'd done the impossible—getting eight teenagers, a group of misfits, interested in their program.

Molly sat at the front of the room, next to Drew. She held a pen and pad of notepaper and started taking down ideas.

Maybe his crazy plan would work after all.

****

While Whitney sat with the other Second Step kids, she felt a fluttering inside her belly, which had nothing to do with the baby she carried. To be honest, her life sucked. She couldn't imagine it getting much worse. She'd been arrested, abandoned by the guy who'd got her pregnant, and her own mom didn't care about her. At school, she was invisible. Both students and teachers avoided meeting her gaze.

But Mr. Atwater and Officer Hernandez were different from any other adults she'd ever known. They looked at her—like really looked. Which was kinda frightening. What would they see if they got too close?

For the first time in a long time, Whitney had a spark of hope. Reality always threatened to snuff out hope. She'd have to protect it like an ember, until the next time she got together with this group. Maybe her hope would have a chance at survival.

After their discussion about fun things to do, they took a break. Whitney stood next to Officer Hernandez at the snack table. For a police officer, she was very friendly. She even smiled when Whitney took more cookies. Usually, the police were only interested in her stealing stuff. Nobody bothered to understand why she needed those things. Did they even take the time to notice the things she'd taken? Shampoo, vitamins, underwear, and food. Never movies, or videogames, or makeup,

Back to the fact people never really took the time to see her—until now.

Chapter Five

At least once a week, Molly went out with her two best friends. Tonight, she met Grace and Colleen for dinner at the Desert Rose. Since Grace's brother owned the restaurant, it was their go-to hang out most weeks. As Molly walked toward the table Grace had already commandeered, she purposely avoided looking at the table by the window. The one where she'd seen Drew sitting at two weeks ago.

Ten minutes later, Colleen arrived and flopped on the booth next to Molly. "Sorry, I'm late. I had a session run over."

Colleen's fair skin flushed pink. She removed her black rimmed glasses and slipped them into a floral case. As a clinical psychiatrist, specializing in the treatment of veterans, she had helped Heath on his journey to overcome PTSD. In Molly's eyes, that made her nothing short of a miracle worker.

"No problem," Grace said. "We just ordered drinks."

"You look like it's been a martini kind of day," Molly said as their waitress approached.

"That obvious, huh?" Colleen ordered a dirty martini with extra green olives. "Working with the government is so frustrating, with so many hoops to jump through. My foundation will help soldiers make a smoother transition into civilian life. But everywhere I turn, I get a door slammed in my face."

"Are you still looking into starting a veterans' retreat?" Molly chose a warm roll from the basket on the table and split it with her thumbs. As she slathered butter on both sides, her stomach growled.

"That's the plan." Colleen glanced down at the menu. "But the details are so much more complicated than I first thought."

Grace turned her head and sneezed, and then pulled out a tissue from her purse. "Sorry, I think I'm coming down with a cold. Maybe you could get a partner to help. Molly and Drew are working together. Their Second Step program is going well."

"I don't know about going well." Molly waited until they'd all given the waitress their dinner orders before continuing. "Both Drew and I have a lot to learn about running this program. We had our first meeting a week ago, which actually went better than either of us expected."

"Drew came over to the ranch yesterday. He seems really happy." Grace glanced over at Molly with raised eyebrows.

A silent question Molly interpreted as, *How are you handling working with Drew?*

Molly answered with a quick shake of the head, meaning *Don't go there.* Grace was the only one outside her immediate family who knew about Molly's cancer. She understood what drove Molly to pursue a career in the DEA. And also why a relationship with Drew was not a risk worth taking.

Drew had a clear vision in his mind of what his future looked like. If Molly ever opened herself to him, he'd reject her. No doubt in her mind. Sure, he'd be sympathetic and let her down easy. Drew was a good guy. But not the type who gave up on his goals. Neither was she. "Drew's doing great with the teens," Molly said. "I have a tougher time. As a cop, they see me as 'the man,' so to speak."

"They'll get over it." Colleen twirled a plastic sword speared with two green olives. "You'll be even more popular than Drew in no time."

"Ha, doubtful." Molly picked up her wine glass to take her first drink when her cell rang. "It's the station. Sorry, I have to take this call."

"No problem. We understand." Grace sipped at her clear soda.

"This is Officer Hernandez." Molly listened to dispatch on the other end. "Tell them I'm on my way. I'm five minutes out." Disconnecting the call, she turned to her friends and sighed. So much for a relaxing girl's night. "Sorry, but I have to respond to a domestic disturbance call. They're requesting a female officer at the scene." And Molly was the only female officer on the Liberty Ridge force.

"Stay safe," Colleen said.

Molly stood. "Always. I hate leaving before we even got started. Save some good gossip for next time. The juicier, the better."

Grace squeezed her hand and smiled. "We'll save you plenty of gossip. Don't feel bad. Go do your job, and get that bad guy."

"I will," Molly said. That part was her favorite.

After a short drive, Molly parked her car behind the two squads already on the scene. The house she approached was small and rundown, with weather-beaten wood siding and flaking yellow paint. Several windows were either cracked or totally broken.

As was her ritual, she patted the Glock resting on her hip. She liked the reassuring weight of her gun. Domestic issues could turn ugly really fast. Molly straightened her jacket.

Officer Dave Foster stepped out of the house. He'd been the first officer at the scene.

"Thanks for coming," Dave said. "I'd like you to talk with the DV victim. She wouldn't give me more than one word answers."

"What's the situation?" She tipped her head to meet the tall man's gaze.

He widened his stance and glanced over his shoulder into the house. "We've made visits here before. Tonight, neighbors heard yelling, and then a loud crash. I guess that's not uncommon coming from this house, but this time the commotion must've sounded worse. Perp is Rich Logan, a white male, mid-forties. He's currently cooling off on the sofa in handcuffs. Victim is his wife, Barbara Logan. She claims Rich didn't hurt her, but the bruises on her face suggest otherwise."

Molly shook her head in disgust and walked into the house. The inside wasn't in any better shape than the outside. The front room was cramped, full of knick-knacks and early nineties furniture. Rich Logan, wearing cut-off shorts and no shirt, scowled from his perch on the sofa. His sweaty face and beer belly were flushed a deep red, making him look like an overripe tomato.

Another cop stood watch over him.

"Hey, man," Rich shouted. He jerked his chin and rose on unsteady legs. "I have rights. You can't keep me handcuffed here. I want to see my wife."

The officer on guard duty, Lee Nelson, gripped Rich's shoulder and pushed him back down. "Shut it," he barked.

She followed Dave into the kitchen. The mingled scents of rotten food and stale cigarettes greeted her. Nicotine-stained wallpaper covered the walls, peeling off like petals on a dying flower. The happy days were long gone.

Cowering at the table was a wisp of a woman. Her dirty blonde hair did a poor job of covering the bruises discoloring her face.

Stepping around a pile of boxes, Molly went to sit on a wobbly chair. She liked to be at eye level whenever talking with a frightened victim.

"This is Officer Molly Hernandez," Dave said. "Tell her what happened tonight." He turned on his heel and left the room.

Molly purposefully relaxed her face and shoulders. "Barbara, I'm here to listen and help."

"My husband didn't do nothin' wrong," Barbara cried out. She slapped the palms of her hands on the table. Fat tears streamed down her face. "Y'all need to leave our house."

The disgust she felt when entering the house was nothing compared to the frustration now twisting her gut. How could Barbra Logan come to the defense of the man who abused her? "You're not being honest. Did your husband give you those bruises?"

Barbara let out a deep sigh and lifted her head.

The sight of her battered face left her fighting for breath. Showing both old and new bruising, Molly could tell tonight hadn't been the woman's first beating.

Both eyes were swollen and discolored. An eggplant-colored bruise marked her cheek. Her lip had split and was crusted over with blood. "Barbara, your husband cannot treat you like this. We can protect you."

"Don't arrest him, please. He didn't do this. I fell down the stairs."

She glanced around the room and noticed a half-opened door, which possibly led to a basement staircase. Though, she highly doubted a fall could have caused the fist sized bruises on Barbara's face and arms. "You need medical attention," Molly said. Rich Logan would see the inside of a jail cell, regardless of his wife's statement. "I can take you to the hospital, or we can call an ambulance."

Barbara slumped in her chair. "I'm fine. I'm not leaving Rich."

"Okay." Molly grew even more frustrated, which stoked her internal temperature. She'd burst into flames with one more denial. "Tell me exactly how you got those bruises." Retrieving her notebook and a pen, she prepared to take Barbara Logan's statement.

"Like I said, I tripped." Barbara's gaze darted everywhere except Molly. "Now, you cops leave my family alone."

Sadly, Barbara would rather be beaten to a pulp than rat on her man. "Are any children present in the house?" Molly was almost afraid of the answer.

Barbara's eyes grew wide, and she lowered her head.

"Barbara," she asked again, ignoring the nausea churning in her gut. "Do you have children?" Molly visually swept the kitchen for any sign of a child's presence. From the way Barbara acted, Molly was sure minors lived in this poor excuse of a home. Her gaze halted on the refrigerator. A school picture hung crookedly from its surface. Molly jumped to her feet to get a closer look. The girl appeared in her late teens and very familiar. Bile rose in her throat. "Is this your daughter? Is this Whitney Milan?"

"Leave my daughter out of this."

Barbara tried to sound harsh, but her voice lacked confidence. The image of the mousy, pregnant girl at the Second Step meeting made Molly turn on Barbara so fast, the woman jerked back in her chair. "I'm asking you one more time. Where's Whitney?"

"She's downstairs. But my husband didn't hurt her," Barbara called out. "She's fine. You'll see."

Molly strode across the sticky laminate floor of the kitchen. Before she got to the staircase, a body slammed into her.

"Get out," yelled a man's voice.

Her body tensed in self-defense. She threw back her elbow, impacting the man's soft middle.

"*Umph.*" He blew out a breath and doubled over.

"I got him." Dave grabbed Rich Logan by the neck. "We turned our backs on him for a second, and he took off." He pushed Rich, who was still handcuffed, into the front room. "Nelson, keep a tight hold on him."

Molly stood at the top of the stairs. She blinked several times to help her eyes adjust to the low light. "Dave, I have reason to believe a minor is living on the premises. I think she's in danger. I'm going down to the basement."

"Got it." Dave stepped back into the kitchen and handed her his tactical flashlight. "You'll need some extra light. I'll take Mr. Logan outside to get acquainted with the back of my squad. Nelson will stay inside in case you need back-up."

Her pulse quickened as she pulled her gun out of its holster and descended with caution. Molly made her way downstairs, and Barbara's cries slowly faded. Beside the glow from one exposed light bulb, the space was dark. She switched on the tactical flashlight and surveyed the room. The musty air made her wheeze. As the beam of her flashlight swept the far corner, she saw Whitney huddled on a stack of pillows. Her anger faded to concern, but she approached with caution. "Whitney, it's Officer Molly Hernandez. Do you remember me from the Second Step program?"

Whitney didn't move. She didn't make a sound.

Was she hurt? Molly slipped her gun back into the holster. She could barely make out the girl's brown hair poking out from underneath a blanket. "I responded to a call about a domestic disturbance. I want to make sure you're all right. Did your dad hurt you?" She knelt next to Whitney.

"He's not my dad," a quiet voice sounded. "No one bothers me when I'm down here."

Molly's heart shattered in a million pieces for the poor girl. Fighting back tears, she sat on the cement floor. "Let me help you. Spending too much time down here is unsafe for both you and the baby." On her short walk over to Whitney, she'd noticed mold growing on the walls.

"Why would it be unhealthy for my baby?" Whitney pushed back the thin blanket and sat.

She looked as delicate and vulnerable as a snowflake in summer. In her current environment, she didn't stand a chance. "Have you seen a doctor since you found out you were pregnant?"

"Mom took me once, but then said we didn't have the money to go again." She wiped her nose with the sleeve of her sweatshirt.

Inside, Molly screamed at Barbara. How could a mother be so neglectful? "Okay." Molly rose to her feet. "Your step-dad is going to jail, so it's okay to come upstairs. I can take you to a safe house, if you still feel threatened living here."

"I can't leave my mom." Whitney carefully rose off the pillows. "She needs me. Plus, I'll be eighteen soon. If I leave home, she'll never let me return." Now standing, Whitney wrapped herself in the pink blanket. One tear streaked down her cheek.

Molly put her arm around the girl's bony shoulders. She wanted to cry herself. "I will give you my phone number. You can call me, day or night, if you need anything. If for some reason I don't answer, call the police station. They'll know how to reach me."

Whitney nodded then tucked a strand of wispy hair behind her ear.

"Another thing," Molly continued. "You need to see a doctor. Not only for your own health, but also for the baby's. I'll give your mom the name and number of a doctor who will see you at no cost."

"I'd like that. I'm always worried if my baby is growing okay, or if I'm doing things right."

"If your mom doesn't take you, I will." Molly ascended the stairs behind Whitney.

Barbara still sat at the kitchen table, her face twisted in a mixture of anger and fear. "I told you she was fine." She crossed thin arms over her chest.

"Whitney is not fine." Her voice trembled as she

fought for control of her emotions. "She's six months pregnant and has only seen a doctor once. She has to hide in a grungy basement to avoid getting hit by her step-dad. She's resorting to shoplifting, because you are not providing the things she needs to stay healthy." Molly could have continued, but she bit the inside of her cheek to stop.

"That girl got knocked up just to spite me." Barbara jumped out of her chair, causing it to tip backward and crash onto the ground.

Whitney slid to hide behind Molly.

Feeling the girl shake, Molly reached back and patted her hand. "Barbara, your husband is headed to jail. I suggest you cooperate with the DA and help provide a safe home for your daughter and grandchild. Take her to the doctor."

"Get out of my house." Spittle flew from Barbara's mouth.

Molly squeezed Whitney's hand. "Are you sure you don't want me to take you to a safe house?"

Whitney's chin trembled when she nodded. "Yes, as long as Rich is gone."

Molly's body vibrated with rage as she walked out of the horrible house. Once outside, she breathed deeply, filling her lungs with fresh air. Inside her car, she grabbed her cell and pulled up Drew's number. Should she bother him? She needed to talk to someone about what had just happened. Drew would listen. He would understand. Before she could second-guess why Drew was the only one she wanted right now, she hit dial.

****

As Drew sat outside, staring off into the darkness

of his backyard, self-doubt seeped into his thoughts. Not because of the spreadsheet opened on his laptop or his lack of success in making any real connections with his dates. He simply wanted what he couldn't have.

Wasn't that a kicker? The only woman who truly intrigued him was out of reach.

A multitude of blinking fireflies floated around the yard, reminding him he wasn't the only one looking for love under the stars tonight. Drew went back to studying the data on his laptop. The first time Heath had seen it, he'd nearly laughed his boots off. The whole idea was super nerdy—to document each woman he dated on a spreadsheet for further review. He'd sorted them by name, the place and time of their date, his overall impression, and a rating. Sure, his spreadsheet was probably one of the weirdest ways of finding a wife, but he was a numbers guy. Data helped him gain a sense of control over the whole process.

Since leaving the Army, he missed the structure. Everything in his life had been tightly regulated—from the clothes he wore to the meals he ate. When he got up and when he went to sleep. He'd been an engineer on an elite Special Forces team. Before every mission, his job was to make sure their equipment was up to the task. Documentation often meant the difference between life and death.

Reading a spreadsheet about all the women he'd dated should inflate his ego. Instead, Drew felt empty, just like the big house behind him. Would his home ever be filled with the family he imagined?

His cell phone rang, causing him to literally jump out of his seat. Sudden, unexpected noises unsettled him. A leftover from so much time spent in war zones.

The caller ID read *Molly*. His poor heart went from shock to elation within a split second.

Play it cool, man. Don't sound too eager. "Hey, Molly."

"Drew."

The inflection in her voice made his name sound more like a question. *Did she call me by mistake?* Disappointment squeezed his chest.

She cleared her throat. "Can I stop by?"

Anytime. "Sure. I'm just having a beer out on the deck."

"Okay, great. I had a rough call tonight, and I'm kind of shaken up. I can be there in ten minutes."

Molly sounded worn down and lacked her usual bravado. "Come around to the backyard when you get here. I'll be waiting." He slapped his forehead. *Could you sound any more lame?* Ten minutes. He had ten minutes to clean up the mess lying around the house. Maybe she wouldn't go inside, but she could still see the dirty dishes and overflowing laundry baskets through the glass patio doors. Drew set his beer on the table and high-tailed it to the house, almost running into the door.

Nine minutes and thirty seconds later, he sat again on the patio chair and took a long drink of warm beer. Hearing a quiet rustling, he glanced up and saw Molly standing next to him. His heart leapt with surprise.

"Sorry for scaring you," she said. "I have a habit of walking lightly. With five older brothers, I learned to move under the radar."

"You really are a pixie. A super stealthy one. How about something to drink, and then you can tell me about this call?"

"A beer sounds perfect." She sat on the padded teak chair next to his.

Drew came back with two cold beers and handed one to Molly.

She twisted off the cap and lifted the beer bottle to her pursed lips.

What he wouldn't give to be that bottle. He ran his tongue across his lower lip. "So, what's got you so rattled?" he asked.

"You remember Whitney from Second Step? The pregnant girl?"

Drew nodded. "Sure. She was very nice but seemed shy."

"I responded to a domestic disturbance at her house. Her step-dad beat up her mom pretty good. I'm so angry over the whole situation. Whitney was hiding in the basement. Her mom refused to give an incriminating statement about her worthless husband. The poor girl has only seen the doctor once during her entire pregnancy! Can you believe that?" Molly waved her free hand through the air.

"No, I can't." In the dim outdoor lights, he saw passion flash in her eyes. He resisted the urge to reach over and hold her.

"I couldn't do much since the wife isn't pressing charges. Said she fell down the stairs. We arrested him, but I've seen enough of these situations to know he'll return home." Molly reclined in the chair and crossed an ankle over her knee.

Although he'd never witnessed domestic abuse firsthand as a child, he'd known kids whose home were battlefields. "We can still help Whitney. When she's with us as part of Second Step, we'll keep an extra close eye on her."

"And to think," Molly continued. "She was the one who asked for self-defense lessons. Why didn't I put two and two together?"

"Don't blame yourself. You had no way of knowing."

"I've never felt so powerless, walking out of that house and leaving Whitney behind." Molly placed her hand on his arm, brushing her fingers over his skin.

The hairs on his arm stood to life underneath her light touch. She must have realized what she was doing because she pulled back, causing him to crave her even more.

For several minutes, they sat in silence.

From the darkness beyond his yard, bullfrog croaks punctuated the still air. Drew watched Molly out of the corner of his eye. Did she know how wonderful she was? Did she have any idea that he found her the most beautiful, tough, big-hearted woman he'd ever met? But she'd leave soon, taking a piece of him when she did.

Chapter Six

Beams of sunlight filtered through the high windows of the horse stable, highlighting the dust floating haphazardly through the air. Molly followed Grace down the main aisle. Today, the Second Step kids would be here at True Horizon Ranch. Molly arrived early to help Grace set up things.

An elderly man had donated a large van for the program. Drew would meet the kids at the community center then drive them out to the ranch. *Better him than me.* She'd gladly let Drew have the privilege of being the group's official chauffeur.

Horses nickered as Molly and Grace walked past the stalls. A horse with a shiny black coat and mane peeked its head over the gate.

"What?" Molly talked to the horse. "Do you think I have a treat?"

"Don't fall for it." Grace reached up to scratch the mare behind the ear. "She has plenty of oats in her stall. Heath just spoils her by always giving extra treats."

"Thanks for letting us bring the Second Step teens out here." Molly leaned her hip against a thick, wooden beam.

"I love the concept of animal therapy." Grace combed her fingers through the horse's long mane. "Working with the animals on the ranch helped Heath. They gave him a sense of purpose and peace. Animals don't judge. They accept you, warts and all. I hope your teens feel the same."

If Molly hadn't been best friends with Grace since kindergarten, she'd be insanely jealous. Grace was beautiful, with long black hair that hung straight to her waist and skin the most beautiful shade of warm copper. Not only was Grace lovely, she had a kind heart. "I'm going to be single forever." She finally voiced the ugly insecurity that had kept her awake some nights.

"Honey, when the time's right then you'll meet a man worthy of your love. You are the most incredible woman, and any man worthy of you would have to be special."

Molly lifted her gaze to a dove perched above the stable door. Its nest rested on a crossbeam. "After my hysterectomy, I put falling in love on hold. I placed all my efforts into my career, which is something I can control. Most days, I'm happy focused on police work and getting into the DEA. But lately, I don't know how to explain it...I'd like someone special to come home to, like you have with Heath." Tears burned her eyes. Saying these words aloud, even to her best friend, took a lot of effort. She hated to talk about her feelings, but if she didn't tell someone, she might give in to the despair that knocked on her heart's door.

"You will find a soul that will connect with yours." Grace wrapped her in a hug. "Then, if you want a family, you can work out those details together."

Molly swallowed, pushing down the lump of melancholy lodged inside her throat. "You know I'm not the type who hinges her happiness on finding a man. I'm content with where my life is headed. I'm probably just going through a phase."

The sound of gravel crunching under tires interrupted their conversation. Drew and the Second Step kids had arrived. Time to focus her attention on helping others, not wallowing in her own grief. The dream of pregnancy and children died two years ago. Only lately had her maternal desire rekindled. A flame doused with ice-cold reality.

Molly exited the barn and approached the assembled group. Drew smiled, the kind that didn't stop at his lips but sparkled in his brown eyes. Now here was a man. He was strong enough to match her step for step, if only he wasn't headed in the opposite direction.

Whitney was there, too. *Good.* Molly walked over and stood beside Whitney. "Welcome to True Horizon Ranch." She glanced around the group. "This is a working ranch, owned by Grace and Heath Carter. They raise Texas Longhorn cattle, along with Quarter horses. You will also see chickens, pigs, a crabby goat, and various dogs."

The teens turned to look around. Their murmurs held a buzz of excitement.

Whitney still looked scared, but Molly noticed a gleam of interest in her eyes.

Smiling, Grace stepped forward. "Hi, I'm Grace. Welcome."

"We will split into three groups." Drew tapped on the screen of his cell to open his stored list. "You will work with each type of animal. I'll tell you which adult you're assigned to."

In an instant, all the kids flocked to Drew, like pigeons surrounding a guy tossing bits of bread. As he read names off his list, the teens sorted into groups.

In Molly's group were Whitney, Derek, and Laura. She led the trio into the horse stable. "Do any of you know how to ride?" Silence greeted her. She stopped walking in front of a horse stall. "This is Daisy. She loves people, carrots, and sugar cubes."

Laura approached with long-legged strides and rubbed the horse's nose. The lanky girl was tall enough to look the horse in the eye. Next, Derek, wearing scuffed high-tops and baggy black shorts, walked over and stroked its mane. Whitney hung back, leaning against the opposite wall.

"Come over and say hi," Molly said to Whitney. "She's very friendly. I promise." Reaching into a plastic container by the stall door, she pulled out three sugar cubes. She placed them on her open palm.

Daisy eagerly gobbled them up with her gummy lips.

Molly opened the stall door and brought Daisy out into the main aisle. Tying a rope on her bridle, she secured the other end to a wooden post. "Here's a currycomb for each of you. Use short circular strokes, working in the direction of the hair growth. For now, only brush the body. We use other types of brushes for the legs and head."

While Laura and Derek worked, Whitney remained about five steps away. "I don't want to," she whispered.

"Have you ever been up close to a horse?" Molly asked.

Whitney's gaze dropped down to the floor. Her beaten tennis shoes swept the hay covering the boards. "No. The horse is so big. What if it hurts the baby?"

The girl showed a strong love for her baby despite growing up unloved herself. Thankfully, Whitney's heart hadn't yet been corrupted by her home life. "I've known Daisy since I was your age. She is very gentle. I promise she won't hurt you or your baby. Just follow my lead."

With tentative steps, Whitney followed her until they reached Daisy's head.

The horse turned to look at them before pricking her ears. She nickered.

"That's her way of saying hello." Molly chuckled. Daisy and her antics were endearing. She hoped they'd get Whitney to lower her defenses and relax. "Just make sure to leave space when you walk behind her, but otherwise you'll be fine."

Very slowly, Whitney raised her hand to touch the mane. "Her hair's so soft." She gripped the brush and began grooming. As she brushed with repetitive strokes, Whitney's shoulders lowered.

Molly showed Derek how to pick the hooves. Laura used a moist cloth and wiped around the horse's eyes and nose. Whitney worked her way around Daisy, using the different brushes Molly showed her. Finally, she combed out Daisy's silky mane.

****

Whitney ran a hand over Daisy's downy soft muzzle. The horse twitched underneath her touch, causing Whitney to laugh. She still couldn't get over how gentle the horse was, considering its large size. Daisy could easily overpower her but instead eagerly submitted. "You are such a good girl," Whitney whispered. She gave the horse a kiss on the side of her broad head. In reply, Daisy turned to rub her muzzle under Whitney's chin.

Was it weird to consider a horse a friend? A best

friend, even? She liked talking to the horse more than she liked talking to most people. An animal didn't stare at her round belly or ask embarrassing questions. Daisy didn't make her feel ashamed of her secondhand clothes or her limp hair.

A huge fly buzzed around her head, and she swatted it away. The bug flew off, probably in search of less-combative prey.

Whitney peeked over at Officer Hernandez, who was assisting Derek and Laura with the wheelbarrows. She wasn't upset about not being asked to clean the stalls. Strong smells still bothered her, and she was sure that dirty straw smelled something awful.

In her mind, she revisited the night Rich had been arrested. She'd witnessed a bad fight, with lots of yelling and crying, which made her flee to the basement—her safe haven in the storm of violence. If she could have helped her mom, she would have. But she could do nothing. Whitney needed to protect her own child. The baby was her number one concern.

When Officer Hernandez found her in the basement, she knew an angel had come to save her. Not only had the petite police officer stood up to Whitney's mom and Rich, she had promised to help her. Officer Hernandez took the time to talk with her. She actually was concerned about Whitney and the baby, something almost too good to be true.

Now Whitney was helping at a ranch, with people who really seemed to care. Mr. Atwater talked with her on the way over. He was a pretty cool guy, for a teacher.

Daisy snorted and shook her head, seemingly to tell Whitney that she cared, too. Giving the horse another kiss, she inhaled the sweet smell of hay, sugar, and apples. Inside her belly, the baby somersaulted.

Maybe her life was finally turning around.

****

Molly's group finished their chores and met the other groups on the porch for a break. Heath served cold lemonade and cracked jokes. On more than one occasion, she forced herself not to laugh. If Heath had an audience, he instantly transformed into a stand-up comedian.

While the teens enjoyed the cool shade, Molly stepped away from the crowd, preferring the quiet view of the cattle pasture behind the house. Whenever she was here, she felt a soul-deep peace. When she moved to Washington DC for the DEA Academy, she'd miss the beautiful nature of the Texas prairie. Then again, after she was assigned to a permanent location.

Her confidence was strong the board would realize her passion and determination. She would be an asset to the DEA.

Drew walked toward her and set his glass of lemonade on the porch rail.

Whenever he was close, she instinctively took a step back. Her body always acknowledged his nearness—her heart beat faster, her breath quickened, and her mind went to thoughts that were totally inappropriate.

"This is fun," he said. "My group loved working in the field with the cattle." His gaze locked with hers.

She saw a flash of hunger. A hunger that had nothing to do with the cookies Grace handed out. Molly looked away but caught the scent of his spicy cologne and sighed. After being out in the field, how did he still smell so good? "Whitney did great with Daisy."

"I wasn't sure at first but once she got going, she loved it. I'd like to bring her back so she can continue to work with Daisy. She connected with the horse."

Drew's smile grew. "You really do have a heart of gold. Whitney's lucky to have you in her life."

Heat crept up her cheeks. She struggled not to stare at the chiseled line of his jaw. Why did he have to be so perfect? "Don't go nominating me for sainthood. I'm just doing my job."

He laughed. "A saint." His voice was deep and husky. "Not exactly the term I'd use to describe you."

As he scratched at the black stubble on his chin, he moved his body to within inches of hers. Molly's brain flashed with panic, commanding her to retreat. The person he wanted didn't exist.

She pictured herself on the job as a DEA Special Agent. *Don't let your feelings for Drew distract you from your goals.* "I need to talk to Grace." She stepped back and began walking away. As she rounded the corner of the porch, she heard Drew's laughter.

"I'm in so much trouble," Drew said in a gravelly voice. "Only a fallen angel could be that seductive without even trying."

Chapter Seven

"How is Devin supposed to learn in this environment, with so many distractions?" A middle-aged mother of one of Drew's students sat across the desk. Her face set in a scowl.

"Mrs. Dover," Drew said, frustration fraying the edge of his voice. "Your son is learning and doing very well in this class. He's also having fun. I don't see the problem." Mrs. Dover was one of 'those' mothers. Weekly, she made the rounds to each of her son's classrooms. Drew had never heard a compliment pass her lips.

"You may have plenty of military experience but little experience teaching children. I'm concerned about how you handled the cheating situation. Rachel Franklin said a few boys were caught passing answers, and you didn't do anything to punish them."

Under his desk, Drew clenched his fist. A sharp stabbing pain radiated from behind his eye sockets. Why didn't anyone warn him about parents like Beth Dover? "I've dealt with the situation in the manner I felt best. Since your son wasn't involved, I frankly don't see how it's any of your business."

Huffing, she crossed her arms over her chest. "Of course, it's my business. The quality of education at this school is my concern."

By now, the pain behind his eyes had spread to his

temples and down the back of his neck. "What are you hoping to accomplish by talking to me today?"

Mrs. Dover wagged her finger at him and stood. "I hope your teaching ability doesn't become a problem." She swung her purse over her shoulder and marched out the door.

Typical. She'd eventually realize she couldn't push him around. Drew didn't play games. He taught the way he thought best. One parent with no teaching experience wouldn't be allowed to run his classroom. The only thing Mrs. Dover had experience with was stirring up trouble.

He closed his eyes and breathed deeply until the pain in his head faded to a dull throb. Then, he began grading the pile of science tests on his desk. While working, his mind kept wandering to how good Molly looked at the ranch. Standing with the group from Second Step, she'd been the shortest one. If he hadn't known better, he would have picked her out as a teenager. But he wouldn't be fooled. He knew from experience little Molly could take down his much-taller body. Grinning at the memory, Drew heard footsteps.

"Hey, loser, stop daydreaming. You look ridiculous." Heath stood in the doorway, laughing. "I'll bet you fifty push-ups I know who you're thinking about."

He shook his head and scrambled for a clever comeback. "I was remembering how pretty your Aunt Linda looked at your wedding."

Heath stepped forward, grabbed a marker off the dry erase board, and launched it at Drew's head. "My aunt is too good for you."

Drew ducked, causing the marker to miss and

bounce off the floor.

Heath pulled up a chair, with the back facing Drew, and straddled it. "Molly Hernandez." His lips twitched into a grin. "You can't get her off your mind."

"That obvious?" He hoped not. Heath knew him better than even his own family, but that knowledge didn't ease his mind.

"Man, everyone can see the way you look at her. What's the holdup?"

Drew tapped his red pen on the desk. "Don't know. She's a challenge, which is part of her appeal. Could be she doesn't like ex-military? Is that why she had a problem with you at first?"

"At first." Heath leaned back and laughed. "She still won't join my fan club. I don't think it's a military thing. With me, she's still learning to trust I'm not the same troublemaker I was when I first came to town. Molly has the hots for you as bad as you got them for her. She just won't act on 'em."

Brushing a hand across the short curls on his head, he sighed and looked up at the ceiling. "Call me Napoleon. I've led a campaign to win Molly and failed. Now I've been exiled to the friend zone. You know, I thought the next part of my life would be easy—get a job, find a girl, get married, and start having babies. I waited so I could do it right. What am I doing wrong?"

"Nothing, man. That's life. Not everything can be managed with a spreadsheet." Heath tapped a finger on Drew's laptop.

"Don't say that. I love my spreadsheets."

"Right there, my friend, is part of the problem." Heath stood and walked to the windows overlooking the grassy outdoor commons area. "In Afghanistan, right before a mission, you'd always hold up the whole show because you'd go over your checklist one last time."

Drew simply nodded. Those days were a lifetime ago, yet they still felt like yesterday.

"Everyone hated waiting until you were ready. But you kept us safe." Heath stared out the window, resting his hand on the frame. "We're not fighting for our lives anymore. You can let go of some control."

"I wake up some nights after a nightmare and wonder if I've really left it all behind." Drew didn't have full-blown PTSD, but he did suffer from flashback nightmares. About once a week, he'd wake up in a sweat. The cold breath of death chilling his skin.

"We're survivors," Heath said. "Don't forget to live."

He tapped his hand over his heart. "Amen, brother."

When Heath turned to face Drew, his face lit with a huge smile. "Well, for a moment I thought we were on one of those touchy-feely talk shows."

The guy never stayed serious for long. "Thanks for stopping by, even if it was to harass me. Is that all you wanted?"

"No." Heath's eyebrows arched. "I almost forgot. Grace is throwing another party on Sunday afternoon. This one's to celebrate the new pool. We'll grill some burgers and stuff. Bring your swimsuit. Molly will be there."

Nice. Another chance to hang out with Molly—the best news he'd had all day. "You could've texted me."

"I know, but I was in town and wanted to see your classroom, which is pretty cool." Heath pointed to the back corner. "I like the skeleton wearing party beads. You name him yet?"

"Yeah, I call him Heath Carter." Drew walked Heath to the doorway and gave him a pat on the back. "See you Sunday." After Heath left, he went back to his classroom with the image of Molly in a bikini swimming in his mind. He wouldn't miss this party for the world.

****

Saturday morning, Molly walked through the front door of the county animal shelter. She only came to look, or at least that's what she'd promised herself. A puppy or kitten might be a good way to take the edge off her loneliness. But she considered the fact her job kept her busy and the DEA Training Academy at Quantico would keep her away for four months. So, she'd only come to the shelter for information.

As she entered the brick building, the overwhelming sounds of barking greeted her. "Hi," she said to the silver-haired receptionist. "I'd like to look at your adoptable animals."

"Dogs are down the hall to your right." The elderly woman at the front counter cupped her hands around her mouth. "Cats are in the cages a little farther down, on the left."

The barking grew louder as Molly advanced down the hall. Once inside the dog room, she couldn't believe the number of kennels. Over half were bustling with activity. A man in a green jumpsuit mopped the floor on the other side, which accounted for the strange scent—a combination of pine cleaner and dog.

Molly did a slow circuit, back and forth down each aisle. Some dogs came up to the front of their kennel to greet her, tails wagging. Others stayed huddled toward the back, on the blanket serving as their bed. All were cute in their own way. Would a dog be a good fit? With her busy schedule, she might not have enough time to devote to him or her. She'd hate to bring a pet into her house then neglect it.

As she approached the exit door, needing a break from the symphony of barking, a white mass of fur caught her gaze. Behind the kennel bars sat a huge dog, matted and dirty. "Hey," she said to the dog lying on the ground.

The man with the mop came up to stand next to her. "This guy's kinda shy. He just got here yesterday. They picked him up as a stray. That's why he's so dirty. The workers haven't given him a bath yet."

"Poor guy." She knelt down to get a better look.

"Don't worry. They'll clean him up soon." He turned from the dog to Molly. "You want to take him for a walk? I'm sure he'd like to get out of doggie jail for a while."

Molly didn't possess much maternal instinct, but this dog was coaxing out the little bit she had. If she took him for a walk, would she become attached? She wasn't ready to make a decision yet.

As the dog continued to look up with sad eyes, her willpower cracked. What would it hurt to give the dog a few minutes of exercise and love? Not like she was obligated to adopt him.

The man in the green jumpsuit didn't wait for her answer but went to get a leash. Once the dog was clipped onto the lead, he handed her the other end. "Have fun, you two," he said before going back to his mopping.

The dog glanced up and cocked his head.

"Come on. Let's go outside." She could have sworn the dog smiled.

With the dog in the lead, she walked to a fenced-in area. Once inside, she let the dog off the leash. After a moment's hesitation, he was off. He ran around the fence line a few times, lifted his leg to pee on a fence post, and then came back to her side, shaking his massive body. Dust and debris flew everywhere.

"What was that for?" she asked him.

He barked and went to retrieve a red ball.

Of course, fetch. Which meant she had to touch the slobbery ball. Once Molly conceded and tossed the ball, the dog went bolting after it.

He could really move for a large breed dog. After a few rounds of fetch, not only were her hands sticky with slobber but so were her shoes. About fifty throws in, her arm ached, and the dog looked like he'd had enough as well.

He plopped down at her feet with his pink tongue lolling out of his mouth.

She found his collar under mats of white hair, clipped on his leash, and took him back inside.

The mop man, who was pulling his bucket down the aisle, raised his head and smiled. "Since he's a stray, the shelter is required to hold him for forty-eight hours. If no one comes to claim him then he can be adopted. Tippy, at the front desk, has the paperwork to fill out. They'll give you a call when he's all cleaned up and ready to go home."

Molly opened her mouth to say she wasn't interested in adopting now, but the words lodged in her throat. A thousand excuses faded with the rise of a new desire—make this dog a permanent part of her life.

"Max is a good dog. He's a nice match for a gal like you." He squeezed out his mop and began cleaning an empty stall. "Don't worry. Even if you fill out the application, you can still change your mind, but I don't think you will."

Back inside his kennel, Max made a mad dash for his water bowl and lapped up every drop. Then, he curled his shaggy body on the floor, glanced upward, and sighed.

So not fair. Max the dog did guilt trips as well as *Mamá.* Molly didn't stand a chance. She went back to the front desk to fill out the adoption application.

"So, which one stole your heart?" Tippy asked.

"The big white one. The janitor called him Max."

"Good choice. When they brought him in yesterday, I said to myself...Tippy, this one won't be here long. Once the waiting period is over, someone will call you."

"Thanks." A weight lifted off her chest, replaced by a tingle of excitement.

"Make sure you buy plenty of kibble. He likes to eat."

As Molly left the shelter, the noise faded. The parking lot seemed too lonely and quiet. Adopting Max felt right. Grace had said an animal could help heal a wounded heart, and Molly agreed. After her battle with cancer, she understood the value of unconditional love. Very few people gave such a special gift.

Chapter Eight

A splash of water jolted Molly out of a daydream. "Hey, munchkins, keep the water in the pool," she said to Grace's twin nieces.

"Sorry, Miss Molly," they said in unison. Both girls kicked off the side of the pool and swam away in their striped orange swimsuits like a pair of clown fish.

Toweling off her wet legs, Molly went back to thinking about her goofy dog. She had one more day to wait and didn't know if she could stand the waves of nerves twisting through her. What if someone else arrived at the shelter to claim him? She'd be happy for the dog but still heartbroken.

The early October sun hadn't received the memo the season was now fall. The hot weather was great for a pool party. Grace and Heath had lucked out.

Sitting by the pool on a plastic lounge chair, Molly dripped with sweat. Despite the nice weather, she almost hadn't come today. For starters, she hated wearing a swimsuit, especially a two-piece that would reveal her scar. The surgeon had placed the hysterectomy incision well below her belly button, but the scar might show if her suit bottom shifted. Grace overruled her objection by taking her shopping for a new suit. The purple bikini they'd picked out had a high waist so she could look cute and feel secure about hiding her scar.

Molly's second reason had to do with Drew, whose presence always unsettled her. She pictured him with his shirt off, climbing out of the pool dripping wet, and his golden bronze skin glistening in the sun. If she was warm before, she was burning up now. The water in the pool looked wonderfully inviting. Maybe a quick dip into cool water would get her mind off the hunky teacher.

The screen door opened, and Grace stepped out holding a tray of hamburgers.

Heath, who was warming up the grill, darted across the deck to take it off her hands. He whispered something in her ear and kissed her sweetly on the cheek.

Something was going on with those two. Heath seemed overly attentive. Maybe he was just being a devoted and loving husband.

"Hey, officer," Heath hollered from his station by the grill. "You know, it's not a crime to get wet."

Molly's good feelings for Heath evaporated. As always, whenever Heath opened his mouth, she instantly remembered why he irritated her so much. "It's not a crime to stay dry, either. Why don't you just concentrate on not burning our meal? I'm getting hungry."

He laughed "Don't worry. While you're lounging around, I'm slaving away by this fiery inferno. But I don't think you should eat until you get wet." Heath's smile grew, showing off his dimple.

He was up to something. Molly's comeback halted on her lips when Grace stepped between them.

"Now, now you two. Play nice." Grace pinched her husband on the rear.

74

Molly closed her eyes, taking in the sounds around her—the splashing water, the giggle of little girls, and a deep, male voice. Her eyes popped open. All she saw was Heath, still standing by the grill. He gave her a wicked smile and nodded.

Before she could speak, Molly found herself lifted into Drew's strong arms before being carried to the edge of the pool.

"Time to get wet," Drew said right before jumping in.

As she hit the water, shock stole her breath. The cool temperature of the water was in sharp contrast to the warm air. Her head went under the surface then bobbed up. Instead of feeling buoyant in the water, her body was firmly anchored against Drew's chest. "Put me down." Her indignation was only surpassed by her rising embarrassment. She tried in vain to wiggle out of his hold but would've had better luck escaping from the grip of a boa constrictor.

Drew's chest vibrated with laughter.

An action which gave her a strong inclination to kick. As much as she wanted to get out of Drew's hold, being pressed against him set her body on fire. One of his hands rested on her thigh, and his chest hair tickled her arm. Heat rose and filled her from the tips of her toes to the top of her head. Seconds passed like hours as he continued to hold her in his arms, the water of the pool lapping around them.

When she raised her gaze to meet his, what she saw jolted her a hundred times more than the cold plunge into the pool. His brown eyes swirled like liquid chocolate. Did he feel the jolt, too?

She needed to stop her growing desire. As she

pushed off his chest with the palm of her hand, he loosened his hold just enough for her to slip away. Molly's feet floated down to touch the bottom of the pool. The water lapped just below her chin.

Drew's face broke out into a playful grin. "I'm sorry. I just couldn't resist. You looked so hot...I mean warm. The idea was all Heath's." Leaning back, he kicked his legs and floated around her.

Did he honestly think he'd get off that easy? "Of course tossing me into the pool was Heath's idea, but you didn't have to play along. Don't partner with me at our next kickboxing class. I play dirty when I'm mad."

"Only when you're mad?" Drew flipped over onto his stomach and took off in a series of breaststrokes, finishing at the pool wall. "I accept your challenge and look forward to getting my butt kicked...again."

So, he anticipated the role of fall guy. She'll make him understand how much she didn't enjoy his and Heath's little joke. Molly waded across the pool, weaving around the twins, until she reached the stairs. As her body hit the warm, dry air, her skin prickled with goose pimples. She squeezed out her hair and water trickled down her back. Taking her towel, she dried off her skin before slipping on her cover-up. Then, she reclaimed her lounge chair.

Behind her sunglasses, she watched Drew swim back and forth across the pool. His back and shoulder muscles rippled under perfect skin. No ugly tattoos like Heath had to spoil it. Hopefully, he couldn't tell her gaze was locked onto him.

Admitting her attraction was easy. What about him was there not to like? The reality of her attraction was like quicksand, pulling her down to a place she couldn't escape. Drew was in the process of settling down. He wanted to fill his big house with a family soon. Not only was he looking for a wife, but also a mother for his kids. With her, that would not happen. Even if she could have children, she'd never be relegated to the nursery.

Stop feeling sorry for yourself. Underneath her swimsuit, her scar itched.

Grace sat in the lounge chair beside her. "Nice view."

"Not bad," Molly said. "Your husband's a trouble maker. You could have warned me."

"Heath and Drew are just having a little fun. Don't be such a sourpuss. You look like you're sucking on a lemon." Grace nudged Molly with her elbow.

"No, I don't." She shrugged. "Okay, maybe a little. I hate being the butt of their jokes."

"I don't think Drew was joking when he held you in his arms. He looked love struck."

"You've been in the sun too long." Molly took a drink of water. "My parents are sorry they couldn't come. They're babysitting for Miguel's kids. Did I tell you his wife is expecting number four?"

Grace's eyes widened. "Wow, that's great."

At any given moment, at least one of Molly's brothers was expecting a baby. Given the birth rate in her family, her brothers had proven very virile. She, on the other hand, was single and childless. The odd duck. Her nieces and nephews loved her as their cool aunt. Her *papá* loved she was a tough-girl police officer. He'd tell anyone who'd listen about how proud he was of his *hija*. Her *mamá* always encouraged her to follow her heart. Molly loved her family. They were her biggest cheering section.

Molly watched Drew exit the pool. As he toweled off, she held her breath. When he slid on a green T-shirt, she finally exhaled. "In other news, I might get a dog tomorrow."

"I didn't know you were thinking about a dog."

"I went to the shelter, just to look."

"That's how true love always begins." Grace laughed.

She rested her hand over her heart. "I met a sweet dog and kinda got attached. He's a Great Pyrenees breed. Huge, with tons of white fur. The shelter workers said someone brought him in as a stray. If no one claims him by tomorrow, he's mine."

"He sounds perfect." Grace rested her hands over her middle. "I'm not feeling well, so I'm heading inside to lie down for a bit."

As Grace rose from her chair, Heath came over to escort her into the house.

Weird. Lately, Heath had been acting even stranger than normal. Was Grace pregnant? *No.* Molly would be the first to know.

With the seat next to her vacant, Drew approached and plopped down.

Great. There went her insides again, all buzzing with nerves. Well, she'd think about her new dog. *Focus on the dog...Molly. Focus on the dog.* He'll be the one waiting at home after a long day at work. Not Drew.

****

"Sorry, Pixie." Drew sprawled out on the lounge chair next to Molly. "I don't know what came over me."

She scowled. "I know what came over you. You and your buddy, Heath, have the maturity of ten-year-old boys." Her dark eyebrows arched over the rim of her sunglasses.

She was so cute when she was mad. "What can I say? It's what happens when you live for a decade with a group of rowdy military guys. Not to mention now I spend most of my days with middle schoolers." His gaze slowly traveled up the entire length of her body. The same rockin' body that was now covered up. But he could still enjoy the view of her legs. Earlier, the sight of her in that purple bikini made his heart stop.

A hint of a smile pulled at her frown. "Fine, I forgive you. Just don't do it again. The consequences will be swift and severe."

"Deal." He reclined farther in his chair. Would one of her consequences be a kiss? Not likely, but a guy could always hope. "Looks like the food's ready. You want to eat?" He escorted Molly over to the deck where a table was set, piled high with food. Hamburgers, chips, pickles, corn on the cob, fruit salad in a watermelon bowl, and a row of desserts were laid out in a buffet. Drew filled his plate and followed Molly to chairs in the shade. "You've said you applied to the DEA," Drew said. "How does the process work?"

"Well." Molly's eyes brightened. "I've completed all the preliminary tests at the Houston division recruitment office. Now, I'm waiting to learn if I've been accepted to the academy. Then I'll be assigned a start date."

He could hear the passion and excitement in her voice. Joining the DEA was her mission, which left him with mixed emotions. Drew was impressed and inspired by her drive. He only wished her goals weren't leading her away. "If they're smart, they'll accept you."

She shrugged.

But he could see pride behind her smile.

"It's been a slow process, but I'm almost at the end. You might not be stuck with me for too much longer."

He'd like to be stuck with her forever. "We need you around here for as long as possible, especially with the Second Step program. I heard back from most of the kids about next Saturday." Drew picked off sesame seeds from his hamburger bun. "The city said a park employee will meet us at Snowfield Park."

"Have you heard from Whitney? I've lost hours of sleep worrying about the girl. She doesn't have a cell phone or internet access at home, so I haven't communicated with her since we were here at the ranch." She held a butter-soaked cob of corn with both hands and took a bite.

Drew was concerned about Whitney, as well. He'd never forgive himself if something bad happened to either her or her baby. "She emailed me Friday while she was at school. Said she wasn't feeling well, but she'd try to come. Can you give her a ride?"

"I can." Molly pierced a chunk of cantaloupe with her fork. "The drive will give us a chance to talk."

"What will happen when she turns eighteen? Does her mom have any obligation to care for her and the baby?" Whitney's situation left him feeling very uneasy. He knew the police could only do so much. Molly's hands were tied by the legal system, and he hoped Whitney's mom would not follow through on her threat to kick the girl out of the house once she became a legal adult. "I know her home isn't the best, but it's better than living in a shelter with a newborn."

Molly turned in her chair to face him. "Social Services would step in. I've contacted a home for pregnant teens. She could live there before and after the baby is born, which might be her best option."

"Well, let's see what the next few weeks bring. She's lucky to have you in her life." He desired to put his arm around Molly and wrap her in a strong hug.

The memory of her skin against his, so warm and silky smooth, drove him to distraction. Earlier, when he'd picked up Molly and jumped in the pool, he'd only been joking around. Now, the joke was on him. The controlled burn he carried had jumped the fire line, breaking out into a wildfire. She was clear that she only wanted him as a friend. Molly had ambitions outside Liberty Ridge.

He understood the dangers of law enforcement. He'd watched his mom struggle with being married to a cop and knew the stress of wondering if your spouse will come home alive at the end of the day.

Molly studied him with narrowed eyes. "Is something wrong?"

"No. Just worried about Whitney." He took a long drink of bottled water. Unfortunately, he had a bad habit of broadcasting his feelings through facial expressions. He wished he could read her as easily.

"Have you seen Grace?" She glanced around. "She went inside a while ago, and I haven't seen her since."

Drew shook his head. "Heath said she wasn't feeling well."

"Maybe I should go check on her."

As soon as she finished the sentence, Grace

appeared at the back door like a ghost who had just been summoned. "See, she's fine. Can I get you a refill on your lemonade?" *Or take you someplace private so I can have you all to myself?*

"You don't have to wait on me. I can get my own lemonade." She tapped a fingernail on the almost-empty glass.

"I'm sure you can." He couldn't help but grin at her stubborn pride. "But since I'm getting up anyway, I thought I'd be a gentleman and offer to serve you."

"Then yes...please." A small smile curved her lips. "Thanks."

He came back with a beer for himself and a full glass of lemonade for Molly. With a flourished bow, he handed it to her. "At your service, ma'am," he said with his best faux-Texas drawl.

Laughing, she clutched her stomach. "You talk Texan like a Yankee."

"I know." He chuckled. "But I'm proud of my northern roots. We have lots of things up north you can't get down here."

"Oh yeah?" She rested an elbow on the table and cupped her chin. "Like what?"

"Detroit is cool." Leaning in toward Molly, he inhaled the sweet scent of coconut sun lotion. "We have Red Wings hockey, which is awesome. And the downtown is filled with classic Art Deco architecture from the city's glory days. Detroit's the Motor City. The Midwest gets all four seasons, and summer's the best. And we actually have a real fall. Winter is snow and ice and days off of school. Then when spring finally comes, we all rejoice because we can leave the house again." He missed Detroit, but after the Army, he'd wanted one last adventure, so he moved to Texas and started the next chapter of his life.

"Sounds nice. I haven't traveled much outside of Texas. Can't tell you the last time I've seen snow." Molly gripped the base of her ponytail and tightened the rubber band holding it in place.

"I've lived all over the world, but there's no place like home." He lifted the glass bottle before him on the table and took a pull of beer. "I moved back after my service ended and earned my teaching degree, but then I got the itch to travel again. When Heath told me about Liberty Ridge, I figured the town sounded like a great place to settle down."

"Have your parents visited yet?"

"They called last night and said they're coming down at the end of the month. My sister is hopefully joining them." Thinking about Julia always left him with a hint of panic. Was she healthy? Had the leukemia returned? Could he donate to her again if it had? As he remembered trying to get back from Afghanistan to donate stem cells, a feeling of helplessness washed over him.

"I can't wait to meet them." Molly wiped her hands on a paper napkin.

Shouts came from the direction of the pool.

"Looks like they've started a volleyball game." She pointed to the group splashing in the water. "You want to join? We could team up and take down Heath."

Spunky Molly was always full of surprises. "Let's go show Heath what happens when he messes with my favorite cop." He stood and reached to take her hand before pulling her upright.

Molly's whole face glowed with excitement, and

she rubbed her hands together. "You might be my new favorite person."

Chapter Nine

Today was the day. Molly had gotten the call that morning. The mandatory waiting period had expired, and she could adopt Max. On her way to the shelter, she made a pit-stop at the pet store. Now, the back seat of her car was filled with dog food, bowls, a pet bed, and various toys. The poor employee who'd helped her had really earned his minimum wage pay.

She was halfway to the shelter when she decided to pay Whitney's mom a house call. As she turned onto Whitney's street, the items in her backseat rattled. She noticed a late-model car parked in the driveway. *Good.* Mommy dearest was home.

Molly walked to the front door and knocked.

A neighborhood dog barked with insistence. Other than the dog, the street was quiet. Because of the time, early afternoon on a weekday, most people were at either work or school.

No one answered the door so she knocked again. "Mrs. Logan, it's Officer Hernandez. I need to speak with you." She waited with no response. *Looks like I'll have to come back another time.*

Molly turned to leave and heard the door creak.

Barbara Logan peeked out. "What do you want?"

"I'm concerned about Whitney's situation." She stepped forward. "I want to make sure she's getting adequate medical care."

Barbara opened the door a little wider. Her face twisted. "Whitney's doin' just fine. She hasn't gotten caught shoplifting again, has she? That girl's always been trouble." She wagged a finger tipped with hot pink polish in Molly's face. "Don't let her fool you. She's not as innocent as she'd like you to think."

Molly's temper was rising—fast. "Mrs. Logan, have you taken Whitney to the free clinic yet?"

"First, you arrest my husband. Now, he can't come back home to live with his family. If Whitney's not doing well, it's your fault."

Molly's anger mixed with sympathy. Barbara was a woman who had no clue how to remedy her life. She was stuck in a cycle of abuse and ignorance. Her husband had too much control, even after being removed from the house. If Molly could do something to help Barbara she would, but short of a miracle, she didn't see any way to get through. But she could make a difference with Whitney. "Barbara, please answer my question. Have you taken your daughter to the doctor?"

"None of your business." Barbara began closing the door in Molly's face.

She kicked out her foot, catching it between the door and frame. "As a police officer, I'm charged with the well-being of all citizens, especially juveniles. So, this matter really is my business." By now, she was so mad she could spit tacks. "Let me tell you how this problem will be fixed. You have one week to take Whitney to the doctor. If you don't, I will have Child Protective Services all up in your business. Got it?" The face on the other side of the doorway drained of color. Even her healing bruises lost some of their sickly hue.

Barbara nodded.

Molly removed her foot, allowing the door to close. Turning on her heel, she strode to her car. Once inside, she closed her eyes and focused on taking deep breaths. She was involved with Whitney as part of the Second Step program, which meant Molly could make sure she received the care she needed. The teen was having a baby soon and still had to finish high school. Even though her own mother didn't give two thoughts to Whitney's well-being, Molly had the power to change Whitney's life for the better. A responsibility she didn't take lightly.

After her heart slowed to a normal rate, she put her car in Drive. Time to pick up her new dog. Ten minutes later, she stood in the lobby of the animal shelter. Her nervous energy was off the chart, first date level high. A brown leash hung from her wrist. The smell of the new leather was refreshing against the strong animal scent permeating the shelter.

While she waited for them to bring out Max, she flipped through potential names for her dog. Max wasn't a bad name, but she didn't think it suited him. Buster, Snowball, Harley? Maybe Flynn, like Flynn Rider from her favorite movie. Although Maximus might work? Which led her back to Max.

No need to make a decision now. She'd give herself a few days and see if the right name came along.

The sound of nails scratching across tile caught her attention.

The door opened, and her dog barreled out, pulling along a shelter volunteer. Max came over to sniff Molly's pants leg and shoes before sitting at her feet. His pink tongue hung out the side of his mouth, and his tail swished across the floor.

Did he know he was going home?

Once his temporary collar was off, Molly put on the new one. When she clipped on the leash, the dog stood at attention, tail wagging. "Thank you for your help," Molly said to Tippy, the elderly receptionist. Then she looked at the dog and scratched the top of his head. "You ready to go home?"

He barked his reply.

When she opened her car door, he jumped into the passenger seat like he'd been doing it all his life. On a whim, she drove past the middle school. She wanted to share her excitement with only one person—Drew.

She found him standing on the edge of the soccer field, wearing black athletic shorts and a white T-shirt. After finding a parking spot, she let out the dog and took hold of his leash. Drew's back was turned to them, so he didn't see her approach.

He blew his whistle and yelled out instructions to the team on the field.

Molly let the dog casually walk up to Drew and sit alongside him. They both watched the action on the field. Still holding the leash, she stood back a few steps and waited for Drew to notice his new partner.

Drew looked down then back up, and then down again, following the leash back to her. His face instantly brightened with a smile. "This is a pleasant surprise. Who's your friend?"

Molly stroked the dog's soft furry head. "Meet the new man in my life, Rider." The name was on the tip of her tongue without even thinking. Rider was the name.

"Hey, Rider. Pleased to meet you." Drew scratched behind the dog's floppy ear. "I didn't know you were getting a dog. Why didn't you tell me yesterday at the pool party?"

Two sweaty boys approached and tossed Drew a soccer ball.

"Three laps around the field," Drew said to his team. "Then you can go."

The soccer team darted away—some as fast as cheetahs, and others as tired and cumbersome as elephants. The noise of rambunctious chatter slowly faded as the bulk of boys made it to the far side of the soccer field.

"I didn't know for sure I'd get him until this morning. He had a mandatory hold at the shelter. I only went there to take a look, but with Rider, it was love at first sight."

"You're a lucky dude." Drew patted the dog's back. "How about we go sit, and you can tell me all about Rider?" He pointed to a group of trees off to the side.

Most of the soccer team had finished running their laps and started toward the school. Several hollered goodbye to Mr. Atwater.

She sat on a shaded patch of grass. Molly kicked off her sandals and wiggled her toes over the soft blades. "Are you done for the day?"

Rider lay down between them and rested his head on her lap.

"Almost. I have a stack of eighth grade tests that need correcting before I can go home. Practice days usually keep me at school later than normal."

Should she invite him to dinner? As a friend, of course. The words stuck in her throat. She coughed, dislodging the mental block. "Would you like to come to my place for dinner tonight? After you're done here."

Acting nonchalant, she plucked at the weeds growing on the ground around her. *So many interesting weeds.*

"Dinner would be nice. I'd just planned on grabbing take-out." He set his hands behind him and leaned back.

"Good," she said. "Rider wanted me to ask you over."

The dog's ears perked up at his new name.

Smart dog. She better be careful what other words he learned.

"Thanks, Rider," Drew said. "Maybe you can give me some tips on how to be smooth with the ladies. You seem to have a way of making them fall in love with you."

"I'm sure he'd share his secrets." She ruffled the shaggy fur on top Rider's head. "I should let you go finish your work. When should I expect you?"

Drew stood and reached out his hand to help her up.

As always, his touch left her dizzy.

"How about six?" he asked. "I'll go home quick and shower."

"Six it is. See you soon." She pulled on Rider's leash and started back toward her car, blinking with disbelief. What in the world had possessed her to invite him over for dinner?

****

Drew rushed through grading his tests. Lucky kids. He probably missed more than one incorrect answer. He didn't care. He was going to Molly's house for dinner. After a quick shower, he stood in his closet, deciding what to wear. He didn't want to overdress, like he was trying too hard. Then again, overly casual would also send the wrong message.

Stop fussing and pick something already! The longer he dwelt on what might happen tonight, the more nervous he became. Finally, he picked out a red polo and khaki shorts. He ran a comb through his hair, thinking it needed a trim. After a splash of cologne, he grabbed his car keys.

On the way over, he stopped at the store to pick up wine and flowers. The flowers were easy. Daisies seemed like something friends would give one another. Because friends was all they were. The wine on the other hand was a bit more challenging. Red or white? Sweet, dry, or semi-sweet? Too many choices. He finally closed his eyes and picked. *Hope she likes Pinot Grigio.*

When he knocked, Molly answered the door with the dog by her side. "Come on in. I just put the steaks on the grill."

In the comfort of home, she looked very pretty. Gold toe rings shone on her bare feet. Her glorious mane of brown hair fell around her shoulders. *Breathe, man...don't forget to breathe.*

She guided him to the kitchen, and he handed her the wine and flowers.

"It's for your dog." The last thing he wanted was her thinking he saw this dinner as a date.

"Really?" She read the label on the wine bottle. "You brought flowers and wine for Rider. He's more of a beef treats and water kind of guy."

He laughed. "No, they're for you in celebration of Rider finding his forever home."

"Thanks." She opened a cabinet and pulled out a vase for the flowers. "They're lovely."

Just like you. Drew bent to pet the dog, which seemed like a safe activity for his overly active mind.

"Good choice on the wine. Pinot Grigio is one of my favorites."

He only had luck to thank for that. "I'll put it in the fridge. Would you mind if I help myself to a glass of ice water?"

"Sure." Molly spread butter on a loaf of French bread. "The glasses are up there on your left."

His mouth felt as dry as dusty paper in an old book. He took a long drink, and the cold water hydrated his throat. "What can I do to help?"

"Go flip the steaks. The spatula is already out there." With a knife in her hand, she pointed to the sliding glass door.

Drew opened the door and followed his nose toward the intoxicating smell of grilled meat. As he opened the lid, heat rose to meet his face. Two T-Bones cooked on the grate, still red on top. He flipped them over and closed the cover. "Mission accomplished," he said when he returned inside. "You have a nice house. How's Rider settling in?"

As Molly tossed the salad, a few pieces of lettuce escaped the bowl. "He seems happy, so far. I'm still working out the details, but I think he'll need walking at least once during the day while I'm at work. Otherwise, he's home a long time without a potty break."

"I could give you some names of kids in my class who I think would be responsible enough to hire as a dog walker." Drew took a seat on a bar stool, snuck a carrot out of the salad bowl, and watched Molly work. She zipped around the kitchen, pulling out this and mixing that. He could easily imagine their children running around her legs as she cooked. Molly unknowingly breathed life into his dreams.

"Can you grab two plates?" she asked. "They're in the cabinet by the glasses."

The smell in her kitchen made his stomach clench with hunger. In his hurry to help, he almost dropped a plate.

Molly came back with the steaks, still sizzling. She set a steak on each plate, and then filled the empty space with salad and a slice of buttered bread.

"Silverware and napkins are already on the patio table. Can you bring our dinner plates? I'll carry the wine." Molly exited the house holding two empty glasses and an opened wine bottle.

He followed her out. After setting down their dinner plates, he took the bottle and opened it, before pouring them each a glass. Sitting, he raised his glass. "To Rider," Drew toasted. "The luckiest guy in the world."

At the sound of his name, the white dog sat up.

If he could be jealous of a dog, he'd be jealous of Rider. Molly opened her heart to him without a second thought. With Drew, she seemed determined to keep him at arm's length. But tonight, she'd asked him over for dinner. For now, he'd enjoy the time with her and not stress about the future. "Was Rider the name he was given at the shelter?"

"They named him Max. I came up with Rider, and I think he kinda likes it."

"I like it." He took a sip of wine, which tasted refreshingly good. "Rider's not the name of an ex-boyfriend or secret crush, is it?"

"Well, kind of. Not an old boyfriend but a secret crush."

The muscles in his stomach tensed. Who was this Rider? Drew would hurt him if he put the moves on Molly.

Her face split into a smile. "It's the last name of a character in one of my favorite movies," she said as she peered over her wineglass and batted her eyelashes. "He's a cartoon, and for a fictional character, he's quite dreamy."

He couldn't hold back his laughter. "You named your dog after a cartoon character?"

Molly swatted him on the arm. "Shut it. The movie is a retelling of Rapunzel, and the story is very romantic."

"I'll take your word." Drew smiled over his glass and took a drink.

"Don't judge until you've seen the movie." Molly crossed her arms.

"We didn't watch those cartoon types on my military bases."

"Well, maybe you brutes should have. A good musical romance is good for morale. After all, love makes the world go round." Her face grew more animated as she talked.

"I'm having a hard time picturing you watching animated movies." If Drew was enamored with her before, his heart was now a complete goner. Underneath her tough exterior lay a soft heart. Maybe that's why she tried so hard to protect it. He began to understand she was more sensitive than people gave her credit for.

"Now that I have Rider, we'll have to plan a movie

night. Would you like to join us?"

Instead of jumping up and pumping his fist like he wanted to, he gently set down his fork and smiled. "I could probably be persuaded."

Chapter Ten

The Damn Yankee bar was packed. Molly, Grace, and Colleen pounced on an empty booth, sat, and ordered drinks.

"So, I finally told Heath." Grace waved a finger in the air. "I will take that motorcycle apart with my bare hands if you aren't more careful."

"That would be awesome." Molly poured a glass of beer from the pitcher the waitress just set on the table. "You sure you don't want any?" she asked Grace.

Grace waved it away. "Clear soda is all my tummy needs. I still don't feel one hundred percent."

"That sucks." Colleen scrunched her nose. "I heard there's this strange stomach bug going around that has people sick for weeks. I hope you start feeling better."

"Thanks." Grace sipped her soda through a striped straw. "So how's the pup, Molly?"

"Rider's good. He's the perfect roommate—doesn't hog the bed, always ready for a walk, and the best listener a girl could ask for." Molly took a sip of beer. The cold liquid slid down her throat. The alcohol went to work, radiating from her core. In minutes, her body relaxed.

"Heath's dog, Shadow, barely leaves his side," Grace said. "Even at night. He sleeps on the floor at the foot of our bed. I can't tell you how many times he's woken Heath out of a nightmare."

Nodding, Colleen scooped salsa on a large tortilla chip. "Shadow may not be a trained therapy dog, but he has a natural instinct for sensing when Heath needs him. Therapy dogs are a blessing for soldiers suffering with PTSD. They can sometimes make the difference between life and death."

"Is Drew seeing you professionally?" Molly asked Colleen. She often wondered how much emotional baggage Drew carried after so many deployments. He didn't seem haunted by the same demons as Heath, but she couldn't imagine anyone could walk away without a few scars.

"Ask Drew." Her face grew serious, and her lips pressed tight. "I'm sure he'll be forthcoming. You two have gotten very close lately."

Molly squirmed in her seat. She never should have brought up Drew's name. "We've been working together with the Second Step program."

"You don't have to pretend around us." Grace leaned forward on the table. "You two radiate a heated energy whenever you're around each other. Are you afraid of getting burned?"

After lifting up her mug, Molly took a long drink. "Drew and I are a non-issue. Is he a great guy? Sure. And he'll make some woman a great husband. But that someone will not be me."

"Why not?" Colleen raised her eyebrows and looked from Grace to Molly.

Resigned, Molly decided to trust Colleen with the truth. In the two years since her surgery, she had only told her family and Grace. She remembered the feeling of the heavy curtain of anesthesia lifting and the struggle to find her way out of the fog. Her body was relaxed and warm, tucked under blankets. As she came to, the beeping next to her bed grew louder.

"*Mi ángel*." *Mamá* put her hand over Molly's. "The doctor said you did well."

Molly opened her eyes to see her parents and Grace standing by her bedside. She moved her free hand to cover her abdomen and touched the bandages. Pain pulsated from her core. "Water," she whispered.

Grace raised a cup and put the straw to Molly's lips.

The water smoothed her dry throat.

How had she ended up in a hospital bed so fast? The fogginess inside her brain began lifting. Only a few months ago, she was diagnosed with cervical cancer. She had just undergone a radical hysterectomy. After her body healed, she'd next start radiation to kill any remaining cancer cells.

The doctors reassured her by saying they recommended an aggressive approach to improve the odds against a recurrence. A radical hysterectomy was a drastic step for someone in her twenties, but after all the clinical evidence and second opinions, Molly was left with little choice. Her dreams of pregnancy and babies were buried in a deeply private portion of her heart. Part of her died the day of her surgery.

But something came alive in her, too. A deep desire to pursue her dreams of being a Federal Agent. Before, joining the DEA had been a far-out idea tucked in the back of her mind. A 'someday' dream. Following the operation, she had a second chance. One she wouldn't take for granted. Her life took an unexpected turn, and she didn't want to grieve for what she'd lost. Molly wanted to celebrate what she had conquered.

After all, she was a survivor.

Now, sitting with her friends, she knew she could trust Colleen's loyalty. Molly wrapped herself in the comfortable coat of fake indifference, one that was threadbare after repeated use. "Two years ago, I was diagnosed with an aggressive form of cervical cancer. I had a hysterectomy and can't have children."

Colleen's eyes glistened with tears, and she leaned in, taking hold of Molly's hand. "I'm so sorry."

"So you understand why a relationship between Drew and I would never work. He wants a big family. Besides, I'm leaving Liberty Ridge, and he's putting down roots." She tapped her finger on the table. "We're heading in very different directions."

A loud shout sounded from across the bar, followed by laughter. Their waitress dropped off another basket of chips.

"Tell him what you just told me." Colleen set her glass on the glossy wood table. Drops of condensation rolled down the grooved sides of the mug. "He might surprise you."

"My cancer and surgery are things I keep very private." Molly could imagine Drew's reaction if she told him. Rejection would soon follow any confession. Why would she put herself through that? In the end, Drew would marry someone else, and she'd move away to pursue her own goals. She didn't see a scenario where sharing her infertility would work to her benefit.

Colleen opened her mouth to speak but snapped her lips shut.

Drew entered through the front door of the bar. He strode across the room, stepping in time to the country song playing on the jukebox, and stopped at an occupied booth at the other side of the room.

Molly's heart squeezed with longing. She held up her hands and narrowed her eyes. "Don't either one of you say a word."

"What about adoption?" Grace asked. "Many people become parents through adopting a child."

A long sigh escaped Molly. "I appreciate you playing matchmaker but adoption takes time, if it ever happens at all. And honestly, I don't know if I want to be a mom." A career in the DEA wouldn't leave much time for a family. Particularly because as a woman, she'd have to work twice as hard as the men. "Drew and I are not meant to be. That's the end."

Thankfully, Grace and Colleen dropped the subject and talked about more lighthearted things—like the new bookstore that just opened on Main Street, Marcy Firestone's fundraising effort for the library, and the chocolate raspberry cupcakes at A Bonnie Bakery.

Molly stuffed her mouth full of chips and salsa, watching Drew approach and stop at their table. The man looked extra handsome tonight, in faded blue jeans, scuffed sneakers, and a red button-up shirt that was a delicious contrast to his coloring.

He slid onto the booth next to her. "What brings you lovely ladies out on this fine evening?"

"Girls' night." Grace smiled at Drew before peering side-eyed at Molly.

An electric pulse tingled across her skin, and she fought against choking while working down the food in her mouth. She needed several sips of cold beer to clear her throat and cool off.

Drew reached across and stole a chip out of the basket. "Cool. I got roped into a party. Heidi, one of the

English teachers, is turning thirty."

With a quick glance over her shoulder, Molly spied a cute blonde wearing a birthday tiara. The expression on the woman's face as she glared back at Molly could have soured a glass of sweet tea. "Looks like someone's setting you up." Molly's stoic expression broke into a smile. "Is it working?"

Drew blushed. "Ummm…no." He swung up an arm onto the back of the booth and rested a hand on Molly's shoulder. "Heidi's a little too happy for my taste."

The guy was cute when he played coy. "Well, you know what they say…happy wife, happy life." Her entire body heated as a result of his touch. If his hand remained on her shoulder much longer, she might spontaneously combust.

"I know the expression, but I get annoyed by someone constantly laughing at everything I say, even when I know what I said wasn't the least bit funny."

Molly stared, expressionless. "Oh, please. Men love a woman who makes them feel like the funniest, most interesting man alive. A real ego boost."

"You are extra prickly tonight, Pixie. What did they put in your beer?" Drew pinched her shoulder. Grinning, he peered into her almost-empty mug.

Heat flushed up her cheeks. Why did he have to use that nickname in front of Grace and Colleen? She could almost see the gears turning in both women's heads.

"Looks like the birthday girl is missing you." Molly gave him a light push. As he moved away, the tightness in her chest loosened. She needed every ounce of self-control to resist pulling him back. "Must be exhausting being constantly pursued by beautiful women." She hoped a joke would take away attention from the heat rushing up her face.

"Why do you think I'm so tired all the time?" He winked at Grace and Colleen. "I'll leave you lovely ladies to your drinks." Now standing, he turned his gaze to Molly. "Don't worry, Pixie. You're not hurting my feelings. I've gotten to know you pretty well, and I've come to a conclusion."

"Please enlighten me." Molly crossed her arms over her chest and raised her chin to meet his gaze.

Drew set his palms on the table and leaned toward her. "I'm getting to you."

Molly huffed. "I have no idea what you're talking about."

He lowered his head to put his lips next to her ear. "I think you do."

****

Drew could have kicked himself. *I'm getting to you.* What a dumb thing to say. He'd been so good up until now, happily hanging out in the friend zone. After flirting with Molly, in front of her friends no less, he was lucky she didn't toss him out on his ear.

With dragging feet, he returned to the group of teachers. Every once in awhile, he snuck a peek at Molly, noticing she kept her body angled so her back faced him. *Yup, still ticked.*

Drew Atwater, socially awkward science teacher, table for one.

After dinner together a few nights ago, he'd felt good about where things stood. But being around her did weird things to his brain. She drove him crazy, in the best possible way, with her sharp tongue and take-no-prisoners attitude. Truthfully, overly cheery women got on his nerves. Heidi, now sitting next to him, with her constant high-pitched laugh, made him want to run away screaming.

Again, he glanced over at Molly. The pink sundress she wore made her glow, and the dim lights of the bar reflected off the waves of her chestnut hair.

Heidi touched his thigh and leaned in. "You want a refill on that drink?"

"No, thanks. I'm heading out." He stood to remove himself from her reach.

"Already? I hoped you'd come back to my place." Her bottom lip curved out.

Inwardly, he sighed. He should have stayed at Molly's table. "Sorry, but I have an early start tomorrow. I'm taking a group of teens to Snowfield Park to help clean up the grounds."

"That does not sound like a fun time." Heidi sipped at her wine. "Weekends are supposed to be our break from kids."

He shrugged. "I have fun, and so do the teens. Enjoy the rest of your birthday celebration." On his way toward the exit, he swung past Molly's table. "See you tomorrow."

"Bright and early. I'll try to be on time." Her lips moved in a slight smile.

No one else would have caught her fleeting expression. But he did—and the signal gave him hope.

Chapter Eleven

"Mark, Sam…take the wheelbarrow and shovels over to those small bushes. Pull out the dead ones, and then toss them into the wheelbarrow. Dump the load on the brush pile behind the tool shed." Drew dished out instructions to the teens.

At first, they complained about doing manual labor, but after a little encouragement, everyone fell in line and pulled their weight. Laura and Charlie were raking out the baseball diamonds. Molly sat with Whitney over by the flowerbeds, pulling weeds.

While he supervised the activity, he worked on the puzzle Molly presented. She'd been friendly this morning, which relieved his anxiety. After their interaction at the bar last night, he'd worried she'd be upset at his flirting. Molly's friendship was important to him, regardless of her romantic rejection.

Rider lay by Molly's side while she worked in the flowerbed. Her dog was the best behaved canine he'd ever seen.

Whitney and Molly engaged in conversation. Every once in awhile, Molly stopped and talked with her hands. Officer Hernandez might be a tough cop, but she had a soft heart.

Whitney was safe under her protective wing. She was fortunate to have such a strong advocate. Her baby bump still looked undersized for being seven months pregnant, but she had a new glow.

He was happy to learn Whitney had visited the doctor and started taking prenatal vitamins. Maybe now the young mother and baby had a fighting chance.

A nice breeze rustled through the large oak and ash trees scattered around the park. Above, the azure sky glimmered. He'd ordered the perfect day. Luckily, the predicted thunderstorms moved farther north, which left them with cool, dry weather.

As he raked old leaves from underneath the brush, he noticed a burn in the muscles in his arms and shoulders. He missed the regular physical labor of the Army. He also missed the camaraderie of working together toward a common goal.

The rumble of an approaching engine broke the peace and quiet of the park. He raised his gaze to see two fire trucks driving into the parking lot. Once they came to a stop, a dozen or so firefighters hopped out and began pulling out equipment.

"What's goin' on, Mr. A.?" Kelly asked.

"Not sure." He studied the activity. "The fire department may be training. We'll have to wait and see." He didn't care what they were doing, as long as they didn't bother his group. But his attitude changed when three of the firemen broke off from the pack and headed straight for Molly. A knot of unease twisted in his gut. As a police officer, Molly would have worked often with the fire department. They were professional colleagues. But something about the way they approached Molly seemed overly friendly.

Even from fifty yards away, he could see their flirty smiles. Two of them even hugged her. All three looked physically fit.

Drew glared at Rider, sending the dog a telepathic message to bite the newcomers. Didn't work. Rider continued his sniff inspection and finally sat at Molly's feet.

Before his common sense got the better of him, he dropped his rake and strode over to Molly. He had no claim on her. No right to be jealous. But he was. A territorial compulsion rose inside his chest. At that moment, he didn't care if he pounded his chest like a caveman. He'd make them aware Molly was with him.

****

A wall of testosterone surrounded Molly. All four men puffed out their chests and straightened their shoulders, and each one seemed to double in size. She was in the middle of a freaking National Geographic wildlife special called *The Territorial Male*.

Two of the firemen she already knew. Matt and Kevin had been with the Liberty Ridge Fire Department for about the same amount of time she'd been with the Police Department. During combined training exercises and numerous calls, they'd become fast friends. She respected the men as professionals and individuals. Since both were married, she enjoyed hanging out with them without the risk of romantic entanglements.

Peter, on the other hand, was new to the Liberty Ridge Fire Department. Tall, with broad shoulders and shaggy light hair, he seemed specially made for the town's annual firefighter calendar.

Whitney gazed up at the men with eyes as large as blue buttons.

"Hey." Drew gave each man a stiff-armed handshake, and then turned his attention to Molly. "Did you pack drinks in the cooler?"

"Yes." She slowly nodded her head. "You were right next to me when I put them in."

Drew shifted his weight back and forth between his wide-set legs. "The kids look thirsty. Now's a good time for a break."

Okay. I'll play along. "Sounds good. As long as you're here, I'd like you to meet Matt, Kevin, and Peter. The Fire Department is running training exercises today." She stopped talking and watched the men size each other up—again.

"Don't worry," Peter said with a grin. "We won't interrupt your gardening."

"We're not gardening."

Drew's voice sounded cool and calm, which she understood as his way of projecting unwavering confidence. A real turn-on. Molly glanced at Matt and Kevin. "I can't believe the Firefighters' Ball is less than two months away. You guys need any help?"

"We have a solid group of volunteers, so I think you're off the hook. But thanks for the offer. Looks like you already have a full plate." Kevin pointed at the teenagers scattered around the park.

Peter sent her a dimpled smile. "Do you have a date for the ball, Molly?"

He held his flirty smile, and her knees actually felt weak. "No date. Not yet, anyway."

Peter would be the perfect date. He was handsome beyond words, but she felt only a shallow attraction. She didn't have to worry about him breaking her heart. Being with Peter would be simple and over soon. He'd be like most men she'd dated, whom grew to dislike her blunt manner and sharp tongue.

The attraction of a tough girl was an illusion. She

learned men often deferred back to a more feminine and cheerful woman. Molly didn't need a man to save her. She could save herself. And that reality, with so many men, was a problem.

"Then how about we go together?" Peter hooked his thumbs in the suspenders attached to his turnout pants.

Out of the corner of her eye, she saw Drew clench his fist. "Sounds fun. We can talk later about the details. Kevin has my number." Another benefit of attending the ball with Peter was showing Drew he was not 'getting to her,' as he'd so eloquently said last night.

"Cool. See you later. We'll try not to get you wet." Peter's blue eyes twinkled. He sauntered back to the fire trucks, along with Matt and Kevin.

"You're seriously going with him?" Drew huffed. "You're lucky a mirror wasn't nearby, or he'd never have noticed you."

"Chill. I'm not dating him. It's only one night." A wave of satisfaction rushed through her. As much as she delighted in his jealousy, she acknowledged both their feelings were unproductive.

"What about me? I don't have a date." Drew frowned and furrowed his brow.

Good thing he didn't realize how adorable he was when he pouted.

He brushed his hand across the top of his head. "I didn't have a chance to ask you, because nobody told me about the Firefighters' Ball."

Whitney was now totally engrossed by the drama happening a few feet away, which did not escape Molly's notice. The teen pulled weeds at an agonizingly slow pace, looking like she gobbled up every juicy word.

The game she and Drew played had to stop. No more push-pull of attraction and dismissal. They were adults, not a couple of high school kids who couldn't figure out the rules of dating. "I'm sure you'll find a date. You have plenty of time." She patted him on the back. "Everyone can grab a drink and then get back to work."

Drew turned his head toward Sam and Kelly sitting in the shade of a tree, doing a little flirting of their own. He mumbled something under his breath and marched off.

"I think Mr. Atwater likes you," Whitney said once he was out of hearing range. "He looked mad when you were talking with the firemen."

Molly knelt and tilled the ground with her trowel. She dumped black dirt, along with a fat worm, onto the earth. "You just witnessed the perfect example of what's wrong with the male species," she said. "For a minute there, I was afraid they'd start head-butting like a couple of bighorn rams."

Whitney sat back on her heels and sighed. "My old boyfriend, the one who got me pregnant, hated when I talked to other guys. Now, he doesn't want anything to do with me."

Sorrow burned the back of her throat. "Does he know about the baby?"

"Oh, yeah. I told him as soon as I found out. He said to get an abortion and leave him alone."

Nausea rolled through Molly's stomach. *What a dirtbag!* He was old enough to get a girl pregnant but wouldn't take responsibility for his actions. "Once the baby is born, you can establish paternity. Then, the court will make him pay you child support." The teen was too young to deal with such complicated adult issues.

Whitney's cheeks flushed pink. "I don't want him anywhere near my baby. Hank's not a very nice guy. He used to hit me."

Molly rested her balled fists on the tops of her thighs. "No one has the right to hit you." Tears dampened the corners of her eyes. "Not a boyfriend, or a husband, or a parent. You are much too valuable of a person, and so is the little one you're carrying."

"Thank you so much, Officer Her—"

"We're friends. You call me Molly."

As they knelt on the ground, Whitney's thin arms wrapped around Molly's neck. "I want to grow up to be strong like you. I bet no one messes with you."

Taking off her LRPD ball cap, she placed it on Whitney's head. "Oh, people try. Strength on the inside is just as important as strength on the outside. You have your whole life ahead of you. Keep making good choices." She smiled encouragingly. "You're headed in the right direction."

Whitney dried her tears on the hem of her shirt. "I don't even know if I'll make it through high school. How will I finish after I have the baby?"

"Have you talked to the school counselor?"

"At the beginning of the year. I got so confused. I don't know what I'm supposed to do."

Whitney obviously needed her guidance. She would need help for the foreseeable future. If Molly followed through on her plan to leave Liberty Ridge, she'd ensure a support system was in place for

Whitney. "How about I make an appointment with your counselor? The three of us can make a plan so you meet your graduation requirements. Does that sound okay?"

"Yes." Whitney's blue eyes beamed.

For the first time since Molly met her, Whitney appeared genuinely happy.

****

At noon, they broke for lunch. The teens congregated on one picnic table, while Drew and Molly ate at another.

"Do you realize we're running the Breakfast Club?" Drew took a long drink of icy cold water.

"What do you mean?" Molly arranged her plate, plastic ware, and napkin before her on the table.

"We're here on a Saturday morning, supervising a group of teenage misfit troublemakers. Don't tell me you've never seen the movie." He inhaled the wonderful smell of roast beef and fresh bread before taking a bite of his sandwich.

Molly cocked an eyebrow. "I have. But the movie takes place in a high school, and we're at a park. Plus, the principal was a big jerk. Does that make one of us the jerky principal?"

His jaw dropped at her outlandish suggestion. "Of course not. You and I are cool. These kids love us." Drew pointed at the other table filled with talkative teens.

She snorted. "Love may be too strong a word."

"Well, Whitney loves you. You're the first person she's probably had in her life who truly cares."

"I'm happy I can make a difference."

Molly had a dot of mustard on the side of her mouth, which made Drew want to lean across and kiss her lips. She must have noticed his stare, because she got a napkin and wiped her face. His thoughts turned to Peter and the guy's smooth moves on Molly. She'd just met the guy and accepted his offer right on the spot. With Drew as a witness.

Until today, he'd never heard of the Firefighters' Ball. He would go for sure, with or without a date. No way would Molly spend the whole evening with backdraft Pete. Drew'd make sure of that.

"What's with the pouty face?" Molly glanced over the sandwich in her hands.

"I don't have a pouty face." Why was his face an open window to his emotions? He'd think about something else besides that stupid ball—and Molly dancing with Peter. His gaze rested on her full lower lip. *Not helping.*

"What's going on with you? You're acting weirder than normal." Molly's lips twitched with a smile.

How would she react if he told her how he felt about her? He couldn't risk losing her friendship. Best to play it safe. "My parents called this morning. They bought their plane tickets."

"So they're coming for a visit? What about your sister?"

"Julia is coming, too. I love my mom, but I'm not ready for the inquisition once they get here." He cleared his throat. "Have you found a nice girl to settle down with yet? Are you eating healthy? Should I start shopping for a mother of the groom dress? How much longer do I have to wait for grandchildren?" Drew ticked off each question on his fingers.

Molly nodded and laughed. "Sounds just like *Mamá*. We should set up our mothers for a lunch date.

They can commiserate about their unmarried children."

With his forearms resting on the table, he leaned forward. "You realize within thirty minutes of meeting, they'll have our wedding planned?"

Her eyes grew wide. "Definitely keep them apart. Don't even let them in the same room together."

He made an honest effort not to be offended and glanced over at the students still hanging out around the picnic table, allowing him some time to recoup his pride. Did she think marrying him would be that bad?

She tossed the last of her sandwich to Rider, who gobbled it down. "Sounds like we've both been blessed with loving families. Not everyone can say that."

"My home and parents were a safe harbor in some very troubled waters. Being biracial had its challenges. Still does, at times." His pulse quickened. "Plus, I was a cop's kid in an inner city school. I was picked on a lot, because I liked school and learning and had big dreams. I wanted to leave Detroit and see the world. So I concentrated on doing well in school."

"All those challenges made you stronger." She sat sideways and stretched out her legs along the bench.

"Definitely." Drew nodded. "In high school, I joined the science club. We were the nerdiest group of kids, but we banded together. We outsmarted and outmaneuvered all those wannabe gangsters roaming the halls." Surprisingly, Molly didn't laugh.

"I bet you made a cute nerd. I'm glad you found a group of kids you could count on. Grace and I have had each other's backs since kindergarten."

"My parents had very high expectations." At the time, Drew hated being held to such extreme standards. Now as an adult, he appreciated all his parents had done. Drew was a strong-willed child, and his dad had been both understanding and firm. They hadn't seen eye to eye on many things. Drew saw the world as either right or wrong. He had an analytical mind and didn't tolerate straying too far from the assigned path.

Dale, his dad, taught him to think outside the box. Sometimes, the world wasn't black or white. The answers for many of life's riddles couldn't be found by following a straight line. Compromise was the key to good relationships. Drew wished he'd paid more attention to his dad's lessons.

"My parents emigrated from Mexico in their early twenties. They worked hard and built a life here, and they expected their kids to do the same."

"Your parents did a great job with you."

"Thanks." She gazed down at her lap.

Her soft smile made her face glow. The intensity of his attraction blasted apart his self-control. All he could think about was pulling her into his arms. Everything inside him ached because he couldn't. "I hope I can do as good of a job with my own kids, someday."

Molly's body stiffened. Her smile faded. "We need to get these kids working." She stood and walked away.

Still sitting at the picnic table, Drew rubbed both palms down his face and sighed. His plan of finding a wife within a year was in danger of running off the tracks. All because of his stubborn, opinionated heart. While struggling with his intense attraction to Molly, he came to the conclusion his dating spreadsheet had grown obsolete.

Chapter Twelve

Rich is back. As she floated from class to class, Whitney replayed those words over and over in her head. If she was a ghost, the people around her would have paid her more attention. As it was, she spent her day avoiding the crowds in the hallways, trying to protect her belly.

Yesterday at school, she'd felt so good, until she'd arrived home. She gotten a B on her math test and couldn't wait to tell her mom. Since Rich had been ordered to stay away from their house, things had been quiet. Her mom acted interested in her. But everything changed when Whitney walked in the back door and saw Rich sitting at their kitchen table, a can of beer in his hand.

Her stomach sickened at the sight. How could Mom have let him back, even after the courts order was issued to protect them? This man was nothing special. He was ugly, fat, and mean, and he didn't even know the meaning of love.

She fled to her room and slammed the door behind her. Not after too much longer, the yelling started. First, the sounds could be blocked out with her head sandwiched between two pillows. Then, something shattered, and all hell broke loose. Whitney heard the door slam, and she let go a sigh of relief. Rich had left. Her mom actually tossed out his sorry butt.

Whitney placed the palm of her hand on top of her baby bump. Inside, the baby moved with shared happiness. She'd protect her son or daughter, no matter what. Her new friendship with Officer Molly gave her a whole new outlook on her life. The future didn't seem so scary anymore. Maybe she'd go to college or a trade school. She'd make sure her baby grew up safe and loved, whether that was with her or another family.

Lost in daydreams, Whitney began humming a lullaby. Hearing the floor creak, she looked over and a frosty chill settled over her skin. A nightmare had returned to life.

****

The Liberty Ridge Police Department bustled with activity. Phones rang in a constant, annoying harmony. Voices from multiple conversations echoed through the room. Every few minutes, someone would clear a throat.

Molly blocked out all the noise and concentrated on completing her tenth report of the day. This one went straight to the Police Chief. He wanted a detailed account of her activities so far as the department's SRO. Since school had only been in session for less than two months, she didn't have much to report. Besides her classroom presentations, she'd handled a few truancies, one call for a disciplinary problem, and an incident of marijuana found on the high school campus.

Finally finished, thank goodness, she hit Save just as her desk phone rang. "Officer Hernandez."

"Molly?" A quiet voice sounded.

Fear settled in Molly's gut. "Whitney? What's going on?" She forced calm into her voice, despite the chill growing inside.

"I'm at school, in the office. Can you come...I mean, if it wouldn't be too much trouble." Sobbing punctuated her sentence.

"I'll be right there." Molly logged off her computer. "Are you hurt?"

"My mom let Rich come home last night. He made bail. A restraining order was issued against him, but my mom didn't care. I'm afraid to go home."

A strong surge of adrenaline increased her heart rate, and Molly fought the urge to either cry herself or kick something, or both. "Hang tight. I'm on my way."

The high school had just dismissed when she arrived. Waves of teenagers exited out of the building, flooding their surroundings, like released water from a dam. As she made her way inside, more than one student gave her an uneasy sideways glance. *It's your lucky day, because whatever you've done, I'm not here for you.*

Whitney's stepdad, on the other hand, would learn the meaning of crime and punishment.

She entered the school's main office and saw Whitney sitting on a plastic chair along the wall.

At Molly's arrival, she uncurled her body to stand. A smile brightened her otherwise cloudy face.

Molly scanned Whitney, checking for signs of injury. All looked normal. No bruising. Relief replaced fear. But as she stepped closer, her gaze lowered to Whitney's exposed arms. Shock turned to red, hot anger. Marking Whitney's smooth skin were a multitude of circular burn marks. So, Rich Logan had moved on to abusing his stepdaughter.

Domestic abusers usually had a pattern and a

favorite victim, but when he or she wasn't within reach, another would serve their purpose just as well. Rich didn't care if that person happened to be a pregnant, seventeen-year-old girl. "Let's find a private place to talk." Molly led her into an empty office.

Whitney sat on a padded metal chair. "Rich got home last night. He started drinking, and my mom ran to the store to buy him more booze. She said he deserved to relax after being in prison." Her body trembled. "I did my best to stay out of his way, honest, but he came to my room and grabbed my arm and pulled me out. Then he took his cigarette and burned my arm, over and over." She bit her lower lip and sniffled.

"Why didn't you call me? I would have come over and arrested him." In an effort to control her voice, Molly tensed, her brow beaded with sweat.

"Our home phone got cut off, because they didn't pay the bill. I thought he would leave me alone once he'd got bored, but he just got more and more mad." She wiped the backside of her hand across both eyes. "I finally kicked him in the shin and locked myself in my room."

Molly's hands shook with fury. "What did your mom do when she found out?"

"Nothing. She looked sad but said she couldn't do anything. If she said something, Rich would hit her."

Molly lifted a few tissues from the box on the desk and handed them to Whitney. "Are you willing to come to the station and give a statement?"

"Uh-huh." Whitney nodded.

"I'll take you to the doctor. They'll check you over and treat your burns." Molly wished the doctors could heal Whitney's emotional wounds as easily. "Rich Logan is going back to jail. I'll personally make sure of it."

"I want him to know I'm stronger than him." Whitney's small chin rose with each word.

At that moment, Molly had never been more proud. "You are very brave." She helped Whitney stand and gave her a hug. "Together, we'll make sure he learns he can't get away with hurting you."

Later at the station, Whitney waited in the conference room, as quiet and still as a Buddha statue. To Molly, she appeared to be steeling her mind for what was to come. After witnessing her mother as a victim for many years, Whitney seemed more than ready to take a stand to protect herself and her child.

Molly found Dave, the officer on duty who was already familiar with Whitney's home situation as well as Rich Logan. After a quick debriefing, she took Dave inside to talk with Whitney.

"Hi there." Dave offered her a handshake. "I'm Officer Foster. I was one of the officers who responded to the call at your house earlier, but I didn't have a chance to meet you."

Dave could easily be mistaken for a former professional athlete, even with the full head of gray hair. He often used his size to intimidate people in the hot seat. But today, with Whitney, he was soft spoken and kind. Molly loved working with him, because he was the best of both worlds.

"It's nice to meet you." Whitney straightened in her seat.

Dave sat across the table. "Can you tell me exactly what happened with your stepdad?"

Whitney's gaze darted from Dave to Molly, and then back to Dave. Inhaling deeply, she rested her hands on her belly and began her story.

Dave took notes and asked questions.

When Whitney told them Rich threatened to push her down the stairs, Molly jumped up off her chair, ready to go deal with Rich on her terms. "I need to get a drink. Either of you want anything?"

Whitney asked for juice, and Dave declined her offer.

Once Molly left the conference room, she headed straight for the women's restroom. A storm of pent-up emotions threatened. Placing her hands on the cool, porcelain sink, she gazed at her reflection in the mirror. Staring back, she recognized sorrow and anger, and also shame. Yes, she'd admit it. Sitting in the conference room, she'd become envious of Whitney's pregnant belly. Why now, when she needed to be at her most professional, did that little maternal voice sound in her head?

Seeing pregnant women usually didn't bother her. She was too busy to wallow in self-pity. Right now, she pushed down the cravings of her heart. After turning on the faucet, she splashed cool water on her face, removing some of her skin's heat.

Taking a few calming breaths, she stepped out of the restroom.

Dave stood in the hall. "Whitney's mom is here. She won't admit she let her husband back in the home or that he hurt Whitney."

"Then we have no choice but to involve CPS." What else could they do? Child Protective Services would ensure Whitney was kept safe, at least until she turned eighteen. If she and Dave did their job right, the DA would prosecute Rich Logan for physical abuse of a minor. And this time, with Whitney's testimony, the judge wouldn't allow bail.

"I'll call CPS right now. But, Molly, did you know Whitney is only a minor for two more weeks? I'm not sure what they'll do after her birthday. She can't move back home." Dave ran his fingers through his hair, making it stick up like silver porcupine quills.

"No, she can't go home, but she does have other options." She'd already been researching places for Whitney to stay long-term.

"I have an idea that would keep her out of CPS." Dave rested his hand on Molly's shoulder. "Someone could take responsibility. Barbara would sign off. She's already said as much. Whitney likes you, Molly, and trusts you. You could become her temporary guardian."

"Did I hear you right?" She rested her clenched hands on her hips. What would make Dave think she'd make a good mother, even temporarily? "You've lost your mind."

He chuckled. "Just think about it. Do you really want her in a foster home, in her condition? Liberty Ridge is a small town. We take care of each other."

One of the front office staff squeezed past them and disappeared into the women's restroom.

The hallway grew smaller, leaving little chance of escape. Deep down, she knew what Dave suggested made sense. On a rational level, she agreed. But right now, as cold sweat dripped down her back, she didn't feel like being rational. "You realize I know nothing about taking care of a kid? I'm just now learning to care for a dog."

"Molly, listen…Whitney's not three years old and needs her diaper changed. She's practically an adult. Think of her as a roommate."

"Why don't you take her?" Two could play at this game.

"You know I already have a full house. We have to fight for the bathroom as it is." Dave laughed then lowered his brows. "Nice try."

How in the world would she handle living with a teenager? And a pregnant one? Waking up every morning and seeing Whitney's baby growing inside her. "Her mom really doesn't care?" Molly asked. "She'll give up her own daughter?"

"Barbara knows she's in trouble and wants to save the hassle of fighting CPS. If you ask me, she's got classic Stockholm Syndrome." He leaned a shoulder against the hallway wall. "Her behavior is a learned survival mechanism and makes her predictable. She'll go back to her husband."

He was right. But in Molly's mind, Barbara had no excuse for the way she'd mistreated Whitney. Molly thought of her own family and her loving upbringing. The Hernandez clan watched out for one another. Even her brothers, who loved to tease her, would drop everything and come to her aid if she called.

Dave cleared his throat. "Whitney's birthday is October 29th. After that, she's considered a legal adult. Think about it, Molly."

Resigned, she closed her eyes. Fate had interceded. She and Whitney shared a birthday. Their bond was meant to be. "All right. If everything gets approved, then I'll accept guardianship. As long as things go well, she can stay with me after her birthday. But this is a short-term solution. We need a plan for after she has the baby."

The lines on Dave's face softened with his broad smile.

He'd told her more than once that he had earned his gray hair and wrinkles honestly. After twenty-five years on the force and four children, he sure had.

"I'm proud of you, Molly. You'll make a great mother someday."

A small tremor moved through her chest and settled in her heart. Locking up the sorrow, she put on a mask of indifference. Dave didn't know her secret, and she wanted to keep it that way. She didn't want pity for something that had been out of her control. "Thanks." She returned to the conference room. Life didn't always play fair. Molly couldn't reclaim what cancer had stolen, but she still had the power to help Whitney.

****

The late afternoon sun streamed into the west-facing windows of Dr. Colleen Gardner's office. Drew sat in a pricey looking, black leather chair and watched Colleen grab his file from her massive mahogany desk.

"Have the nightmares subsided since your last visit?" She lowered herself into a chair and crossed her legs.

"No, but they're not as intense. The journaling before bed helps." His folded hands fidgeted on his lap.

"Retraining your brain takes time. Have you ever considered yoga? At first, turning your focus inward is scary, but with practice, the meditation skills you learn in yoga are very beneficial." Colleen opened his file and pulled her reading glasses off the top of her head before resting them on her nose. "Last week, you didn't want a prescription sleep aid. Is that still the case?"

"I'll only take medication as a last resort." Today was Drew's fourth session with Colleen. Simply having someone to freely talk with helped lessen the issues he'd experienced over the past year. His nightmares were the worst. What he saw in his dreams was like reliving the worst parts of his deployments, over and over again—the panic and loss of control of being on the run, and the fear of not getting home in time to save his sister.

"I agree," Colleen said. "So, how's teaching going? Is it what you expected?"

"Yes and no." Drew laughed. "I like teaching. I'm happiest when I'm making a difference with my students. Dealing with the parents is difficult."

"What about outside the classroom?" Colleen studied him. "How's your personal life?"

Even her black-rimmed glasses couldn't diminish her penetrating gaze. Drew squirmed in his seat, wearing a rueful smile. "That's a whole other story." He took one deep breath to collect his thoughts. No doubt, he could trust Colleen and her professional ethics. She wouldn't share any of what he said. But the topic of his love life, or lack thereof, made him uncomfortable. He hated admitting his failures. "When I was in the Army, I devoted everything to the service. I made the decision to put off marriage and family, because I wanted those experiences to be separate from my military life."

"You did what you felt was best. I understand why you waited."

He unfolded his hands and rested them on his knees, causing his body to lean forward. "I've found starting my new life isn't as easy as I assumed. I guess you'd call me a romantic. I imagined I'd meet the love of my life, we'd marry, and live happily ever after. Just goes to show how naïve I am."

"Not naïve, maybe overly optimistic. Love doesn't work like a computer program." Colleen smiled. "Don't panic. Let love happen naturally. Finding that special someone may take longer than you expected, but it will happen." She jotted down notes on a sheet of paper inside Drew's folder. "Are you concerned about being alone?"

Being alone—exactly what he feared the most. In the Army, he'd been surrounded by his brothers, who were his other family. Since moving to Texas, he'd been separated from almost everyone he knew, besides Heath. Truthfully, a part of him panicked at the thought of being alone for the rest of his life.

"Yes." He swallowed, dislodging his rising discomfort. Sweat beaded on his brow. "Loneliness is a fear. See, I compartmentalize things. It's how I survived in the Army. I'm a planner and hyper organized. When I went on a mission, I focused on every detail. I'm having a hard time letting go of that vigilance in civilian life, especially when things don't go as planned."

Drew wiped his hand across his forehead. "I have these big plans and expectations, but none matter because the one woman I want doesn't want me. Every time I think I have a shot, she pushes me away."

Her eyebrows drew together. "Are you talking about Molly?"

The back of his shirt was now drenched in sweat. Did Colleen have heated seats? "Molly is a wonderful woman. I feel the most like myself when I'm with her. She makes me laugh. She forces me to be the best I can be."

"Force is a good word for Molly." Colleen chuckled.

"She's a little spitfire. I compare every other woman I meet to Molly. No one measures up. What am I supposed to do when she's been crystal clear she's not open to a relationship?"

Colleen took off her glasses then reached over to pat his knee. "Be the best friend any woman could ask for. Don't expect anything more than what she's offering. I can't speak for what Molly's reasons are, but you have to accept her feelings. You have a preconceived notion of how you should fall in love. Romance should be as easy as baking a cake, just follow the recipe and everything will turn out perfectly delicious. With Molly, the recipe is all jumbled up. Maybe you've dropped a few eggshells in the batter. That's okay. You don't know what the future holds. Just don't waste time and energy analyzing things that are out of your control."

"That's asking a lot from someone like me. I live to over analyze."

"I know." Colleen smiled. "Don't forget the lessons you learned in the Army about strategic planning."

How could he forget? The Army had drilled preparedness until the mindset became second nature, even a year after separation. "Always have a backup plan. And then a backup plan for your backup plan."

"Right. Stay flexible and willing to change."

"I'll try, Doc." Drew noticed the time. His session

was over. "Now that we're off the clock, I want to ask you if you're going to Molly's birthday party."

Colleen's blue eyes widened. "I am. But I thought Grace and I were the only ones invited outside her family. Molly gets funny about being the center of attention."

"Oh, uh." Drew crammed his hands into the pockets of his pants. "Mrs. Hernandez called last night and invited me. I said I'd come, but maybe I shouldn't. I don't want to show up someplace I'm not wanted."

"Please, come." Colleen grinned and rubbed her hands together. "You have to meet Molly's brothers. You'll get a better understanding of why she's so strong willed. Her family is awesome. They're big and loud, and her brothers love to tease her. They'll be thrilled to meet you."

A picture formed in his head—Drew surrounded by five large men, all threatening him bodily harm if he hurt their baby sister. Then he imagined Molly, ready to bury him alive for causing her grief, and his stomach grew queasy.

"Can't wait." He'd soon find out if he really meant it.

Chapter Thirteen

Molly twisted the shower faucet handle, heating the lukewarm water spraying over her body. She'd been in the shower for the past fifteen minutes in an attempt to rebury her emotions. To the world, she played a tough girl who didn't let anything or anyone get in her way. She did a good job of hiding her pain. But at times she needed to let out her emotions, or her hard shell would crack.

Two weeks ago, Whitney moved into her townhouse. Rider loved the extra attention. *Greedy, spoiled dog.* Whitney fell easily into the rhythm of Molly's life. She helped with the cooking and cleaning, and even made omelets that morning for breakfast.

Earlier, as they sat out on the deck eating breakfast, her pair of Mourning Doves stopped by for a visit. Probably for the last time before flying farther south for the winter. They both enjoyed watching them for a while until Whitney winced in pain.

"Are you okay?" Molly stood, pulse racing, ready to get her cell and call the doctor.

Whitney covered her mouth with her hand and laughed. "The baby's kicking up a storm. Come feel." She took Molly's hand and rested it on her abdomen.

The movement Molly felt could only be described as other-worldly. The baby twisted and turned, making Whitney's belly churn like the sea during a storm.

Molly experienced a sense of wonder mixed with an incredible feeling of loss. She masked her pain with a wide smile. She'd kept secret how much that moment emotionally cost her.

Now, in the solitude of her shower, she let the stinging tears run free. Her hand moved down her chest to her own flat stomach, and her finger traced the line of her scar. Its rough ridge stood out in contrast to her smooth skin. The incision healed quickly. Her muscle and tissue expertly knitted back together. The cancer cells were expelled, no longer a threat. But her heart— she didn't know if that could ever completely heal. Would one day she be totally absolved of cancer's true cost? Most likely, not.

Molly's shower slowly cooled, which meant the hot water was gone. Time to stop hiding and face the day. Her parents were throwing her and Whitney a combined birthday party in the afternoon. Thank goodness Whitney's presence would deflect some of her family's attention. Plus, Whitney was turning eighteen. She deserved a fabulous party.

Molly, on the other hand, hated her birthday. Or more like she hated the added attention. She'd made *Mamá* promise only to invite family, plus Colleen and Grace, and unfortunately Heath.

She slipped on a light blue sundress. After a touch of makeup and a brush through her hair, she grabbed a sweater and descended the stairs. She found Whitney sitting at the kitchen table, clutching a worn, leather purse. "You look very pretty, birthday girl."

Whitney wore a colorful sundress, which billowed around her body. She'd pulled her hair in a pretty up-do.

A stark difference to the pale, sickly girl Molly had first met at the initial Second Step meeting.

"Thanks. You look pretty, too. I like your dangly earrings. They look like aqua raindrops." Whitney grabbed Rider's leash and headed outside to Molly's car.

A short car ride later, they arrived at Molly's childhood home. Her parents had raised six children in their fifteen-hundred-square-foot ranch-style house. Growing up here had been crowded, full of rowdy children, and also full of love. The property sat on three acres of land, which gave the energetic kids plenty of room to run. Many days, Molly spent building forts, climbing the Ash trees, or playing in the small creek at the back of the property.

When Molly opened the back door of her car, Rider took off toward the activity. A few of her nephews played football in the front yard. They waved as she made her way to the front door with Whitney in tow.

"*Hola.*" *Mamá* met them at the door. "You must be Whitney. What a sweet girl. Come inside and make yourself at home. You call me *Mamá*, okay?"

No one could make someone feel more welcome than Maria Hernandez. She was even shorter than Molly but boasted a personality four times her size.

A slow smile spread over Whitney's face. "Thank you."

"Silly me. I didn't wish you happy birthday. We'll have such a fun party. Eighteen years old." She stepped back and shook her head. "Good thing everyone's getting older but me."

Whitney stared with wide eyes, like a kid who had

seen bubbles for the first time. "I'll take Whitney out back to introduce her to the family." Molly sniffed the air, and her stomach growled. "You need any help here?"

"No. I have everything under control. You go out and have fun." With a wave of her hand, *Mamá* scurried back into the kitchen.

The smell of tamales filled the air. Conversation and laughter drifted through the open windows. Judging from the volume, all her brothers were already here.

Ready, set, go. She opened the screen doors and stepped onto the patio. She no longer worried about her brothers teasing too much, because over the years, she'd learned to dish it out as well as take it. She counted again and saw six men, and the extra person was not *Papá*. Molly's stomach dropped to her feet. Drew turned and smiled like he didn't have a care in the world.

Just wait. Your fun has only begun.

Her oldest brother, Manuel, stood beside Drew and followed his gaze. A slow smile spread across his face. "Hey, Molly. We finally met your boyfriend. You've been holding out on us."

Her vision blurred red. She turned on her heel and marched back into the house. What in the freakin' world was Drew doing here? "*Mamá*, did you invite Drew Atwater?"

Mamá stopped chopping cilantro. "*Sí*. He's your friend."

"You should have asked me before inviting him." Molly picked up a sprig of cilantro and sniffed.

"No, I don't have to ask because the party is at my house. You shouldn't be so unsociable. He is Whitney's *amigo* as well." *Mamá* smiled and resumed chopping.

Her voice held no hint of remorse. "You know what the boys will say." Molly again inhaled the spicy scent of cilantro filling the kitchen, which helped calm her temper.

"*Hija*, I have no doubt you will put your *hermanos* back in their place. Now, go outside and make Drew feel welcome. He seemed so excited to meet your *familia loca*. Go." She shooed Molly with her free hand. "Wipe the frown off your face and smile."

As she went back out on the patio, Molly tried not to growl. Drew stood talking with her brothers, and *Papá* had joined them at some point. Miguel must have said something funny, because Drew tipped back his head and laughed.

Whitney, whom she'd left on the patio, wandered over to a table where her nieces colored. Even at eighteen, Whitney didn't look much older than the preadolescent girls she sat beside.

Taking a beer out of the cooler, she walked past her sisters-in-law, who were deep in conversation regarding the high price of diapers. One subject Molly wanted to avoid. She joined her brothers and took a seat on a lawn chair. "Hi." She made eye contact with Drew. "I didn't expect to see you here."

"Blunt much?" Michael scrunched his face. "Geez, M, you sure know how to make a guy feel welcome. But don't worry, we've already made him an honorary member of the family."

"Great," she mumbled, and then turned to Drew. "I offer a standing apology for my brothers. They can be a bit overbearing." Her brothers yelled in feigned offense. "And loud." She rolled her eyes.

Drew leaned in. "Don't worry about me, Pixie. I'm former Army Special Forces. Handling a woman's big brothers is child's play," he whispered into her ear.

She couldn't stop the smile creeping on her face. But as soon as she noticed her brothers' silence and stares, she frowned and narrowed her eyes.

"You owe me twenty dollars, Marco," Miguel yelled and held out a large hand, palm up. "I told you our sassy, baby sister has fallen in love."

Grabbing the nearest weapon—a bag of potato chips—she hurdled it like a missile at Miguel.

Miguel caught the bag flying toward his head and laughed. "Calm down, sis. Don't be so touchy."

"Do you remember when you were fifteen and brought Renee Baumgartner home for dinner?" she asked Miguel, whose dark hair was gelled into a trendy Faux Hawk. Her youngest older brother had always been concerned with style and fashion. Proven by the expensive, name-brand boat shoes covering his unsocked feet.

He reclined farther in his chair and rested a foot on his knee. "You bet I do. You put a spider in her cup."

Molly had loved playing pranks on her brothers—payback for their harassment. "Do you remember why?"

Miguel paled.

And the rest of the group quieted.

About time they used their ears instead of their mouths. She turned her attention to Drew. "Miguel was the baby of the family until I came along. When our *mamá* brought me home from the hospital, he was so jealous. Then, when I got a little older, he'd take me out of my crib and hide me in the closet in hopes *Mamá* would forget about me." Molly took a drink and let the cold liquid slide down her dry throat. "Once I got a little bigger, I learned to fight back. The spider incident was pure retaliation. Earlier, Miguel had roped me to a big oak tree." She pointed to the hundred-year oak at the back of the field. "I spent three hours wiggling my way out."

"The constrictor hitch knot took me a long time to perfect." Miguel grinned and pointed a finger at Molly. "But man, that sucker was impossible to untie."

"Tell me about it." Molly snorted, remembering her ordeal. "When I finally did get out, I was angrier than a Diamondback rattler. I knew Miguel had invited a girl over for dinner, so I hatched a plan for revenge."

"Which I still haven't forgiven you for." He shook his head. "I really had the hots for Renee. After spiders appeared in her food and drink, she begged me to take her home. She never talked to me afterward."

"So be warned, my beloved brothers, do not underestimate my lust for vengeance." Hopefully, her reminder would help them lose some of their eagerness to tease. So thankfully, when Drew put his arm around her shoulder and gave her a hug, not one of them uttered a word.

****

Pride radiated off Drew as he listened to Molly. *If I'd only known her back then.* She was a thorny rose who refused to be pushed around by her brothers. As he held an arm around her, he felt her tense. He unhooked his arm from her shoulders, folded his hands, and set them in his lap. So far, he'd stayed out of Molly's line of fire. The last thing he wanted was to put himself back in.

The Hernandez brothers, with their contagious good humor, made him feel like part of the family. They reminded him of his brotherhood in the Army. Beneath the teasing was a deep respect. Molly benefited from their combined protectiveness, even though he was sure she didn't see their teasing that way.

When he'd arrived, Mrs. Hernandez gave him the royal treatment, which led Marco and Miguel to question him about his relationship with their sister. Drew insisted they were colleagues and friends who shared the occasional kickboxing class. Of course, her brothers didn't buy his dispassionate sales pitch. Then once Molly arrived, all politeness and pretense evaporated.

When she'd exited the house, every cell of his brain became filled with her. Molly's sundress fit perfectly over her compact body. He wanted to tangle his fingers in the loose waves of her mahogany hair. Did her brothers miss the look of desire burning in his eyes? Not likely.

Drew glanced over his shoulder at Whitney, who seemed happy coloring with Molly's nieces. He'd come today for her as much as for Molly. An eighteenth birthday needed to be celebrated. Sadly, Whitney's own mother didn't care.

Soon Grace, Heath, and Colleen arrived to join the party. Grace still wasn't feeling well, and Heath continued to be flustered by her illness. He kept a close watch and rarely left her side.

Finally, the dinner bell rang, and everyone lined up to eat. Molly placed herself well away from him—two table lengths to be precise. But he wouldn't let sixteen feet get in the way of watching her throughout dinner.

Colorful lights hung in the tree branches overhead. Lively conversation and delicious smells filled the air. For the first time in a long time, Drew felt like he belonged. Until he glanced up and saw Heath sitting across the table, shoving a *tamale* into his wide mouth. "Slow down, man." Drew laughed. "The thing won't run away."

Heath finished chewing then gave him a crooked smile. "You never know. How did you finagle an invite to this shindig? I expressly remember Grace saying tonight was for family and close friends only."

Drew set down his fork and leaned forward. "Then why is your ugly mug here?"

"Didn't you get the memo? I'm her new best friend." Heath scooped a pile of *poblano* rice onto his fork.

"You're funny. Molly's mom called and invited me. She said Molly's family was eager to meet me."

"I bet they were." Heath kicked him under the table and jerked his thumb toward Molly. "But is she happy you're here?"

The sharp toe of Heath's boot left Drew's shin throbbing. If he wasn't at a social gathering, he'd have Heath in a headlock by now. But the guy did have a point. Was Molly glad he'd come? "Don't be fooled by her frown. Deep down, she's excited by my presence." He took a bite of cucumber salad, and wonderful flavors exploded on his tongue. "You're the one she's giving the stink eye to."

"You're most likely right. I need to check on Grace. She looks like she needs to lie down." Heath left and escorted Grace inside the house.

After Drew finished eating, he grabbed an open

chair next to Molly. One abandoned by her niece who'd run off to play with Whitney on the tire swing. "So, when do we get to sing the Happy Birthday song?" Resting an elbow on the table, he angled his body to face her.

"*Mamá* will bring out the cake later." She sighed and crinkled her nose. "Then you can torture me with your singing."

"How do you know my singing is torture? I may have the voice of an angel."

"I didn't mean your voice would be torture. I hate the attention." Frowning, she slouched in her chair. "Everyone should sing for Whitney and leave my name out of the song. She's the one who should feel special today."

"I think she already does." Drew turned his gaze to the wide backyard.

Whitney pushed a little girl on the tire swing, laughing loudly. Surrounding her were a half dozen other girls, waiting their turn.

His worry over her was replaced by happiness and joy. "She's really good with kids."

Molly nodded. "I felt the baby move today. She doesn't have much longer to figure out things. I'm taking her to meet with the head of a local crisis home for pregnant teens. Hopefully, they can take her in."

He stole a pickle off her plate and quickly ate it.

"Thief." She slapped his hand. "Get your own."

"You know your family is pretty awesome, right? I'm sorry if my presence has caused you grief. Guys, especially big brothers, have a weird way of showing affection."

Her smile lit up her eyes.

His heart fluttered in response. Each one of her smiles still had that effect on him. Luckily, she didn't give them away very often, or he'd end up with serious heart palpitations. Try explaining his lovestruck heart condition to a cardiologist.

"I love my family." Molly placed a flat hand over her heart. "My brothers live to tease me, but I know if anyone ever hurt me, they'd hunt down the offender to the ends of the earth."

"Point taken." Drew swallowed hard. "Is that why you don't date? Too afraid of brotherly interference?"

Her smile faded. "Why I don't date is none of your business."

Great. Now her defenses were back up. He'd only been joking. "Maybe I should go see if Whitney needs help with the swing." Drew stood. "She looks tired." He walked across the yard and joined Whitney by the tire swing. At least, she didn't resent his company.

No matter how hard he tried, he was always left spinning his wheels. He'd made a mistake in thinking Molly would want to be his friend, let alone his lover. He'd made a mistake in coming here today.

Chapter Fourteen

Sometimes, Molly hated her mouth, which liked to cut ties with her brain and take on a life of its own. Mostly, her mouth went rogue whenever she was around Drew. He made her feel entangled in a web, and while she struggled to escape, she used her words as weapons. Slicing through affection and attraction until only a few silky strands remained, blowing in the wind.

Drew didn't deserve the way she'd lashed out. He'd proven himself a good friend. Why couldn't she just accept the olive branch he held out, over and over again? Soon, he wouldn't extend another offer.

She considered a life without Drew, causing panic to swell in her chest. As much as she hated to admit—and she hated admitting weakness—she needed him. He kept her balanced. He was one of the few men in her life, besides her family, who didn't shy away from her strong personality. He actually liked her because of who she was.

Molly turned her attention to the pickup football game in the back yard. Day had turned to evening, and the sun looked like a fireball sinking into the earth. Large, puffy clouds transformed into watercolor shades of purple, pink, and orange. She propped up her feet on the seat of a chair and enjoyed the view.

Grace stepped through the door of the house and joined her on the patio. "What a beautiful evening."

"You feeling any better?" Molly rubbed her arm. Grace's normally healthy-looking skin was pale and tinged with green.

"My stomach has settled." Grace sipped at a glass of ice water.

"I told her she should come outside for some fresh air." Colleen sat next to Molly. "Maybe you could eat something. Your body needs nourishment now more than ever."

Molly sensed a hidden message. *What am I missing?* "You should see a doctor and find out what's making you sick all the time."

"I have gone to the doctor. Not much they can do." Grace pointed to the backyard. "Looks like the guys are having fun playing football."

With the football in hand, Drew took a few stutter steps backward. He scanned the field for an open receiver, cocked back his arm, and tossed the ball high in the air.

The football landed in the arms of Molly's nephew, who took off running. Unfortunately, his dad, Marco, cut him off and tackled him to the ground.

The game quickly became competitive, and shouts filled the air. Drew and Heath were on opposite teams, which meant Molly and Grace cheered loudly for their respective sides, vying to outdo one another. Colleen stayed neutral, encouraging both teams.

"Good luck getting them to stop for cake," Grace hollered above the noise of the cheering.

As Heath barreled toward their makeshift end zone with ball in hand, Drew swept his foot and sent both of them sprawling onto the ground. They spent several seconds in good-natured arguing, and then stood, dusted themselves off, and went back to their opposing teams.

Whitney pulled up a chair next to Grace and joined the fan section on the patio. "Your family is the best, Molly." Her eyes sparkled. "I just made an escape from your nieces' beauty parlor. Selena offered to do my hair and makeup, but I had to decline. Sorry, but I'm not letting a four year old give me a makeover, no matter how much I need it."

Molly laughed. On past occasions, her nieces had enjoyed styling her hair. But tonight, she stayed clear of their small combs, barrettes, and sparkly headbands.

The cool air brushed her shoulders, and Molly slipped on her sweater. The extra layer, as well as Whitney's animated discussion, warmed her. She witnessed the transformation of a fearful teenager into a confident young woman.

"Are you feeling better, Mrs. Carter?" Whitney's brows drew together.

"Call me Grace." She patted the teen's hand. "The nausea comes and goes. I feel better now. Food smells bother me most."

Whitney nodded and smiled. "I know. The smell of food bothered me, too, during my first few months. Don't worry, though, you'll feel better soon. After the third month, you'll eat anything that moves."

The earth dropped from under Molly's seat. All the pieces came together. Grace was pregnant. Molly's best friend since grade school was expecting a baby and hadn't told her. Did everyone else already know? The air left her lungs, and she struggled for breath. Did Grace really believe Molly would let her own infertility stand in the way of happiness for her best friend? "Why didn't you tell me?" Molly stuttered.

"I wanted to." Tears welled in Grace's eyes. "I could never find the right time. I didn't want to cause you any pain."

More disappointed than angry, Molly stood. She needed distance between herself and this situation before she said something she'd later regret. "I'm sorry you felt you couldn't come to me with such happy news."

Despite her best efforts, her own jealousy bubbled to the surface. She was surrounded by children and pregnant women. Whitney, Grace, and her sister-in-law, Karen, all carried inside them the blessing she'd been denied. She needed a quiet place to clear her head. As she headed toward her favorite spot by the creek, a bitter taste filled her mouth. When a small patch of wildflowers came into view, she gazed at their beauty, wrapped in a comforting peace. Sinking onto the tall grass by the stream, she curled into a ball.

She couldn't block out the sympathetic looks of Grace and Colleen. Molly wished she could jump into the slow-moving water of the creek and let her body float weightlessly toward a world without sickness and loss.

The water trickled over rocks, making a soothing music, and soon Molly's body and mind relaxed. She focused on the rhythmic bellows of bullfrogs warming up for their nightly serenade. Resting her head on her raised knees, she closed her eyes. Her mind went to work, sorting out all her tumbled-up emotions—a basket full of grief, shame, jealousy, and anger.

Grace was more than just a friend. She was like a sister. Sure, they'd had their disagreements, like

Grace's relationship with Heath, but they'd always been honest. How could Grace have kept quiet about her pregnancy? Finding out she's to become a mother was one of the most joyful moments of a woman's life.

Only Grace knew how much Molly had struggled with her loss of fertility. And now, her feelings for Drew brought back memories she'd rather forget. Molly sat in the still peace of nature and refused to shed one more tear. Her life had an endless supply of possibilities.

The sky was the limit. All she had to do was reach up and take what she wanted.

****

When Drew noticed Molly sneak away from the party, he'd wanted to follow her. She probably thought no one spotted her stride toward the trees at the back of the property. What had upset her? If he asked, she'd most likely push him away. His intentions were good, but with Molly, intent never seemed enough.

The football game ended with his team winning by one touchdown. When Mrs. Hernandez came outside with the cake, the whole family moved like a flock of birds in her direction.

"Where did Molly run off to?" Heath tossed the football into the air then caught it with one hand. "I'm ready to dig into the cake."

"Not sure. I'll go find her. If we're not back soon, tell Mrs. H to sing to Whitney and start eating. I'm sure Molly wouldn't mind." Drew followed the trampled grass marking Molly's path. He'd learned enough in the Army to track a wayward woman. As the sounds of running water grew more pronounced, he saw a head of dark hair set in the middle of a sea of golden tall grass.

From his vantage point, he observed Molly sitting with her knees against her chest. She was so still, Drew thought maybe she'd fallen asleep. He took a step forward, rustling the grass.

Molly turned to face him. The corners of her mouth curved downward. "How did you find me?"

"For someone so small, you leave quite a wide trail." He sat next to her and folded his legs.

Her eyebrows rose up her forehead. "Wide, huh? Didn't your mother teach you not to use the term 'wide' in reference to a woman?"

"What can I say?" He shrugged. "I'm a slow learner."

"Do you track women often?"

"Nah, you're the first. I tracked while in the Army. My favorite experience was Robin Sage, part of the Special Forces assessment. We parachuted into the middle of a fictional guerilla-style war. In order to succeed, I had to read nature and look for signs easy to miss if you weren't paying attention."

"Sounds like fun." Molly's mouth lifted. "So, you're saying I can never hide from you?"

"Nope." He leaned toward her. The unmistakable floral scent of Molly filled his nostrils. "Who are you hiding from, Pixie? Your family or me?"

"No one, really. I needed a quiet place to think."

"You look very pretty today. I should have told you earlier." Drew reached over and tucked a silky strand of hair behind her ear. His finger lingered, trailing along the smooth skin of her face and ending at her small chin.

"You don't look half bad yourself."

Had she just given him a compliment? Maybe he

hadn't made a mistake coming to the party. "They're ready to cut the cake. I told them to sing to Whitney and dig in. I hope that's okay."

"Thanks. They all know I hate the singing."

Fireflies danced around them. Their flashes of light blinked a secret code—a search for love in the darkening twilight. Two bodies finding one another, just when the world turned quiet and dark.

Molly rested her head on Drew's shoulder.

He feared with the slightest move on his part, even a breath, would disrupt the moment. Only a soft breeze moved through the tall grass. "Your family is worried about you moving away." He'd heard from almost every family member how they wished Molly would stay close to home instead of joining the DEA. She was the youngest. The baby of the family. Drew agreed the best place for Molly was in Liberty Ridge.

"I can't stay here *and* pursue my career goals." Molly twirled a yellow flower in her fingers. "I don't mind being an SRO, but the job is not where my passion lies. I need more excitement. I want to put an end to drug trafficking or at least curb availability of the drugs."

He couldn't let her walk away without a fight. "You're doing a lot of good in our small town. We need you here." Drew paused to clear his throat, opening a path for a more heartfelt plea. "I need you here."

"I can't make my decision based on what everyone else needs." She lifted her head from his shoulder and straightened. "I want to spread my wings. To be my own person—not what everyone in this town, or my family, thinks I should be."

He understood her drive. Respected it. But his

selfish desire for her was stronger. "You have people who love you here. Why do you want to leave?"

"You don't understand." Molly lifted her chin.

He placed his fingers underneath her jaw line and tilted her face until she met his gaze. "Then enlighten me."

****

When Molly was younger, she'd imagine tiny fairy creatures, flitting among the water and grass, using their magic dust to make merry mischief. People would fall under their spell and do things they otherwise would never do—like kiss a handsome man.

Magic was the only reasonable explanation for why she kissed Drew. Her attraction was too strong to resist. When their lips met, a powerful surge pushed through every vein inside her. Drew's arms wrapped around her and brought her into the protection of his warm body. His lips tasted of beer and the tang of spices.

She didn't remember folding her arms around his neck, but her fingers now worked eagerly in the short curls of his hair. Drew pulled her even closer. She melted into him like hot wax being poured into a mold.

When his lips left hers, she almost cried. But he moved down to her neck and worked his way up behind her ear, and then back to her mouth. Everywhere he touched seared her skin.

He laid her back down onto a bed of tall grass and wildflowers. The earth below cradled them in a protective cocoon.

His fingers traced along her collarbone. "I need you." He gazed trancelike into her eyes. "Stay in Liberty Ridge."

Along with conscious thought, unwelcome reality

flowed in. She set the palms of her hands against his chest and pushed. But Drew wasn't giving up. He kissed her again.

"Drew." She turned her head. The effort took every ounce of her willpower. The loss of his body heat left her shivering. "We shouldn't have kissed."

"Why?" Drew sat beside her. His cheeks were flushed, and several blades of grass stuck out of his tousled hair. "I like you. You like me. A simple math problem with an easy solution."

She scooted away, needing more distance. If he reached over to kiss her again, she didn't know if she could pull herself away a second time. Her heart wanted him so bad. Her chest ached from the self denial. "You and I will never work. My life doesn't revolve around getting married and having babies. I know you waited until you were out of the Army to start a family. You told me you want to settle down in Liberty Ridge and fill your big house with lots of kids."

His face fell, and his gaze dropped to the grass. "I still don't understand why you won't give us a chance."

"I'm not having kids." There, she finally stated the truth. Well, part of it. The most important part. "I wouldn't ask you to compromise on something so important."

"You can work in law enforcement and have a family. Take my parents, for example."

His voice was quiet, sounding like he'd lost most of his fight. "Understand that my job as a female DEA Special Agent will be tough and all consuming. And that's my dream, Drew. I can't let anyone get in the way."

He tossed a stone into the creek, creating a

plopping sound when the stone broke the surface.

Molly raised her hand and caressed his cheek. Her palm moved over the light stubble covering his face. His eyes stared back, branding her soul. "You are a very good friend." Sadness pierced her heart.

"A poor consolation prize." Drew pushed to his feet.

The sound of soft footsteps cut through the quiet.

"Oh." Grace placed her hand over her mouth. "I didn't mean to interrupt."

"I was just leaving." With his head held high, he strode away.

"Drew looked upset." Grace sat and stretched out her long legs. "What's going on?"

"We finally had an honest conversation." Pain throbbed in her chest from the knowledge she'd hurt him. "I told Drew things he didn't want to hear."

"Speaking of being honest." Grace angled her body to face Molly. "I'm sorry for not telling you about my pregnancy. You should have been one of the first to know. I was afraid of making you unhappy. I know you've been struggling lately, with your feelings for Drew and now living with a pregnant teenager."

"You don't have to apologize. I'm the one who should say sorry." She rested a hand on Grace's arm. "You're my best friend, and I shouldn't have reacted the way I did. Can I still be your baby's favorite auntie?"

Grace laughed. "Yes. You are allowed to spoil him or her rotten."

"Come on." Molly stood then reached down to pull Grace to her feet. "Let's get back to the party."

As they walked to the house, the heat of Drew's

kiss lingered on her lips. She locked away the memory of their kiss in the deep spot of her heart, reserved for things she'd rather forget but couldn't.

When they got back, Whitney and Rider were both indulging in a slice of cake. Everyone looked to be having a good time. But under the festive glow of the party lights, Drew's absence was palpable. The hole inside her ripped open a little more. Guilt seeped in. He'd left without saying goodbye.

Chapter Fifteen

The bag swung back at Drew, and he went in for another punch. This morning's kickboxing class served as a safe outlet for his frustration. After almost a week, he could not get the taste of Molly off his lips. Her floral smell wouldn't leave him, either. He'd catch a whiff of roses mixed with honeysuckle and transport back in time, to the bed of the creek, when he held her in his arms.

Drew experienced a glimpse of what his future could be, but their love was only an illusion. His and Molly's goals were two pieces of a puzzle destined to never fit together. He should man up and accept a life with Molly was not meant to be.

Molly stood at the far end of the gym, having partnered today with someone else. He missed the feisty gamesmanship they'd developed. She kept him on his toes, proving herself a worthy opponent—both on and off the mat. Molly might be little, but she was strong. She knew what she wanted and didn't let anything, or anybody, get in her way. Too bad she didn't want him with such passion.

Drew poured his energy into every kick and punch.

"Time out," Bernie, his new partner, hollered from the other side of the bag. "You're killing me."

"Sorry, man. You want to switch? I can hold the bag for you for a while." Drew took a long, cold drink of water from his sport's bottle.

"Nah, you can keep going. Give me a minute to rest my arms." He tipped his head to the other side of the gym. "Why aren't you paired with Molly today?"

Drew shrugged. "She'd partnered up before I got here. Guess she was antsy to get going."

"I'm glad I've never had to spar against her." Bernie wiped a towel over his bald head.

"She is a handful." Drew's gaze was drawn to Molly, who was flawlessly working the bag. Her partner shouted something, and she smiled. Then she kicked even harder.

"You should see her when she really gets fired up." Drew took a deep breath. "She's unstoppable." After class, he toweled off, picked up his duffle bag, and headed toward the door.

Molly cut him off. "How'd your new partner hold up?"

"Bernie made a poor substitute." His heart hitched. "I missed you."

The corner of her lip curled up into a small smile. "Well, if nothing else, we make a good kickboxing team."

Drew followed her outside, and then hesitated. Was he safe to ask her out for a post work-out snack? As friends, of course.

Molly turned to face him. "We should talk about what happened last weekend at my party."

"How about we go grab a bite to eat?" What was there still left to say? She'd been very clear about the direction her life was headed. Her future did not include Liberty Ridge, or children, or him. In an uncomfortable silence, he walked at her side. "I'm sorry I left without saying good-bye. I was upset, but my mood didn't justify acting like a jerk."

Molly tipped up her head to look at him and shielded her eyes from the sun with her hand. "No, you're not a jerk. If anything, you're too nice. Always tell me the truth, Drew. Stop worrying about offending me."

Right now, he didn't feel like being nice. He wanted to tell her the truth—she was driving him crazy. Instead of walking side by side, he wanted to grab her, push her up against the wall, and kiss her until she forgot everything but him.

She stopped and took hold of his hand. "I hope we can find a way to stay friends, even after I move away."

"Me, too." His pulse quickened. "I don't want to lose you." He'd grown used to having her there, whenever he needed someone to talk to. Or a workout partner to help blow off steam. His life would be dull without her.

"Great, now let's get something to eat. I'm starving." Molly sniffed the air. "A Bonnie Bakery always smells divine."

They couldn't be lovers, so Drew had to be satisfied with friends. Hanging out on a Saturday morning over a doughnut and coffee was a good start.

Molly ordered black coffee and a chocolate-frosted long john almost as long as her arm. As she took a bite, she closed her eyes and moaned.

In an effort to maintain control, he gripped the edge of the table. "Got a sweet tooth, huh?" Drew unclenched his fist and lifted his cup of espresso to his lips. The deliciously strong coffee helped calm his nerves. Molly called him a coffee snob, and he owned his quirk. While deployed, he'd learned the finer points of coffee prep. Those little pleasures, like a good cup of coffee in the middle of the desert, made his life bearable. His Special Forces team had insisted on taking with them an espresso machine and coffee grinder to every base.

Molly smiled with a brown spot on her upper lip. "Bonnie's doughnuts are my guilty pleasure."

He pulled away his gaze from her chocolate-covered lip and pushed away memories of their kiss. Besides the owner, they were alone in the bakery.

Bonnie stood over at the bakery counter, reorganizing a row of cookies. Her pink apron was streaked with flour.

Drew considered how Molly felt as a cop serving the small town where she'd grown up. He understood she'd want to start over someplace new. A new city would offer more excitement. He just wished she wasn't so hell-bent on pursuing a career in Federal law enforcement at all costs. The woman sitting across from him was stubborn to a fault.

For years, Drew had spent countless, long nights planning his perfect, quiet life—a house full of children and love. Then Molly came along and shattered his heart. All he could do was put the pieces back together and move on.

****

On Friday, Molly picked Whitney up from school for a meeting with the director of the Mid-Texas Pregnancy Resource Center, or the MTPRC. The girl had been quiet for most of the ride, seeming content to watch the landscape roll by outside the car window. Molly knew she was nervous. If everything went as planned, Whitney would move into the privately funded home for pregnant teen girls over the weekend.

Whitney was now legally an adult but still very much a child. She had several important decisions to make about her and her baby's future, and Molly wasn't qualified to be a good source of information. The women who staffed the MTPRC had the resources and the experience to guide Whitney. They knew the right things to say to a scared, pregnant teenager.

She wondered if Whitney had considered adoption but didn't feel comfortable asking. The center would help facilitate an adoption, if that's what Whitney decided. If not, they would house her and her infant at the center's home until she learned a skill and could support herself and her child.

Surprisingly, over the past weeks, she'd grown used to having Whitney around the house. Both Molly and Rider would miss her when she moved out.

When she arrived at the center, Molly was pleasantly surprised. The main building was a white farmhouse. The rural location provided both security and privacy for the girls who lived there. Plus, they had plenty of outdoor space to enjoy. Fields of golden wheat surrounded the property, as far as the eye could see. In the distance, a lone harvester moved slowly across the horizon.

Molly led Whitney onto the front porch and pressed the doorbell. A high-pitched chime sounded from somewhere deep inside the house.

Soon, a young woman with a baby straddling her hip answered the door.

"Hi," Molly said. "I'm Officer Molly Hernandez, and this is Whitney. We have an appointment with your director, Mrs. Coleman."

"Come in." She smiled at Whitney. "Follow me. I'll take you back to her office."

Molly entered a house full of activity. To the left of the entryway sat a large sitting room, full of comfortable chairs, toys, and a television. On the other side was another brightly decorated room. Several toddlers, along with their mothers, played on a colorful mat.

She followed Whitney and their escort down the hall, listening to their conversation. Whitney's shoulders relaxed, and her gait appeared more natural.

"This is a really great place." The girl hitched up her baby on her hip. "So don't worry. They take good care of you. I know having a baby so young is super scary."

"I don't know what I would have done without Molly." She jerked her thumb over her shoulder. "Your baby is a cutie."

When Molly entered the director's office, she saw a petite woman walking out from behind her desk. She was about as tall as Molly, with black hair laced with silver. Her clothes were casual—jeans and a button-up shirt.

She smiled and approached with a hand outstretched. "I'm so glad to meet you." Mrs. Coleman shook Whitney's hand. "Welcome to our home."

Mrs. Coleman turned to Molly. "Thank you for bringing Whitney today so we can get acquainted. I'd like some time to talk just with her. Afterward, we'll join you for a tour of the center."

"I'll be on the front porch, enjoying the view." Molly squeezed Whitney's hand for reassurance and noticed sweat on the girl's palms. "You got this." She patted Whitney's shoulder then left the office, closing the door gently behind her. Once outside, she took a seat on an old, wooden rocking chair. As she mindlessly rocked back and forth, the floorboards underneath creaked. Her gaze followed the movement of the harvester out in the distant field. Its purpose was singular and clear. If only her life could be so simple.

Her thoughts drifted to Drew. His handsome, chiseled features were clearly visible in her mind's eye. The memory of their kiss still left her weak with regret. She wanted to be with him all the time. He was one of the few people who made her laugh. A touch from him reduced her natural defenses to a mound of smoking ash.

Those feelings didn't matter. She and Drew weren't meant to be. He wanted things she couldn't give. And Molly was following her own path—toward her own career goals.

Yesterday, she'd heard from the DEA recruiter. She'd been officially accepted into the program. They would assign her a Training Academy date soon, which meant four months in Quantico, Virginia. After graduation, she'd be assigned to a field office, anywhere in the country. There, as a Special Agent, she'd have a fresh start. She could finally be her own person. Not a little sister, or friend, or cancer survivor. She'd shape her life the way she saw fit, and then maybe someday find a man to love. A man who'd marry her because he couldn't live without her. Not because he had a preconceived notion of family. Her heart lifted along with her determination.

After she'd ended the call with the DEA recruiter,

she'd itched to dial Drew's number. Instead, she called her parents then Grace—all whose excitement matched her own.

The screen door opened, and Whitney stepped out with Mrs. Coleman. "Are you ready for the tour?" Whitney asked.

Whitney's smile was so broad Molly was afraid her face would crack. "You bet. Lead the way." Molly stood and stretched her legs. For now, her troubled heart was comforted. From the look of joy on Whitney's face, Molly knew she'd had found a new home.

****

Whitney was so happy, tears flooded her eyes. The teen pregnancy home was the answer to all her prayers. Mrs. Coleman explained the center's mission—providing a safe place for teenage mothers and their children. She'd said sometimes staying in the family home was not an option. Boy, could she relate. Right now, the last place she want to be was in her mom's house.

Molly's place felt comfortable, and she hoped this group home would soon feel similar. Maybe someday, she'd buy a house of her own. Whitney sat in the playroom with two other girls while Molly talked with Mrs. Coleman in her office. One of the girls, named Angela, was pregnant, like her. The other, a slightly built young woman with large blue eyes, rocked her baby boy.

"When are you due?" Angela twirled her black hair, which was pulled back into a long, full-bodied ponytail.

"January fourth." Whitney's cheeks warmed, and

she looked at the floor. She shouldn't be embarrassed talking about her pregnancy with these girls, considering their shared circumstances.

"I'm due in four weeks, not that I'm counting down or anything." Angela laughed and rested folded hands on her round stomach.

Lisa kissed her baby on the forehead and chuckled. "I hear ya. When I was in my last trimester, I marked off the days on a calendar. A countdown to the big day. This little guy was a week late, though. He took his good ol' sweet time."

"How does it feel…to hold your baby in your arms?" Whitney raised her gaze to rest on the tiny infant.

"Totally amazing." She pressed a kiss on top of the baby's downy head. "Except in the middle of the night, when he's crying and all you want is to go back to sleep."

Guess she better stock pile quiet time in bed now. With a curious mind, Whitney sat quietly and listened to the ongoing conversation between the other girls. They both seemed happy here. The weight of worry lifted off her heart and floated away like dandelion fluff in the breeze. Being around girls like her gave her a sense of security. For the first time since she found out she was pregnant, she saw the end of this journey wasn't shrouded in darkness and mystery. Things would be all right.

****

As a group of rowdy sixth graders filtered out of his classroom, Drew said a prayer of gratitude his next period was free. Blame the kids' craziness on a full moon, because he didn't have another excuse. Just that morning, he'd sent four students to the vice-principal's office for disciplinary problems. Under normal circumstances, he would have handled the little troublemakers himself, but his patience had run dry. Time to call in backup.

His whole day had sucked—until Molly walked into his classroom. The sight of her in her police uniform sent his blood pressure soaring. Something about a woman in uniform, well this woman, made him want to challenge authority. Maybe she'd have to handcuff him.

His gaze involuntarily flitted down to her duty belt, and his mind went straight into the gutter.

"You look like the cat that ate the canary." She approached the podium wearing a grin.

Needing to control his dirty mind, he focused on straightening the papers on his desk. "I had a rough morning, that's all. What brings you here?"

She took a seat behind his podium and rested her forearms on its surface. "Suspected drugs on the campus. I did a sweep and couldn't find anything. The police really need a drug dog. These kids are too good at hiding things they don't want found."

Drew agreed. "Did you get a tip?"

"A student reported on another student selling prescription drugs."

No surprise, but he sickened at the thought kids were dealing drugs right under his nose. "I hope you catch him or her."

"Me, too." As she sat on his stool, she swung her feet, which hovered about five inches off the ground. "Whitney's moving into the Mid-Texas Pregnancy Resource Center. Actually, she's there right now."

Her news lifted Drew's spirit. Not that living with Molly was bad for Whitney, but she needed a more permanent solution. Especially after the baby arrived. "I'm relieved she liked the home. How are you handling being an empty nester again?"

She shrugged. "My house seems empty. I'll miss having her around. But this arrangement is not about me. The director really went out of her way to make her feel welcome. The other girls seemed nice. They'll help her make an informed choice to keep the baby or seek adoptive parents."

"I hope they don't pressure her into doing something she'll regret."

"They won't." Molly stood and hooked her thumbs in her duty belt. "I also wanted to tell you my news. I've been officially accepted to the DEA Training Academy. I'll get my start date soon."

"Very exciting." Drew glanced away, not wanting to show his disappointment. He knew nothing he could say would make her change her mind. And why should he, if the DEA was where her heart was leading.

"I'll tell you the date as soon as I know. You'll need to find another volunteer for Second Step." Molly walked toward the classroom door.

"Thanks for stopping by and sharing your news. Will I see you at the Bluebird Trail cleanup on Sunday?"

Molly turned and smiled. "Of course. What time did we say the kids should be there again?"

"Ten o'clock, on the dot."

Molly's smile widened. "You are the picture of punctuality."

He pointed to his chest. "I'm a planner. I like to be

on time. Blame my obsession on the Army."

"Heath is always late, and he was in the Army." Molly cocked her head and smirked.

Her handcuffs came to mind again. "Heath's a bad example."

"You can say that again. But I can't blame him for losing track of time. As a newlywed, he has quite a few distractions. Probably why Grace ended up pregnant so quickly."

Drew laughed. "I honestly wasn't surprised when he told me. Both Heath and Grace have had baby on the brain for quite a while." He was both excited and envious of his friend. Heath's life was everything he wanted for himself—first comes love, then comes marriage, then comes a baby in a baby carriage. Where did the memory of that nursery rhyme come from? He must have baby on the brain as well.

She rested a shoulder on the doorframe. "This really pains me to say but you could take a lesson from Heath. Don't hold yourself to such a rigid schedule. Loosen up and see what happens. They say spontaneity can be very satisfying."

Swallowing hard, he dislodged the boulder-sized lump in his throat. "I don't know how to be spontaneous."

Molly straightened her spine and rolled back her shoulders.

As if she'd just accepted a challenge. "Let's see what we can do about that."

Chapter Sixteen

"How about this one?" Grace asked. Seconds later, a yellow dress appeared over the top.

Molly stood inside the changing room of My Sister's Closet, wearing nothing but her bra and panties. She took hold of the hanger, pulled it down, and examined Grace's selection. As she held up the dress, the chiffon fluttered over her body. *Too frilly.* Plus, the color gave her skin a jaundiced tone. "Not for me. Sorry, Grace."

"Will you at least try it on and let me see?"

Exasperation sounded in Grace's voice. They'd searched every rack in the store for a dress for Molly to wear to the Firefighters' Ball. So far, she'd dismissed each and every one.

Molly grumbled and put on the yellow dress. Opening the door, she saw Grace gazing in the three-way mirror. A beautiful black dress draped over her body. The dress was loose enough to accommodate the slight swell of her belly.

Grace turned with wide eyes and raised eyebrows then let them fall. "Oh...you were right. The dress is horrible."

"Finding a dress is hopeless." Molly hated the thought of stopping at another dress shop, but she couldn't go to the dance in her police uniform, which she found more preferable than a frilly dress.

Colleen peeked out her head from a changing room. "Don't worry, Molly, you'll find something." She stepped out into the aisle and did a twirl. Creamy silk billowed around her calves. "What do you think?"

"It's a winner." Grace gave two thumbs up.

Which left Molly the only one holding an empty bag. Her shoulders slumped. Shopping, in general, was not in her wheelhouse. And looking for a formal dress left her head spinning. She didn't know what she wanted, but definitely not any of the dresses she'd tried on so far.

The Firefighters' Ball was only a few weeks away. She'd seen her date, Peter, around town a few times. One Friday night, they'd hung out with a group of friends. He was good looking and fun. For most women, he was a dream come true. But not for her. Peter was not Drew.

She'd heard through the grapevine Drew had asked Ann Deauville to be his date for the Ball. Ann was as smart as she was pretty. A veterinarian, no less. Molly took Rider to see her right after she'd adopted him. Drew and Ann would make a good couple, and he deserved to be happy. So, why did the thought of Ann making Drew happy leave her so depressed? No matter how hard she tried, she couldn't let go of her useless feelings for Drew.

Molly went into the changing room and put on her jeans and T-shirt. Moving on would be easier once she left for Quantico, which hopefully would be right after the holidays. But more and more, she doubted her chosen path. Was she wrong to give up on love for the sake of her career goals? Hadn't she told Drew to be more spontaneous while she was being anything but?

She did one more lap around the store. My Sister's Closet was the only dress shop in town carrying formal gowns. If she couldn't find the perfect dress here, Grace would surely drag her to another town in continuation of the hunt. *Please, no more shopping!*

The storeowner waved Molly toward the back. "I have a few dresses that just arrived."

Molly flipped through the rack, not overly impressed. Not until the very last dress. She gasped. The crimson masterpiece was exquisite. As she ran her hand along the dress, the silk shimmered and flowed like molten lava. Back in the dressing room, she held her breath as she slid the garment up her body. She was afraid to look in the mirror. The dress made her feel like a queen, and she didn't want reality to spoil the illusion.

"Come on," Grace whined from the other side of the door. "We want to see."

When she stepped out, Grace took her by the elbow and led her to stand before a large mirror. Looking back was a woman Molly didn't recognize—more siren than cop.

The boat-neck neckline rested on her collar bone. The straps were wide, almost covering her shoulders, and when she turned, she saw the back dipped low. Stitched into the red silk was an intricate vine design. The A-line waist was slightly cinched then gave way to a full skirt, which pooled onto the floor. The hem would definitely need to be taken up—one of the curses of being short.

"Put you in a room full of firemen and watch out." Colleen touched Molly's arm and made a sizzling sound. "You'll burn down the whole place."

"Drew will have a hard time keeping his eyes on

his date." Grace took Molly's hand and spun her.

A nice perk. "How much?" Molly asked the owner. She imagined this purchase would put a small dent in her savings, but this dress was so worth it. "I didn't see a price tag."

"Five-hundred-sixty-dollars, which is a steal for such a well-made, designer dress."

Excitement made a sharp U-turn and headed toward disappointment. The dress cost as much as her monthly car loan, insurance payment, and food budget combined. "Over my budget."

Grace cut off the path to the changing room and set her hands on her hips. "Molly, you wouldn't find another dress this perfect. Splurge on yourself. You deserve it."

"Why should I pay so much money for a dress I'll wear once?" A reality that bummed her out a little. She didn't see any other fancy gatherings in her immediate future. Not with DEA training looming.

"Sell it to a resale shop after the Ball." Colleen stood beside Grace, and they looped arms. "I'm not letting you walk out of here without that dress."

Out of the corner of her eye, she once again caught her reflection in the mirror. She imagined herself in Peter's arms, being twirled around the dance floor. Then, Drew would approach for one last dance. He'd hold her close. She could almost feel his strong arms around her waist, sending her pulse soaring. "Fine. I'll buy it, but only to get you two off my back." Molly shook her head at the squeals coming out of her friends' mouths.

She wished she was a big enough person to let Drew enjoy his evening with Ann, with no interference from her. But who was she kidding? She wasn't so nice. Molly was dropping a lot of money on a red-hot gown to not only capture Drew's attention but also make a lasting impression.

****

Drew stood at the head of the Bluebird Trail, shovel in hand. Molly was farther down, leading a group of teens outfitted with trash bags and garbage pickers. Sunlight filtered through the heavy foliage, leaving dappled golden spots on the gravel trail.

They'd only been there fifteen minutes when Molly approached, holding an empty trash bag. She'd taken off her sweatshirt and wrapped its sleeves around her waist. "Here's the deal. The trail is already clean. How about we take the group on a hike instead?"

"We can't take a hike." Drew adjusted his baseball cap and peered down at Molly. Was she even looking for trash or just an excuse to change their plans? "Our schedule says we work on trail clean up until noon, followed by lunch at the park's picnic spot."

"Who cares what the schedule says? The weather is beautiful, and we should enjoy it." She pointed down the trail. "The Ferris River is about a mile away. Let's bring the food, and we can eat lunch there."

They'd made a schedule for a reason. A schedule served a purpose. "We can always plan a hike for another day."

"Ugh," she groaned. "Listen, you need to r-e-l-a-x." Molly stretched to set her hand on his shoulder and squeezed. Smiling, she tilted her head. "Come on. We can come back another day when the trail really needs cleaning."

Man, she could turn from bad-cop to good-cop in

166

the flip of a switch. Probably a trick she learned from growing up with five older brothers. Molly did have a strong argument, but in his experience, if people didn't stick to the mission plan, they could get hurt or killed. He closed his eyes in order to refocus. The Second Chance group was not a military unit in a war zone. They were at the Bluebird Trail, with a group of teenagers. No one would die if they went for a hike.

He opened his eyes to see her beautiful face. The feel of her hand still resting on his shoulder burned through the fabric of his shirt. "You win. Let's go for a hike. I don't want you saying I can't adapt."

She narrowed her eyes. "I would never say you're rigid and inflexible."

"Yes, you would." Drew laughed, knowing for a fact that's exactly what she would have said if he hadn't acquiesced. "Now, are you chit-chatting all day or are we hiking?" She looked so cute, standing there in her gray shirt, little shorts, and work boots.

Molly's eyes widened, and a grin spread across her face. "Let's tell the kids and grab the coolers. Good thing we brought the light, soft-sided ones."

Twenty minutes later, they walked side by side down the tree-lined trail. The kids walking ahead made a lot of noise but were having fun.

"Thanks for agreeing to do this." Molly bumped him with her hip. "See, being flexible didn't kill you."

"The day's still young."

"Have you always been so resistant to change?"

"Have you always been so blunt?" Drew asked with a laugh. He and Molly were finally at a good place in their friendship. No more flirting. No rebuttal. Just two people enjoying each other's company.

"I came out with my fists in the air." Molly raised her hands to the sky.

The image of baby Molly, born ready to take on the world, endeared her to him even more. "I believe you were a fighter from day one. For me, I've always liked consistency. In the Army, my life was very regimented. I thrived in a strict environment." He rubbed the back of his neck. "But after Afghanistan...I have a hard time giving up control. Sometimes, the act makes me physically sick."

Molly stopped walking and took hold of his hand. "I'm sorry. You know I run my mouth, and my foot ends up there on occasion, but I'm a good listener. You can always talk to me, however much you want to share."

The soft look in her eyes sent a beam of warmth to his heart. He'd seen a lot of darkness during his deployments. Many things he'd never told another soul. A few people, like Heath and his family, knew about his darkest moments. Maybe, the time had come to trust Molly with the story.

As they continued to walk, she kept hold of his hand, offering him a lifeline. "I was sent all over the world, but my Unit spent the most time in Afghanistan serving Operation Enduring Freedom. One day, another soldier and I went out to do recon in a small village close to our firebase. We were dressed native and had an Afghan interpreter. On our way back to base, we came under attack. My partner was fatally shot, and our interpreter ran off. My radio communication wasn't working so I couldn't call for back-up." An ice-cold shiver ran over his skin at the memory of red blood soaking into brown dirt.

He remembered the ringing in his ears from rapid rifle fire. The sounds around him faded to the background. Instead of the scent of autumn leaves, the metallic smell of blood stung his nose. Drew tasted acrid smoke on his tongue. "I dragged my deceased partner to a hut and covered his body. I could hear the rifle fire grow closer, so I ran for my life. I spent days on the move, staying one step ahead of the Taliban. Luckily, having dark skin worked in my favor. I blended in. The worst part was I was scheduled to leave for Detroit to donate stem cells for my sister." His mouth grew sticky and dry. "Julia had leukemia at the time. I knew if I died, she'd probably die, too."

"How horrible." Molly stroked his hand with her thumb.

All he could do was nod. He'd spent fifty-two hours on the run with nothing under his control. Food, shelter, and his life were at the mercy of fate. "Sometimes, I can act a little weird about being on time and sticking to a schedule. I panic when I don't know what will happen next or if I don't have a plan of action."

"Understandable," she said. "You had a traumatic experience where you lost all control. I'm sorry I teased you."

"Don't stop now." A bark of laughter escaped his tight throat. "I'd hate for you to be too nice." The comfort of holding her hand helped ease the tension in his body. A glance over at Molly made him feel grounded. She had a good effect on him—she held him steady when anxiety crept into his analytical brain.

"Thanks for telling me. The knowledge helps me understand what makes you tick."

"I don't think even Colleen has figured out that one. I see her once a week to work through some lingering issues." He picked up a stick off the gravel trail and twirled it in his hand. "Nothing serious."

"I'm not judging." Her eyes glittered with tears. "Colleen is a great resource for veterans. She does good work."

"Yes, she does. I want nothing more than to put all those memories behind me." Starting over was his purpose for moving to Liberty Ridge. He'd had his fair share of adventure in the military. Now, he wanted stability and consistency—a safe, boring life. No more wondering where tomorrow would take him.

Molly had told him she craved her independence too much to be tied down. Someday, she might have a change of heart, but he couldn't wait for someday. If circumstances had been different, if his sister had never become ill, he just might have waited.

Unfortunately, he couldn't put his life on hold to follow Molly as she pursued her dreams.

****

Being teenagers, the group complained about being hungry ten minutes into the hike. Once they found a spot by the river, Molly opened the coolers and let the kids dig in.

When the teens' stomachs were satisfied, the topic of conversation turned to grievances against their parents.

Molly shook her head at some of the kids' perceived injustices. In this group, those who had parents who cared enough to discipline their children should be grateful.

"One day, you'll appreciate your folks." Drew tied

a bag holding their lunch trash and tucked it inside a cooler.

"Doubt it," muttered a flushed face boy wearing a black hoodie.

At Drew's deep inhale, Molly laughed. He appeared as frustrated as she was amused.

He placed a foot on the picnic table bench and rested folded arms on his thigh. "My parents are coming to visit in ten days. I haven't seen them since I moved to Texas."

Several kids looked wide-eyed at Drew like they were surprised he had parents. She shook her head. Geez, how old did they think she and Drew were? Molly couldn't wait to meet Drew's family, which was only fair since he'd gotten the full initiation rites with hers. "What do you have planned?"

"I'm opened to ideas." Drew glanced around.

"You could take them to a football game." Jake combed back his long, blond bangs with his fingers. "Our high school varsity team plays in College Station on Friday night."

"Friday night lights. Good, anybody else?"

"You should take them to Heath and Grace's farm," Whitney piped in.

Her smile had brightened when she'd said Heath's name. Molly let out a long sigh. Great, another one lost to his charms.

Drew lifted his face to the sun. "I should put you guys in charge of entertainment."

A few boys brought along a football and started playing catch in the field. The rest seemed content to sit and talk.

Molly's mind returned to the story Drew told her

on the hike. All the time she'd known him, she assumed he'd left the Army mostly unscathed. But to have lost a friend in combat then spend days on the run in hostile territory—the traumatic experience must have left emotional scars.

She assumed his highly structured lifestyle was a personality quirk. Maybe he had a natural tendency to be that way, but his experiences overseas sent his instincts into overdrive. She now understood his one-year memorandum to find a wife. His time in the Army had taught him life could be cut short in a blink of an eye.

Above them, the sky turned from bright blue to steel gray. They packed up and headed toward the trail. The walk back was fairly quiet. A brisk wind picked up dried leaves and swirled them on the ground. Tree branches rustled with the movement of birds and other small animals.

When Molly raised her head to gauge the weather, a fat water droplet landed on her forehead. At first, the rain fell half-heartedly. She wasn't concerned. Until the harmless sprinkle escalated into a downpour.

Everyone ducked for cover. Molly found a spot under a mulberry bush. She scooted over to let Drew squeeze in beside her. "Where did this storm come from?" She wiped rainwater from her eyes. "They weren't predicting rain for today."

"The weather forecast was wrong. I'm shocked." Drew's eyebrows arched over his chocolate brown eyes.

She lightly punched him on the arm. Their bodies were pushed together, in an attempt to stay dry. Being so close to Drew made her light-headed. The scent of his spicy cologne filled the air around her, intoxicating her brain. Adrenaline pulsed through her, causing her to tremble. She scooted over and put some distance between them but couldn't go far, unless she wanted to go back out in the rain. *Please don't notice how incredibly crazy you're making me.*

Drew cleared his throat and grinned. "Whose bright idea was going for a hike, anyway? Our teens are probably miserable right now."

Shouts of laughter filled the air.

"Yes, they look miserable." She pointed at the trees and bushes providing shelter for their group. "Admit it…this is so much more fun than cleaning up trash."

"You couldn't torture those words out of me." Drew ran a finger down her arm. "Won't you miss this? Tell me once you get to Quantico you'll miss us."

Doubt clouded her resolution to leave. Being here with Drew felt right. And even though the teenagers in the Second Step program could get on her nerves, she enjoyed her time with them. Was moving away the right thing to do?

Yes, she had to leave. Molly wouldn't stick around and watch Drew fall in love with another woman and get married. Her focus would remain on her future with the DEA. The Training Academy wasn't for sissies and the dropout rate was high. As long as she didn't get sidetracked by her feelings for Drew Atwater, she knew she'd make it through. "Sure." She constrained her emotions and put on a pleasant smile. "I'll miss ya'll."

"We'll miss you, too."

"I'm sure your new police co-leader will be better equipped to handle teenagers."

The rain slowed to a sprinkle, and the giggling kids

came out from underneath the trees and shrubbery like they'd been playing hide and seek.

The corners of his mouth lifted. "But we work so well together. And I'm sure whoever I get stuck with as co-leader will not be as cute as you. He'll probably be tall, hairy and stinky."

"Just your type." She nudged him in the ribs and walked back toward the park.

"*Naw*." Drew caught up with his long strides, taking one step for every one of her two. "The feisty pixie variety are more my style."

Chapter Seventeen

Ten days later, Drew drove to the Austin-Bergstrom International Airport. He parked his car in the passenger pick-up lane, and the sound of plane engines roared in his ears. Sliding glass doors opened with a *whoosh* and out stepped his parents and sister.

His mom gave an enthusiastic wave with her free hand while his dad maneuvered toward him carrying two suitcases. Julia tagged along behind.

His family was a welcome sight. Trying not to be obvious, he visually examined his sister. She was still stick thin and pale, making him fear her cancer had returned. But she wouldn't hide a reoccurrence. Not after everything they'd been through to beat leukemia the first time. His mom pulled him into a very strong hug for such a slight woman.

"Oh, Drew. I've missed you." On tiptoes, she planted a kiss on his cheek.

Once he was released from his mom's sumo hug, he got another one from his dad.

"You look good, son." He patted Drew on the back.

"What have you guys been eating?" Drew stepped away from his parents to catch his breath. "I think you may have cracked a few ribs."

His mom swatted him on the arm. "We've just happy to see you."

Julia looked at him with a gleam in her eyes, which told Drew she was healthy. "Hey, sis." He gave her a kiss on the cheek. "You happy to see me, too?"

"I only came along to keep these two out of trouble." Julia gave him a gentle hug. "Of course, I'm happy to see you. I'm curious about what life is like deep in the heart of Texas." She leaned over to whisper in his ear. "How's your plan going? Have you found the one?"

"Did Mom put you up to this?" *I wouldn't doubt it.*

"No, I don't think she knows about your one-year plan." Julia shifted the purse strap over her shoulder.

"Good, let's keep it that way." Even without the knowledge of his plan, he was sure his mother would be on a one-woman mission to wrangle him a fiancé by the end of her visit. After the suitcases and his family were loaded into the car, Drew headed back toward Liberty Ridge.

What would his family think about his new home? They'd been disappointed when he'd told them he wasn't staying in Detroit. He was away for a long time with the Army, and they hoped he would settle close to home. Maybe now, once they got a chance to see the town and the great people who lived there, they would understand his desire for a quiet life in a small, southern town. Drew merged onto U.S. Route 183 heading north. "How was your flight?"

"Uneventful." Dad's deep baritone voice filled the confines of the car. "Had a little disturbance over Oklahoma. Nothing too bad."

"We almost didn't make it to the airport on time because Mom left behind a suitcase." Julia leaned to rest her forearms on the back of the driver's seat. "She didn't realize it until we were halfway to the airport, so we had to turn around and go back home."

"Your dad was rushing me, so leaving behind my luggage wasn't my fault." Mom breathed out a sigh.

"One suitcase should have been enough. We're only staying for the week." Sitting in the front passenger seat, he turned to Drew. "You know how she is—had to take everything but the porcelain toilet."

He missed the free verbal exchange and teasing resulting from a close family. Kind of like the relationship he'd developed with Molly. She was a kaleidoscope, a unique and vibrant person, and she pushed him to be a better man. He realized why spending time with her was so comfortable. Molly felt like family.

On the drive back to Liberty Ridge, he engaged in small talk with his family. From the highway, Drew pointed out tall oil rigs and the expansive ranches dotting the Texas prairie. After an hour in the car, he pulled into the driveway of his large house. He hoped his parents and sister saw the structure as he did—a down payment on a long-held dream.

"You have a wonderful home." His mom exited the car. "Planning to fill it up anytime soon?"

Julia snorted with laughter.

"And here we go." Drew shook his head. He'd hoped for a few more hours before he had to explain why he'd bought such a big house but was still single.

"Mary Anne, remember…you promised not to pester Drew with marriage talk for at least twenty-four hours." Dale wrapped an arm around his wife's waist. "Our boy's gonna kick us out onto the street if you start already."

"You mind if we take a walk?" his mom asked after the luggage was brought inside. "My legs could use a good stretching."

"Go ahead. Julia and I will catch up." Drew took his sister outside and pointed to a patio chair. "Take a seat. I'll bring out something to drink." Moments later, he placed a tall glass of lemonade on the side table by her chair.

"You have a great place." She raised her glass. "The yard is huge."

"Thanks. I like it." His property was just over an acre. A wooden swing-set sat off in the back corner, looking neglected. Large oak trees edged the yard, making a natural border. "Over the summer, I weeded the flower beds." He'd worked hard to replace all the dead plants with colorful blooms. But a large garden stood out in dull contrast to the surrounding vegetation. "I ran out of time to plant vegetables, but maybe next year I'll get in a few tomato plants, green beans, and zucchini."

"I can't wait to come back next fall and help you eat your garden produce." Julia sipped at her lemonade.

As she glanced around the back yard, he studied her. Her hair had grown out and was styled in a cute, curly bob. The last time he'd seen her, she instructed him not to worry. *Easier said than done.* Julia's health was something he thought about every day.

"You seem very relaxed." Julia covered his hand with hers. "Are you happy?"

He never lied to his sister. Long ago, they'd promised one another not to dish out platitudes in order to spare each other's feelings. "Most days, yes...I am happy. I like teaching and working with the Second

Step Program. I've made a few good friends, and Heath's here. He understands the transition of going from Army to civilian."

She pressed her lips together. "How's your dating spreadsheet working out?"

His temples ached at the mention of his failed attempt. He never should have created the stupid spreadsheet. "I've learned affairs of the heart are never simple."

"You don't have to tell me." Julia sighed. "I thought I had it all when I lived in Chicago. Sometimes, what we build up in our head is totally opposite of reality. On my wedding day, I never would have guessed Burt could cheat on me, but he did. Life doesn't always play out like a movie script."

Drew remembered how hard the divorce had been on Julia. Then shortly after, she'd become easily fatigued and achy. He never forgave himself for not being there to support her. She was alone in a doctor's office in Chicago when she received the diagnosis—Acute Myeloid Leukemia or AML.

Stationed in Afghanistan, he'd begged for permission to go home on the first transport plane out of Bagram. His request was denied, so his mom kept him up-to-date on Julia's treatment through emails and phone calls. Those nuggets of news had been the only things keeping him sane. "What about you?" Drew asked. "How's life in Michigan?"

"I found a cute little bungalow in Ferndale to rent. I'm moving out of the house at the end of December. Horrible time to move, I know, but I need my own space." She tucked a dark curl behind her ear. "I'm doing really well, thanks to you."

Tears burned his eyes and the back of his throat. "You fought cancer and won."

She nodded. "I saw my hematologist last week. A year has passed since my last treatment. She said everything looks good. My cell and platelet counts are within the normal range."

"That's good news." Some of the weight of his worry lifted from his chest. But he also heard what she wasn't saying. The threat of a leukemia recurrence hung like a blade, ready to tear her life to pieces all over again.

Julia put her head on his shoulder. "I've missed you."

"I've missed you, too, Speedy." He'd given her the nickname back in their teens. Julia had been a track star in high school and college. Now, because leukemia had ravaged her body, she became winded just walking up a flight of stairs.

"You never answered my question. Have you met anybody special?" She nudged him with her knee.

Not wanting to talk about his troubled love life right now, Drew stayed silent.

"What about Molly, your police friend who helps with the teenager program? Any sparks flying?" She watched him through narrowed eyes. "Ha...I knew she was the one."

Darn his love struck expression at the mere mention of Molly's name. Plus, Julia had always been nosy. A trait Drew had learned to tolerate over the years. "Molly and I are friends." He prayed Julia would drop the subject. "She's moving away soon. Plus, she's too involved with her career to think about having kids, which is a deal breaker for me."

"Can't or won't?" Julia's smile faded.

"Either way, my feelings for Molly don't matter."

"Molly sounds like me five years ago. When my work was my life. Burt and I wanted kids someday, but much later in our lives. So I understand where she's coming from. But I also know you've put off having a family for a long time." Julia shifted in the chair to sit on her hip and face him. "Is there any room for compromise?"

Drew stood and began to pace. "I've put my life on hold for ten years. I've seen men I care about die. Then there's your illness."

"Don't you dare make this about me." She raised her chin and glared.

Her fiery eyes burned right into his soul, causing him to flinch. "What if your leukemia comes back, and I can't donate?"

"I don't live by 'what ifs' and neither should you. We have no guarantees in this life."

"But my child could be a match." Conflicted feelings tore Drew's heart apart. If only he could see into the future. Then, he would know which plan to follow.

"Just because you were a match doesn't mean your child will be. The odds are very low."

Pushing down a lump of emotion in his throat, he took hold of Julia's hands and pulled her to stand next to him. Then he wrapped her in a tender embrace. "I don't want to lose you." He'd been in Afghanistan when he'd been tested the first time and learned he was a match for a stem cell transfusion. At that moment, he'd finally had some control over the situation. He could do something to help. Then, when he'd come under attack, forcing him to run for his life, he'd felt both his life and Julia's slip out of his grasp. He never wanted to experience that helplessness again.

"You need to follow your heart. I want to be a bridesmaid at your wedding."

Drew smiled. "I can't wait to see you wear an ugly, hot pink bridesmaid dress."

She punched him on the arm. "I would wear the most hideous dress, you know, but only because I love you."

****

Molly had just ended a phone call when a deep, unfamiliar voice echoed from the police department entrance. Then, the Police Chief said something in response and laughed. *Wow*. The Chief had actually come out from behind his desk. Curiosity got the best of her. She walked through the bullpen and took a peek into the lobby. A tall, African American man stood by the front desk, talking to the Police Chief. Next to him was Drew, who stood unsmiling, until he spotted her.

He waved and nodded his head toward the other man. "My dad," he mouthed.

The elder Mr. Atwater was an impressive man. His height, well over six feet, combined with his muscular build made him resemble a football lineman. He'd surely intimidate the most hardened criminal when dressed in uniform blues. Drew's dad turned his head as she approached. "Hello, Mr. Atwater. I'm Molly Hernandez." She reached out to shake his hand, tensing with the expectation of feeling her bones pop, but his big hand was gentle and warm. "Welcome to Liberty Ridge."

"Call me Dale. You're Drew's friend, right? He

said you work as the Department's SRO."

His dark eyes assessed her, standard for any cop meeting someone for the first time. "I do, sir." Molly couldn't stop glancing from Drew to his dad. No denying they were father and son. Both men were the same height, with Dale having a wider build. Drew's skin was a lighter shade of brown and his hair had a looser curl, but they shared a strong, square chin and expressive almond-shaped eyes.

Dale's smile widened. "SRO is important work. Officers in the school make things easier for everyone out on the street."

She nodded. "Drew said you are on the Detroit Police Force. Which department?"

"Homicide for the past fifteen years. I'm a Sergeant." He hooked his thumbs into the front pockets of his dark blue pants. "Tough work. I've seen a lot of bad things I wish I hadn't."

"I can imagine." She pictured herself in Dale's position. How would she handle the stress of working the inner city streets? The question left her more excited than afraid.

The Chief, who stood next to Dale, shook his head. "I worked in Fort Worth right out of the police academy. Lasted only five years there before I opted for a job in a small community. I give you a lot of credit for staying with Detroit for so long."

"Detroit faces many challenges." His brow furrowed. "We have a good mayor, and he's making some real improvements. Take the abandoned house problem."

"I'm sure Molly has work she needs to do." Drew nudged his dad's arm.

"Oh, nothing that can't wait." She smiled, enjoying her time with the two Atwater men.

"Detroit is filled with empty, rundown buildings." Dale smiled at Drew before returning his attention to her. "The only purpose they serve is providing safe zones for the bad guys—gangs, drug dealers, hookers...you name it. The city now has made demolishing the blight a top priority. The process is slow, because money is tight."

"Dad." Drew cleared his throat and crossed his arms. "I'm sure Molly doesn't want a lecture on the revitalization of Detroit."

Dale laughed. "I could talk all day, and poor Drew's listened on more than one occasion. Looks like he's ready to drag me away." He shook her hand again. "I enjoyed meeting you, Molly. Hope we'll see you on Sunday at Drew's house for the party."

Drew's face paled before his cheeks blushed crimson. "I meant to invite you."

Yeah, right. Her first reaction was anger but she quickly burst the bubble of her temper. "I look forward to meeting the rest of your family, Drew. Let me know what I can bring." Molly went back to her desk, while Drew and Dale followed the Chief for a tour of the station. Why hadn't he invited her to his family's little get-together? Maybe they were keeping the gathering small. Could be Drew didn't want to introduce her to his matchmaking mom.

Did the reason really matter? She'd go, if only to repay Drew for all the teasing she'd taken from her family when they'd met him.

A half an hour later, her shift ended, and she went to the locker room to change. Back in civilian clothes, she grabbed her bag and headed for the back door. As she exited, the bright sun forced her to squint. Today, she'd driven her car to the station. She fumbled for her keys then hit the keyfob to unlock her car. A large shadow moved in front of her.

Molly's heart leapt from her chest. The smell of unwashed body wafted over her, making nausea rise from her stomach to her throat. She inhaled deeply through her mouth and turned to see Rich Logan standing behind her. "What can I do for you?" Her voice was as hard as steel.

He leered, and his bulky arms crossed over his chest. "Nothin'. Just thought I'd come over and say hi."

How did a justice system let this scumbag out of jail—twice? Sensing a very unpleasant confrontation looming, she planted her feet wide apart and firmly held her ground. No way would Rich see her retreat. "Unless you want another arrest, I suggest you move along."

He stepped to the side and stuck out his foot, blocking her access to her car. "You listen to me. My old lady's upset she ain't goin' see her grandbaby. Now that Whitney's living in the place for knocked-up girls, she talkin' about givin' the baby up for adoption. We don't give our babies away around here."

Molly swung her arm and hooked her hand behind Rich's neck. Pushing down his head, she placed it on the hood of her car. "I'm giving you ten seconds to get out of my sight. Go." She released her hold.

After a slight hesitation, he took off.

Once Rich was gone, she breathed a sigh of relief. As she pulled the door handle, a hand landed on her shoulder, causing her to jump. On instinct, she swung her fist.

"Whoa, it's me." Drew stepped back with his hands in the air. "Sorry, I didn't mean to scare you. I saw Rich and wanted to make sure you were all right."

"You want us to go after him?" Dale stood next to his son, peering downward.

"No, thank you. Rich Logan is a complete idiot," Molly hissed. "I should have thrown him back in jail, but he'd most likely be out within a few days. If he approaches me again, I will arrest him."

"That's my girl." Drew bit his lip and frowned.

Dale opened his mouth and let loose a deep, baritone laugh, which immediately lifted her mood.

"Glad you're okay," Dale said. "Come on, son, let Molly go home now. Have a nice evening, Officer." He waved as they walked away.

Molly fought a smile while she watched them disappear around the front of a building. *His girl, huh*? Have fun explaining that one to your family over dinner tonight.

Chapter Eighteen

Okay, he was in serious trouble. As they drove away from the police station, his dad sang along to the radio.

"*All the single ladies....*" Dale boomed out in tune with Beyoncé.

Drew was left with the overwhelming desire to bang his head on the steering wheel. His dad had definitely caught the meaning behind Drew calling Molly his girl." *What a stupid thing to say.*

The small get-together he'd planned for his parents and sister had grown faster than James' giant peach. Ann, the woman whom he'd been casually seeing, would be there. They'd gone out a few times to dinner and a movie. So far, things were going well. Ann was very nice and very smart. She was the woman he was trying to fall in love with.

Molly was the woman he couldn't stop loving.

And they'd both be at the BBQ. The hits just kept on coming.

Fortunately, with Julia here, he hadn't fretted much over his love life. She still appeared drained of energy—sleeping nine hours at night and still napping in the afternoon. He knew if the leukemia was back, she would have told him. But he still worried about the long-term effects of the treatments they'd used to rid her body of the disease. "How's Julia doing?" Drew hoped his dad might have some fresh insight.

Dale turned his head to look over. "Your sister's a fighter. She's strong and healthy. We have no reason to think her AML will come back. I know you worry, son, but have some faith."

Drew did have faith. But he also believed in preparation. He'd done tons of research on stem cell transplants between family members and crunched the numbers on the likelihood of his child being a match. The percentage was low but still a possibility. The medical community had made great strides in the development of new treatments for leukemia. He'd even learned cord blood could be used for stem cell transplants. Something most hospitals just threw away after a birth.

"Thanks for coming down to visit." Drew really meant the sentiment, despite his parents inviting half the town to his house. He didn't realize how much he missed them until times like this—talking with his dad in the car, just like when he was younger. But now, Drew was the one driving, and his dad was in the passenger seat, turning up the radio volume and singing along.

Once home, he went upstairs to change into workout clothes. He'd head over to the gym and see if Molly was around. Inside his bedroom, he stripped off his shirt and tossed it on the bed. An unwelcome chill crept in and settled deep in his chest.

His dream from last night pushed into his consciousness. He'd been in bed, but his mind had been back in Afghanistan. He was on the run, unable to find his way home. A shiver ran over his skin at the memory.

He hid in a hut, with his dead buddy lying under a pile of dried hemp leaves. The sound of rapid rifle fire sounded in the distance, echoing in his head. The hut was a death trap, and he had to escape. Darkness gave way to the dim light of dawn. Again, he replayed his plan—head west, keeping the rising sun at his back. A Forward Operating base sat in the foothills. If he could get there, he'd make it to Bagram, and then onto a plane to Detroit. He had to get out alive—for Julia.

Just as he was getting ready to sneak away, he heard the door to the hut burst open and rifle fire erupted. Strong hands grabbed his arm and pulled him outside, into the bright sunlight. Surrounding him were Taliban, their AK-47s pointed at his chest. Alarm sent adrenaline surging through his veins, which stoked his determination. He couldn't die here. He had to live.

That image was the last thing he'd remembered from his dream. With his heart racing in panic, he'd awaken in the safety of his own bed. The same dream visited him often, warping his mind. In reality, the Taliban had never found him. He made the journey safely to the firebase, and then on to Bagram. He'd gone home to save Julia's life.

The facts were small comfort when he was shaking and dripping with sweat after a nightmare. The memory of those days in hell washed over him, again and again, relentlessly chipping away at any security he claimed.

Now, he stood at his bedroom window and looked over his backyard. He saw his parents sitting on the back porch and imagined children running through the soft grass, laughing and playing tag. He had to focus on the present and the future. The past was a monster hiding in the closet. *A beast only scary if you acknowledged it.* He'd learn someday to close the door, once and for all.

****

Stepping through the doors of A Bonnie Bakery always left Molly giddy with anticipation. The sugar in the air and the smell of warm bread released an overload of endorphins in her brain. Being here made her happy. She deserved a little happiness every once in awhile, even if she found the joy in the filling of a frosted doughnut.

Molly's eager gaze followed Bonnie's hand as she reached for a chocolate doughnut, pulled it off the tray, and handed it to her on a small ceramic plate. With a tall cup of black coffee, she sat at a small table by the window. Downtown Liberty Ridge was waking up, with shop owners flipping their Closed signs to Open. She'd taken one bite, savoring the sweet pop of flavor, when her phone beeped. A text from Whitney.

—Mrs. Coleman is taking me on a tour of the hospital maternity ward. I'm so scared!—

—You'll be fine...don't worry. Call me later. I want to hear all about it.—

She really missed Whitney's easygoing presence around her house. Luckily, she had Rider to keep her company. Looking back, she wondered how she hadn't gone mad with loneliness before both dog and girl entered her life. Then there was Drew. The benefits of his friendship also had taken her totally by surprise.

The bell on the bakery door rang, and two women entered. The first was a blonde woman, mid-fifties, petite and very pretty. When Molly saw the second woman, she nearly choked on her doughnut. She was tall and thin, with wavy hair and a very familiar pair of brown eyes. So, these women were the rest of Drew's family—his mom and sister.

As they ordered, she scoped them out from her seat by the window, trying not to draw attention. They probably wouldn't know who she was anyway, but better safe than sorry. Turning her attention back to her coffee, she took a drink.

"Excuse me. Are you Molly?" Drew's sister stood beside Molly's table wearing a smile. "I'm sorry. I didn't mean to interrupt. Drew showed us a picture of you with some of the kids from your program."

Molly returned the smile. She'd never win the award for Miss Congeniality, but she didn't want her reserved persona to come off as rude. "Hi. Yes, I'm Molly."

"I'm Drew's sister, Julia." She pointed a thumb at the woman standing beside her. "This is our mom, Mary Anne."

Both women took a seat at the table next to her.

The unexpected company was surprisingly nice. "Pleasure to meet you. How are you enjoying Liberty Ridge so far?"

"The town is wonderful." Mary Anne took a sip of coffee. "I see why Drew likes living here. He took us to a high school football game last night. We're visiting a cattle ranch today. I might even get to ride a horse!" Her blue eyes gleamed. "You know, I had hoped Drew would live closer after being away so long in the Army. I should have known better. He always had to do things his own way."

"Drew told us you're a cop." Julia picked off peanut pieces from the top of her doughnut. "What's your job like in a small town?"

"I don't see much action. Maybe an occasional speeder." *Usually Heath.* She laughed. "I spend most of my time working in the schools."

"I'm glad this is a safe town." Mary Anne said. "I've been married twenty-five years to a Detroit cop. I say a prayer every day Dale walks out the door to go to work. All I want is for him to come home at night, safe and sound."

"I had a chance to meet your husband at the police station." Talk of police work was familiar territory. With a shared connection, she felt like she'd known Drew's mom and sister for longer than a few minutes. "Dale seems very proud of Detroit and the progress the city is making."

Julia let out a loud laugh. "He could literally talk your ear off about that subject. And I'm not kidding. When he finished, your ear would be dangling off the side of your head, begging for mercy."

Drew's family was pretty cool. She could see bits and pieces of Drew reflected in them. He was a wonderful person with a kind and generous heart. She liked that about his family, too.

Julia leaned toward Molly. "Okay, since you know my brother pretty well, I need to ask…now that he's living in the south, has he finally learned to loosen up? Please tell me he's let go of his spreadsheet obsession."

"He's loosened up about a micrometer." Molly indicated a paper's width space between her thumb and index finger and smiled. "He is trying. I got him to agree to a change of plans during our last Second Step kids outing."

Mary Anne gasped. "A miracle. Even when he was young, he hated any type of change. I honestly don't know where he gets that attitude from."

"Remember our trip to Lake Michigan?" Julia asked her mom then turned to Molly, wearing a wide grin. "Drew was probably seven, and Mom and Dad planned a trip to Lake Michigan for the weekend. On the trip there, we passed a u-pick orchard and stopped."

Julia lifted the tea bag out of her steaming mug and placed it on the saucer underneath. "Drew got upset because he was told we were going to the beach. He refused to get out of the car, so Dad yanked him out. Then, he had a meltdown and refused to walk out to the orchard. By this point, my dad was livid. Those two had a showdown in the parking lot. You've seen my dad, so you know he's a big guy. But Drew wouldn't budge. He wanted to go to the beach, just like we'd planned."

Molly imagined the scene in her mind, which melted her heart. Sweet little Drew, throwing a world-class temper tantrum. How endearing.

"He sure was a handful," Mary Anne said. "He finally went to the orchard with us, but only after I threatened to turn around and go home. Looking back, I think I could have been more understanding. That's just how he's wired...very structured and organized. Once he grew older, he was a little better at going with the flow, but I'm afraid after what happened in Afghanistan..." Mary Anne took a deep breath and looked at Julia.

"Do you mean when he was ambushed, and then chased by the Taliban?" Molly sensed the shift in their previously jovial conversation.

Julia nodded. "Drew's disappearance was a very bad time for our family. He doesn't like to talk about what happened, but the experience still haunts him.

Drew is the reason I survived leukemia. He came home to save me."

Her eyes, which looked so much like her brother's, shone with tears. Molly's own eyes welled with emotion. "Your brother is an amazing man." She'd even say a hero.

"Yes, he is." Mary Anne patted her daughter's hand. "Whoever wins Drew's heart is a lucky woman. He may have his faults, don't we all, but he always takes care of the people he loves." She narrowed her gaze at Molly.

Is the air getting warm in here, or is it just me? Her body heated under Julia's and Mary Anne's scrutiny. Surely, they didn't think she was said lucky woman.

"Don't mind us." Julia smiled. "We love pestering him about his love life. Drew's been through a lot. He deserves happiness."

Mary Anne slid back her chair, the metal legs squeaking against the vinyl floor. "My husband is across the street. I'll see what he wants from the bakery. Be right back."

Once Mary Anne exited, Julia turned her attention to Molly. "My brother's in love with you."

She choked on a bite of doughnut. *Well, let's get straight to the point.* "I care about Drew, but we don't want the same things."

"Like what?" One dark eyebrow arched. "Marriage and kids?"

Molly wondered if she could trust Julia to understand. Cancer had also ravaged her body, like a thief, with no remorse. "I'm a cancer survivor, too. The disease stole a lot. I can't have children. But I'm here— alive. I have a second chance to chase my dreams. I have things I want to do and experience."

Julia reached over to rest her hand over Molly's, compassion and understanding flowed between the two. "Thank you for sharing your survival story. I know how personal a history with cancer is. I won't say anything to my brother. He doesn't know, right?"

"Only my family and best friends know. I haven't told Drew. He should get his full house—kids coming out of every nook and cranny. You were right. He's a good man and deserves to be happy." Molly swallowed back tears.

"Sometimes, men are too thickheaded to know what will make them happy. Drew has become fixated on his dream of having the perfect family. But what does that really mean? A family can come in many forms. He needs to accept that." Julia paused to take a breath. "I know he can be inflexible but think of him as a plank of wood. Add some steam and he will bend, with the right motivation."

Chapter Nineteen

Molly hit the gas, propelling her car through the intersection in order to beat the yellow light. Guilt nudged her that she was speeding, so she eased up. She was on her way to Drew's house with a store-bought cake riding shotgun in the passenger seat.

Her poor stomach had twisted itself in a tight knot. After spending the past months waiting and wondering, she'd finally gotten the call that would change the direction of her life. Her Training Academy date was set. She'd report to Quantico on January third. After eighteen weeks, she'd graduate and become a DEA Special Agent. All her preparation had paid off.

Her goals were now a reality, so she should be excited, right? Instead, her strong convictions cracked. Nervousness and self-doubt seeped in. Why now, when she was just about to take the big leap, did she question herself?

Part of her worried about Whitney. Molly would leave town right when her baby was due. Sure, Whitney had care and support at the MTPRC. But Molly knew she filled an important role in the teen's life—a big sister, of sorts.

During her time on the Liberty Ridge Police Force, she'd assumed because she was serving a small town, she wasn't making a big difference. But after seeing the affect she'd had on Whitney, she wondered if her beliefs were wrong. Sure, Molly wasn't arresting big-time drug dealers, but the impact she had on individuals like Whitney and the other kids in the Second Step program changed lives.

Then there was Drew. She loved working by his side, whether kickboxing at the gym or wrangling a group of teenagers. He accepted her, smart mouth and all. But the part of her he couldn't accept, the fact she was career-driven with no plans of a family anytime soon, was a deal breaker. Was Julia right about Drew's ability to accept change? If Molly was the one he wished to spend his life with, would he compromise? What was she willing to give up in order to be with him?

As she parked on the street in front of Drew's house, she halted her spinning mind. Judging by the number of cars parked along this street, she guessed most of the town was here. She reached over to pick up her cake and ripped off the price tag. Not that she'd fool anyone. The clear plastic container was a dead giveaway she had not spent the day baking.

With quick steps, she walked down the sidewalk toward Drew's house. The sound of familiar voices stopped her in her tracks. In the driveway stood Drew and Ann, the woman he'd asked to the Firefighters' Ball. As Molly watched from around the corner of the house, Ann reached up to rub Drew's shoulder. She whispered something in his ear, which made him laugh.

Molly was an intruder, a witness to their intimate moment. So, Ann was why Drew hadn't invited her. Why he'd acted so nervous when his dad had asked her over. He didn't want Molly ruining his chances with his new girlfriend.

She didn't miss the look in Ann's eyes. Molly was sure she'd worn the same expression of hopeful love at some point around Drew.

Turning on her heel, she hustled away. Once inside the safety of her car, she tossed the cake back on the passenger seat. Minutes later, she pulled into the gym's parking lot. When she was in pain, she didn't spend time crying. Instead, Molly punched things. The gym was probably the safest place for her right now, if she intended to stay out of jail.

After taping her hands, she slid on her gloves and went to work. She sent blow after blow, kick after kick, punishing the floor-mounted bag mercilessly. The muscles in her legs and arms burned. The strain sent a fire coursing through her body. She didn't want to feel anything but physical pain. Sweat dripped down from her face, making the mat's surface slick. She pushed her body until it folded onto the floor. Lying down, she took deep breaths in and out, trying to recover. Her head spun, and her muscles quivered.

Seeing Drew with Ann shouldn't hurt. Molly'd been the one who'd pushed him away. She told him to look elsewhere—they had no future.

After talking with Julia, she'd been given a small flicker of hope. But she'd spent enough time with Drew over the past few months to understand his deep-set ways. His new relationship with Ann was for the best. Even so, doing the right thing still stung.

Her workout left her once again calm and centered. The effort drained her, even of emotion. Drew was moving on, and so was she. Molly didn't have the right to be jealous of something she never had.

The memory of their kiss at the riverbank stirred in

the back of her mind. A kiss that told her Drew still possessed her heart.

****

Drew glanced at his cell phone for probably the hundredth time. Where was Molly? Last he'd heard, she was coming to his 'not so little' get-together. Had she been called in to work? Had talking to his mom and Julia yesterday at the bakery changed her mind? And if so, why?

When he'd seen them through the window of A Bonnie Bakery, sitting together and talking, he'd wanted to sneak inside and listen in. Women talk was equal parts curious and scary.

Heath tossed him a beer. "You've spent the past hour watching the driveway. Who're you waiting for?"

"Thanks." Drew turned his thoughts from Molly to his friend. He twisted the cap off the bottle and took a drink. "Molly. She's not coming."

"Maybe she's running late. Couldn't decide what to wear or had to style her hair."

"When have you known Molly to be concerned about fashion?"

"True, true." Heath nodded. "She called Grace this morning. Said she got the start date for the DEA Academy. She'll leave right after Christmas." He slapped Drew on the shoulder. "For what it's worth, I'm sorry things didn't work out between the two of you."

The information about Molly leaving for the DEA Academy drained his remaining hope. The kiss they'd shared the night of her birthday party had been electric. A feeling stronger than anything he'd ever experienced. The memories didn't matter—not the sweet taste of her lips, or the floral scent of her hair, or the way her smooth skin shivered under his touch. "You win some, and you lose some." Drew shrugged. "Molly has big dreams. I can't compete."

"Ann is nice." Heath tipped his head in the direction of the auburn-haired beauty currently chatting with Drew's mom. "And she seems into you."

He shuffled his stance. Ann was nice. Too nice, and too agreeable. What was the matter with him, that he didn't find those qualities desirable? "Not much chemistry between us. Maybe our connection will grow with more time."

With a shake of his head, Heath lost his smile. "Time won't solve that problem."

Drew ran his fingers through his hair, which had grown out into short waves. "I have to stop thinking about Molly." His frustration evolved by the second. "I've waited on the sidelines and watched other guys settle down and get married because when it was my turn, I wanted to do it right. I'm finally ready, and I won't sit around and wait on a woman who may never get married and have a family."

"Because Molly would rather spend her day chasing drug dealers than driving carpool?" Heath asked.

"I'm in love with Molly, but I won't sacrifice my own dreams in order to be with her."

Heath placed one hand on Drew's shoulder and, with the other, gave him a light slap upside the head. "Man, I'll tell you this only one time, so pay attention. Molly's a very driven lady, and not every man has the strength to mold his life with hers. Now, you have your one-year plan, and that's fine and dandy, but it will never jive with Molly. No matter how hard you try. That woman's determined to be a Federal Drug Enforcement Agent, and the drug trade has no idea the storm that's coming. Don't stand in her way."

Drew stood dumbfounded. What in the world had just happened? Heath was right. Molly did need a man who would unconditionally support her goals, not the other way around.

Heath clinked beer bottles with him, tipped his head, and walked back to the party.

And all this time, Drew wanted Molly to fit into his mold and, in the process, change the things that made her so unique.

He could picture her in her new position, running down the bad guys and taking dangerous drugs off the street. She was ready to light the world on fire.

Hanging his head, he sighed. Unfortunately for Drew, her passion made him love her even more.

Chapter Twenty

Molly was in the middle of a really good dream when a loud chiming yanked her back into consciousness. "Hello," she mumbled into her phone. After no reply, she realized she hadn't pushed the right button to answer the call. *Ugh.* "Hello."

"Molly, I'm at the hospital. The baby——" Whitney broke off with a groan.

"What's the matter?" Molly's heart raced with growing dread. Whitney wasn't due for another three weeks.

"The baby's coming early. I really need you."

Molly's feet hit the carpeted floor. "Are you at Memorial?"

After a pause, Whitney answered, "Yeah."

"Just stay calm. I'll be right there." She ended the call then rummaged for the jeans and hoodie she remembered tossing on the bedroom floor. Once dressed, she pulled up her hair into a ponytail and let Rider out to do his business.

"Sorry, boy," she said when he came back inside. "No dogs allowed at the hospital, but I'll tell you all about the baby when I get home." She gave him a kiss on top of his furry head and grabbed her car keys.

The drive to the hospital only took five minutes but felt like an eternity. Once there, she headed straight to the maternity ward and flashed her badge for quick access. As she approached the birthing room, she heard Whitney's groans of pain echoing in the hallway. Molly entered the room with a flutter of nervous excitement. "I'm here." The sight of little Whitney lying on the hospital bed sent her emotions into overdrive.

Mrs. Coleman sat beside Whitney, holding her hand. "You're wonderful to get here so fast."

Whitney opened her eyes, and a ghost of a smile flickered on her face. "My little rascal is impatient."

The nurse standing at the heart rate monitor came over and patted the girl's hand. "You're doing great. I'll be back to check your dilation again in a little bit. Relax between your contractions and drink some juice."

Mrs. Coleman stood and approached Molly. "I'm needed back at the center. Can you stay with her for the duration?"

"I'm not going anywhere." Molly smiled at Whitney. "We got this."

After Mrs. Coleman left, Molly sat beside Whitney's bed. Other than the beeps on the baby's heart monitor, the room was calm and quiet.

Too soon, Whitney tensed as another contraction seized her body. She moaned and rolled on her side.

What do I do? Molly took hold of her hand. The seemingly weak girl squeezed so hard, Molly swore her bones cracked. "Ride it out." She matched her breathing with Whitney's long deep breaths in an attempt to stay calm, but truthfully, she was scared to death.

"Oh…they're getting worse." Whitney panted after the contraction released. "They told me in the birthing classes labor would hurt, but this is beyond pain. I feel like an alien's inside me, ripping me apart to get out."

That image left Molly's stomach queasy. "Luckily,

you're not giving birth to an alien. You'll meet your baby soon. What do you think—boy or girl?"

"A boy. I think the baby will be a boy." Whitney paused to take a sip of juice. "I didn't want to know before, you know, at the ultrasound. I didn't want to become too attached."

"Have you made a decision yet about the baby?"

Whitney wiggled up into a sitting position. "I've decided on adoption."

She searched for doubt in Whitney's face and only saw strong conviction. She took hold of the girl's small hand. "That's a brave decision." As well as selfless. Somewhere, a couple would soon get a call that would change their lives in the best possible way.

"I've given it a lot of thought and talked to the women and other girls at the home. I need to get my life together before I can be a good mother. My baby deserves to have a safe, stable home."

"I'm proud of you." She put her arm around Whitney, whose body seized with another contraction. They were coming more often. The nurse had told her close contractions meant progress. And progress meant a baby would soon be born. "I'm here. Whatever you need, just ask. We'll get through this, together." She wrapped both arms around the girl and held her like a mother would a small child.

Sobs burst out of Whitney. "Thank you, Molly. I couldn't do this without you."

The nurse entered and checked her progress. "You're at six." She smiled calmly. "You're doing great. Now relax and let your body work. The pain will be over soon."

"How can I relax knowing I still have four

centimeters to go?" Whitney let her head fall back on the pillow.

Molly checked the time—2:15 am. She placed her hand over her mouth and yawned. Maybe she had time to sneak away for a cup of coffee. No one in this room would be sleeping any time soon.

****

Nothing in any of Whitney's childbirth classes prepared her for such pain. Her body was well beyond her control—the squeezing, the back-breaking pain, the pressure. She wanted to die.

"Molly?" Her voice sounded barely above the beeping of the monitors.

Molly straightened in the chair beside Whitney's bed. "What do you need?"

She groaned as her lower abdominal muscles contracted and pushed down. "Baby…is…coming."

After disappearing from the room, Molly came back with a nurse, who again checked her dilation.

"I'm getting your doctor," the nurse said. "Don't push until she arrives."

Yeah, right. With each contraction, her body did what her body wanted. No amount of deep breathing could slow down this train. Her baby was coming, and fast.

Thirty minutes later, her son arrived into the world. *My son.* The person she'd loved since the moment she'd found out she was pregnant. Whitney turned her head at the sound of the baby's cries. Tears blurred her vision.

Molly stood by the nurse who cleaned the baby. She glanced at Whitney and smiled. "He's beautiful. Do you want to hold him?"

"No." She could barely get out the words. "Keep

him for me."

"Whitney, are you sure?" Molly's smile faded.

Right now, she wasn't sure about anything. If she held her son in her arms, she'd never give him up. "Yes, I'm sure. I love him so much. Please watch over him for me." Exhaustion hit her, and she closed her eyes. She imagined her mom at her side, loving her as much as Whitney loved her own child. Finally, after holding in her emotions for so long, she allowed them to fully release and began crying.

****

Class had just started when Drew's phone chimed with a text message. Normally, he kept his cell on silent mode during the school day, but early that morning, Molly called him from the hospital with the news Whitney was in labor.

Most of his students were concentrating on their chapter test, so he picked up his phone and opened the message.

—It's a boy! Mom and son are healthy. 5lbs 11oz with a head of dark hair—

—Tell her congrats from Uncle Drew—

—Will do. She's decided to put the baby up for adoption. The couple will arrive tonight. Can you come to the hospital after school?—

—I'll be there ASAP—

What a relief to learn the baby had been born healthy, with no added trouble for Whitney. Her decision to give her son up for adoption was brave and filled with plenty of heartache. Drew couldn't imagine giving up his own child. Though, he hadn't spent time in Whitney's shoes.

Over the next six hours, the school day dragged.

When the end-of-day bell finally rang, he packed up and headed for the door. He couldn't wait to get to the hospital.

Molly must be exhausted, having been up most of the night. The woman could be as tough and hard as a diamond but encased inside was a nurturing heart. In his eyes, she sparkled with a brilliant multi-dimensional color.

Once he arrived at the hospital, he checked in and went to the maternity ward. On his way to Whitney's room, he stopped by the glass window shielding and showcasing the hospital's newborns. Sitting in a wooden rocking chair was Molly, dressed in yellow scrubs and rocking a tiny bundle in a blue blanket. To keep from falling, he rested his hand on the window frame.

His ears rang with the sound of his pulsing blood. In his tunnel vision, all he saw was Molly's face turned down, looking sweetly at the baby. She made a beautiful picture of maternal love.

Molly lifted her head and caught his stare. Slowly standing, she handed over the baby to the nurse. After exiting the nursery, Molly came to stand by him at the window. "You're here earlier than I expected."

"I left right after school let out." Drew looked again at the tiny baby now placed in a plastic crib. The name Baby Boy Milan was written on blue paper and placed above his head. His skin was a rosy pink, brighter on the patches on his chubby cheeks. The baby's face wrinkled with effort and, then after several seconds, relaxed back into a deep sleep.

"Looks like I got out of there just in time." Molly crinkled her nose. "I'm not changing a poopy diaper."

Drew laughed. "I can't believe he's really here. He's perfect. How's Whitney holding up?"

"She was brave. Her labor was long and hard. When the baby was born, Whitney didn't want to hold him. I started crying. I was blubbering worse than the baby."

Sadness ached inside his chest. "Did she name the baby?"

"No." Molly crossed her arms and slouched against the wall. "She wants the adoptive parents to name him. She's resting now, or at least trying to. I know her decision is tearing her up."

Drew instinctively pulled Molly into his arms. She seemed totally drained, both physically and emotionally. Allowing him to hold her, she relaxed against him, placing her head over his heart.

"He's a sweet boy," she sighed.

"The baby looked good in your arms." Drew felt her body stiffen.

"He was fussing, and the nurses were busy. Once I got him rocking, he went back to sleep." Molly stepped away and gazed at the baby. "I wish things could be different."

"What do you mean?" He saw a tear form in the corner of her eye, which she quickly wiped away.

"For Whitney." She took a deep breath. "I wish she was at a place in her life where she could keep and care for her baby."

So did he, but the reality of the situation was just the opposite. Despite his heartache, he felt pride for Whitney's proven maturity. "When will the adoptive parents be here?"

"Around eight. Whitney requested a blind adoption

so she won't meet them. The adoption agency is handling all the legal paperwork. The couple will take the baby home tomorrow, if the process goes as planned and the baby receives a clean bill of health."

"Is Whitney sure adoption is what she wants? She could change her mind in a month and regret the adoption." Had the Pregnancy Center pressured her into that decision?

"Go talk with her," Molly said. "Ask her those questions for yourself. I'm confident she's really weighed all the options and is not taking this decision lightly."

Drew followed Molly down the hall toward Whitney's room. He matched his normally long stride to her pace, despite the fact he was anxious to see Whitney.

She stopped before entering the hospital room. "How do you feel about adoption?"

"I think adoption is a wonderful way for a baby to find a loving home."

"What about you?" Her wide brown eyes stared up at him. "Would you consider adopting a child?"

He took several seconds to respond, thinking over the question. "Adoption is something I never personally considered. I'd like to see a bit of myself reflected back in my child."

"To have a part of you live on is important for most guys." Her back straightened.

"I suppose." By the serious expression on her face, he knew he was walking on very delicate glass. One false step, one wrong word, and the conversation with Molly would shatter. "For me, I not only want that connection, but I also have Julia to consider. A blood relative provides another possible stem cell match."

Her eyebrows lowered. "But she's in remission now, right?"

"Yes, but I like to have a plan, though, in case her leukemia comes back."

"You and your plans." Shaking her head, Molly opened the door and stepped into Whitney's room.

Whitney's eyes lit when she saw Drew. "Did you get to see my baby boy?

"I did, and he's beautiful." Whitney appeared so young and, yet again, to have aged years. He supposed the strain of childbirth had that affect.

Molly stayed by the door. "I'll head to the cafeteria for a cup of coffee and give you two a chance to talk."

After she left, Drew pulled up a chair and sat next to the bed. He took hold of her small hand. "I'm so proud of you. Molly said you did great."

"Really?" Her light eyebrows shot up her forehead. "I wanted to give up. Molly encouraged me through each contraction. Then, when the time came to push, she got really intense. I was kinda scared." She chuckled.

"I understand. I've taken kickboxing classes opposite her." Drew shared a smile with the slender teenage girl.

Whitney blinked and looked away. "Did she tell you about the adoption?"

Drew nodded. "She did. Are you sure adoption is what you want?"

"I want both of us to have a better life. I know what it's like to grow up in an unstable home."

He couldn't relate, but he could understand. "People will help you, if you want to keep him."

"I know." Whitney set her lips in a firm line. "I want to go to college and become a police officer like Molly. Someday, I want to help others, the way you and Molly helped me. I want to start my family when I'm married and ready. My baby will grow up with a mom and dad who will love him and provide him with a wonderful life."

Reassuring warmth spread through Drew's chest. Whitney had become a smart, strong, young woman. A few more trials for her lay ahead over the next days, and both he and Molly would be there to see her through.

****

After lingering in the cafeteria and nursing her coffee, Molly decided she should head back up to Whitney's room. As she came back into the hospital lobby, she was shocked to see Barbara Logan standing by the front desk.

"Whitney Milan is my daughter," she shouted at a hospital employee. "I have to see her."

Molly approached from behind and flashed her badge at the woman sitting behind the information desk. "Mrs. Logan, please come with me."

Barbara's face paled. "Please, Officer Hernandez. I want to see my daughter and grandson."

Molly led Barbara over to a private alcove and sat her on a chair. She took a calming breath. "Why are you here?"

"Whitney called me this morning from the hospital and told me what she's planning to do with the baby." Barbara sniffed back tears. "I want to tell her I'm sorry for being a horrible mom. I sent Rich packing. I promise he's never coming back to my house. Whitney can come home. I'll help her raise the baby."

Although Molly didn't doubt Barbara's conviction, she'd need more than pretty words. She'd need to see some tangible, long-lasting action. Only time would tell if Whitney's mom was committed to her daughter's well being. "I'm glad you have removed your husband from your life. That's a start. Your daughter has a bright future ahead, and more than anything, I want her to succeed."

"Let me help her." Barbara raised her folded hands. "You've gotta believe me."

"Here's my suggestion." She widened her stance and folded her hands behind her back. "Get help for yourself first. Go to counseling. Gain emotional strength so you won't be tempted to let your husband, or anyone else for that matter, abuse you. Then, when Whitney comes back into your life, you both can move forward, together."

"I'm so sorry." Barbara pulled a tissue out of her pants pocket and blew her nose.

"I'll take you upstairs." *Please don't let this be a mistake.* "Then I'll ask Whitney if she wants to see you. You can go in only if she agrees. You have a chance to start the healing process. Whitney needs support for her decision, so don't question her motivations or suggest she can move back with the baby. If you do, I will remove you. Is that clear?"

Barbara raised her head but avoided eye contact. "Crystal clear."

After checking with Whitney, Molly escorted her mother into her room. Their conversation was strained at first. Molly stood with Drew off to the side and observed the reconciliation without being intrusive.

Her mind wandered back to her earlier conversation with Drew. No surprise he didn't consider adoption an option for building his family. Although, his words still stung her heart. If and when she was ready to start a family, adoption would be a lifeline to a child who'd need her as much as she needed him or her. But for now, she had other dreams to chase.

Leaving for Quantico would be easier if she hadn't fallen in love with Drew. He made her a better person and for that, she'd always be grateful. One tear escaped her eye and rolled down her cheek. As the saying went—the passage of time healed most wounds. Molly wondered how many years she'd need to mend her broken heart.

Chapter Twenty-One

By the time Molly left the hospital, she could barely put one foot in front of the other. Earlier that evening, both she and Drew had been with Whitney when she'd met with the adoption agent. Molly had asked her friend, a lawyer, to come to the hospital and look over all the forms before Whitney signed. After she was assured all the forms were in good order, Whitney signed them with a shaking hand.

On Whitney's behalf, Molly also met with the adoptive parents. They'd explained that after years of trying, they'd been unable to conceive. When they'd received the call that morning, they broke down with tears of joy. After spending almost an hour talking with them, Molly left confident they would make wonderful parents to Whitney's son. A weight had been lifted off her heart.

On the way out of the hospital, Drew escorted Molly to her car. "Are you all right to drive home?" He stopped and held her shoulders. "You can hardly walk straight."

"I guess the day finally caught up to me. I'll make it home fine." She yawned. "Only a short drive." After fumbling for her car keys, she dropped them onto the ground.

Drew bent to pick them up. "I'll drive you home. You've been awake for almost twenty-four hours. I won't let you fall asleep behind the wheel and crash."

"I'm fine. I won't fall asleep before my head hits the pillow. I promise." She reached out to grab her keys out of his palm.

Drew closed his fist, hiding her keys. "Come on, Pixie, let me take you home. I'll even tuck you in and read you a bedtime story."

She couldn't stop her growing smile. The man was incorrigible, as well as way too cute. Against her better judgment, she followed him to his truck, dragging her feet in exhaustion.

When Drew set his hand under her arm to give her a lift into the passenger seat, she didn't protest. "Thanks," she muttered. Trucks were not made for people of her height. Of course, Mr. tall, dark, and handsome had no problem sliding into the driver's seat.

"I'll bring you back to the hospital on my way to school tomorrow morning."

Inside the warm comfort of his truck, her eyes grew heavy. She inhaled and caught a whiff of his cologne. "Whitney will be released from the hospital around noon. She'll need a lot of emotional support. The adopting couple will be there about that same time to take the baby home."

"You know, instead having to pick you up, you could stay over at my house." Drew's suggestion hung in the air, and then he laughed. "Oh wait, on second thought, Grace told me that you snore."

Heat crept up her face. "She never said that."

"She did, just in case things got serious between the two of us. Grace wanted me to know what I'd get myself into."

His sexy smile appeared again—a playful curve of

his full lips. Her tired body could not resist his charm. "Please." She rolled her eyes. "You're extra full of yourself tonight. And I don't snore."

He laughed. "Guess I'll never know the truth."

Way too soon, he pulled into her driveway. Drew jumped out and jogged over to open the door.

As he reached out to help her down, dizziness gripped her. The heat of his touch left her struggling for breath. With her feet now on the ground, they stood toe to toe.

Drew's hand cupped her elbow. His other hand rose to play with her hair, wrapping a strand around his index finger.

Her gaze locked onto his. Those warm, brown orbs held her captive. She couldn't stop the slow burn. All was quiet, except for the hum of insects. She stood with him in the dark, under a blanket of stars.

Drew put his arm around her waist and pulled her close. "You are so beautiful."

Her sleepy mind jolted back to life. Adrenaline pumped through her, awakening every nerve in her body. She lifted up on her tiptoes and pressed her lips to his. Her traitorous hands found their way around his neck. They linked together and pulled him closer. She dug her fingers into the hard muscle of his shoulders. Drew's breath smelled minty and fresh. She couldn't get enough. Sparks shot through her veins.

He trailed his thumb along her jaw line and rested on the tender spot under her chin. His other hand tightened its hold around her waist. The full length of Molly's body pressed against him. "Bad idea," she squeaked out while her head continued to spin.

"Not the way I see it. Since your birthday party,

kissing you is all I think about." Nipping at her lower lip, he moaned. "You taste more delicious than a cookie from A Bonnie Bakery."

"What about Ann?" Molly took a step back. Her body chilled at the loss of contact with Drew. "You should be thinking about Ann."

Drew groaned. "Ann and I aren't serious."

"I don't want to interfere with your relationship with Ann or any other women. You need to stop kissing me." Molly continued her retreat with small steps.

"You kissed me, remember?" Drew advanced. "If you don't like kissing me then why do you keep doing it?" He leaned in close and grabbed her around the waist, securing his hold once again.

His breath warmed the top of her head. "My enjoying kissing you is not the point." If her willpower slipped, she'd take him inside and continue. Drew's lips were heaven. When they kissed, the ground underneath her felt like tectonic plates colliding—two solid forces pushing against each other to form something larger than she could have imagined.

But tonight, even in her sleep-deprived state, better judgment ruled. "Ann's a good person. You belong with her."

Drew's dark eyes flashed. "What makes you think you can dictate who I fall in love with?" His posture was military straight, and he crossed his arms over his chest.

"That's not my intention." Her temper heated, with her anger directed at herself as much as him. Despite her words, all she wanted was to be back in his arms. "I'm only saying you shouldn't go around kissing every girl in town when you're finding someone to settle down with."

"Do you seriously think I'm chasing skirts?"

"Of course not." All her energy drained out of her body. The long day had caught up to her with full force. "I'm tired, and I don't want to stand here arguing. Good night. Thanks for driving me home." Heading toward the front door, she climbed the front steps and put the key in the lock. The door creaked open before she had a chance to slide in the key all the way.

Her front door was unlocked and open. She'd locked it when she'd left. Had the dog sitter forgotten to close the door behind her? But Bridgette always used the back door when she took Rider for a walk. A sickening dread uncoiled inside her. She pushed Drew to the side and flattened her body against the wall next to the front door.

A muffled barking sounded from somewhere inside, and a vile smell wafted out, causing vomit to rise in her throat.

Someone had violated her house. *Where is Rider?*

****

"I've got your six." When Drew noticed Molly snap to high alert, he moved behind her. Something was very wrong.

She used her foot to swing the door all the way open. "Police. Step out so I can see you. Hands up."

The house was completely dark, not even the ambient glow of electronic devices helped light the way. The power must have been cut. Rider's deep barks were the only sound coming from inside. The smell reminded him of the disgusting odor of a garbage dumpster.

Molly crept through the front room with Drew

following close. Going into a office at the front of the house, she went to a small safe, pressed in the code to unlock it, and pulled out a handgun. Then she went to the basement door. After reaching for the handle, she twisted the knob and swung open the door, gun drawn.

Rider came charging out.

Thank goodness, the dog was all right. While Molly swept the rest of the house, he stayed in the kitchen petting Rider, who was panting heavily.

"All clear," Molly said as she entered the kitchen.

He released Rider, who went bounding over to Molly, pawing and licking her like a furry doctor examining his patient.

Drew stepped into the front room and got a good look at the mess he'd walked through earlier. What he saw left him more nauseous than before. The outdoor streetlight through the front door shone over the extensive damage.

Furniture had been slashed and soiled. Red paint covered the beige carpet. On the wall, the intruder left a profane message. Precious family pictures were broken and strewn on the ground, with shards of glass poking up like tiny mountain peaks. Trash was scattered everywhere. The rotten smell became so overpowering, he had to step outside.

Molly and Rider joined him on the front porch. With her gun in her left hand, she pulled out her cell phone with the other and dialed. "Hey, it's Molly. I had a break-in at my home and need a squad sent over right away."

As she listened to the dispatcher on the other end of the line, she paced back and forth like a caged tiger.

"Will do. Thanks."

She turned her attention to him. "Processing and clean up might take a while. You can go home and call it a night. It's getting late."

Outwardly, she appeared calm, but he knew inside was a very angry and upset woman. "I'm staying here. No way am I'm leaving you right now."

"Dispatch said officers are enroute."

He pulled her into his arms, needing the comfort of contact. As he rubbed her back, the tension in her body softened. She relaxed and leaned into him. The floral scent of her hair tickled his nose, and he kissed the top of her head.

"You should stop doing that." Her voice was quiet and subdued.

"Admit it, you needed a hug. And that kiss was totally innocent."

She chuckled and wrapped her arms around his waist.

"I'm staying here until the cops are done," he said. "Then you're coming to my house."

Her head jerked up and nearly clipped his chin. "Whoever did this is long gone. I don't need a babysitter."

No doubt, she could take care of herself, but he didn't want to leave her alone. "Come for my peace of mind. I won't sleep unless I know you're safe. You and Rider can stay in my guest room. I promise to tuck you in and walk away."

Her lips turned up. "No bedtime story?"

Before he could think of a humorous reply, the glow of headlight beams announced an approaching vehicle. A second followed close behind.

Molly greeted the officers and walked them inside

the house.

Standing in the doorway, Drew watched them take stock of the damage. Restoring the room would take hours of hard work.

One of the officers gave a long whistle. "Who'd you tick off, Molly?"

"Rich Logan." She folded her arms across her chest. "His wife finally enforced the restraining order and kicked him out. He's currently awaiting trial for multiple charges, one of them being the physical abuse of a minor. But he thinks all his problems are my fault."

"He approached Molly outside the station last week." Drew stepped forward. "I witnessed the exchange. He wanted to start something."

"I've called in a tech from the county to process the scene." The stocky officer brushed a hand over his buzzed black hair and looked around. "And we'll need the power company out here to get these lights turned on. I suggest you find somewhere else to bunk for the night."

"Don't you need me here?" She lowered her gaze to the dozens of photographs littering the floor.

"Go pack a bag, Molly, and let us handle this. As the victim, you can't be involved. You want these charges to stick, right?" The taller of the two officers gave her a hug. "We'll nail this guy, don't worry."

Back in the kitchen, Drew packed Rider's bowls and put some dog food in a plastic bag. He clipped Rider to his leash, and then met Molly on the stairs with an overnight bag in hand.

After a few parting words, she left the police to their task.

Drew opened the truck door and let Rider jump

onto the back seat. He turned to see Molly looking pale and her hands trembling.

"Would you rather stay at Grace's?" He took the heavy bag from her hands. "I'll take you there if you'll be more comfortable."

"No." She sighed. "The ranch is too far away to drive at this time of night."

As he backed out of the driveway, she started to laugh—the kind of hysterical laughter that only happens when exhaustion takes over the brain.

"I can't believe this. I just met with a realtor to put my house on the market, and now it's trashed."

Don't think about her moving. Focus on the fact she's sitting next to you, right now. "They'll nail Rich Logan to the wall. Don't worry about your house. I'm sure a team of cleaners can take care of the mess within a few days."

"I hope so." She covered her mouth with both hands, yawned, and then rested her head against the window. Within seconds, a quiet snore sounded.

In sleep, with her guard lowered, she looked so angelic. He was tempted to take a photo with his cell phone to capture the moment, but he restrained the impulse. The memory of her, so peaceful and beautiful, would have to be enough.

****

During the ride in Drew's truck, sleep claimed Molly fast and hard.

Once the ride ended, Drew shook her awake and wiped a spot of drool off her cheek.

How embarrassing. She gathered all her energy and dragged herself into his house. Molly followed him up the stairs and shuffled into the guestroom. Her feet caught on a stack of books on the floor, and she would have done a face plant if Drew hadn't caught her around the waist.

"Sorry about the mess." His cheeks flushed crimson. "I never cleaned up after my family left for Detroit."

Besides a bed, dresser, and a few deadly piles of books on the floor, the room was almost empty. "Thanks for letting us crash here tonight." She flopped onto the bed. A soft mattress never felt so good.

Ryder sniffed around the room before finding a comfortable spot to lie down.

The security of being with Drew helped ease her mind. Sure, she didn't think of herself as a woman who needed a man's protection, but tonight, she'd accept Drew's help with gratitude. "I want to know how Rich got past Rider." Molly put her head back on the pillow and closed her eyes.

"Thankfully, Rider wasn't hurt, and neither were you." Drew picked up a blanket on the edge of the bed and covered her.

Encased in a cocoon of warmth, she drifted back toward sleep. "Thank you," she whispered.

He kissed the top of her head. "Sleep tight, Pixie. See you in the morning."

She thought about getting up to change into her pajamas but couldn't find the energy. Instead, she fell into a dream world, where Drew filled his empty house with a family they created together. Inside her mind, she saw their children—a beautiful fantasy.

Chapter Twenty-Two

The man could cook.

Molly took another helping of breakfast casserole and settled back onto the kitchen chair. Earlier, she'd arisen to the smell of coffee and bacon. She took a hot shower and went downstairs to find Drew working in the kitchen. He looked adorable in his 'kiss the cook' apron.

She glanced at him now, across the table, and decided she needed to get out of this house, and soon. Molly imagined him sitting at this very table, eating breakfast with his future wife. The food on her plate suddenly looked unappealing. Her stomach soured, and the bacon in her mouth tasted like cardboard. "Thanks for breakfast but we should get going." Molly picked up her plate and set it in the sink. "I'll clean up while you get ready."

He smiled cheekily and handed her his empty plate. "Is that all you're eating? Don't you like my cooking?"

"Yes, you're the next Bobby Flay. Now, get moving." Molly flicked the dishtowel at him, just missing his rear. She really needed to leave. His house represented everything that made her wrong for Drew. Big—meant for a large family. Permanent—he wanted to put down roots here in Liberty Ridge. Right now, the house was almost empty. Drew waited for a wife to begin filling each room. Her being in town only got in the way.

Molly cleaned the kitchen while Drew showered and got ready.

"Okay, dear, let's go." He descended the stairs.

Drew looked handsome in his teacher uniform—polo shirt and khaki pants, with a leather messenger bag in hand. So much so, she wanted to kiss him on the cheek and tell him to 'have a good day at work.' Instead, she picked up her bag, said goodbye to Rider, and went out to his truck. If she stayed in his house any longer, she'd drive herself crazy.

Her dream was a mirage. An oasis in the middle of the desert. From a distance, the palm trees and water looked like heaven, and a wanderer pushed themselves to reach paradise. But ultimately, they'd be left with nothing but emptiness.

Drew drove her to the hospital and stopped in front of the main entrance. "I'll call you at lunch to check in. Keeping Rider at my house is not a problem. You, too, by the way."

As she hopped out of the truck, Molly grunted. Why did they have to make these things so high off the ground?

"Maybe I should buy a step stool." Drew smirked.

"You're hilarious." She went to close the truck door and paused. "Thanks for everything last night. I'm really glad you were there. I owe you one."

His teasing smile faded. "That's what friends are for. See you later."

"Bye." She closed the door, and then went inside the hospital. Her thoughts turned to Whitney. How was she holding up emotionally? Today, she'd leave both the hospital and her baby. Was she second-guessing her decision? After stopping at the nurse's station, she walked into Whitney's room. "Morning, sunshine." Glancing at Whitney, who sat in bed, she noticed the girl's cheeks were streaked red. "What's wrong?"

"I tossed and turned all night. I hardly slept," Whitney said between sniffles. "After I took my shower this morning, I went for a walk down to the nursery. I saw him. I saw my son. He's so small and helpless. What I am doing, giving him to someone else?"

Poor, sweet girl. Molly sat on the bed and wrapped her arms around Whitney, who broke down into sobs.

Her body shook with each gasp for breath.

"Doubts are a natural part of a decision this important. Your baby's adoptive parents will love and care for him. They are very nice people, who have been vetted by the adoption agency. I still believe you're doing the right thing, but you can still change your mind."

"Are you sure they'll love him?" Whitney's glossy eyes were puffy and red.

Molly handed her a tissue. "Yes. Now, let's get you some breakfast. You'll need your strength today." She knew how easily emotion could take over. Once that happened, rational thought disappeared, and despair crept in. After her hysterectomy, she'd spent days grieving for the future she'd lost. Even surrounded by loved ones, she'd felt alone. Her only comfort had been the echoes of the voices in her soul, telling her that she was strong. She was a survivor.

After Whitney ate a little eggs and toast, the corners of her mouth lifted in a small smile. "My breasts are so full, I'm afraid they'll burst!" She wrapped her arms around her chest and winced. "They never told me how painful drying up is."

"If they explode, don't do it in my car. I just got it detailed." Molly took the hairbrush off the nightstand and began combing Whitney's tangled hair, until her locks were as smooth as velvet, just like her own mother had done for her as a girl. Sometimes, the smallest acts conveyed the deepest love. Molly was not Whitney's mother, but she loved her with maternal protectiveness. Similar to the deep emotions that motivated Whitney's sacrifice.

When a nurse came in with Whitney's discharge papers, Molly left the room to meet with the social worker, who appeared in the doorway.

Once Whitney was cleared to leave, Molly walked alongside her. She held her hand as Whitney rode in a wheelchair. When they exited through the hospital doors into the crisp outdoor air, the tension in Whitney's body appeared to melt away.

"I'm proud of you," Molly said when they pulled up to the MTPRC house. "I know your heart is breaking, and I'm sorry I can't do anything to make that hurt less."

Whitney stared off into the distance. "I didn't think I could leave the hospital without him, but I did. I will finish high school, and then college. I will become a police officer. And someday, a wife and mother."

Pushing back tears of her own, Molly said a prayer that all Whitney's dreams would come true. After all she endured, she'd earned it. "Give yourself permission and time to heal, both physically and emotionally. Allow yourself to grieve. Just remember that I have faith in you." Molly reached over and gave her a hug.

She got out of the car, moving slowly. Five teenage

girls poured out of the front door of the house and surrounded Whitney. Her temporary family at the MTPRC would see her through these rocky days. Then once she got back on her feet, Molly knew the girl was destined for great things.

"Watch out, world." As she observed Whitney hug her new friends, Molly smiled. "You can't keep a strong girl down for long."

****

Whitney's body ached, every part of her was sore, including her heart. Tonight was her first night back at the center since giving birth. Everyone had been real nice, but right now, she needed to be alone. Nothing anyone could say would make her feel better. Molly told her to give herself time to grieve, and that's what she would do. Earlier that morning, she'd said goodbye to her son. She entrusted him to strangers, who would love and provide for him. *Please let them love him they way I would have.*

Looking up at the dark ceiling, Whitney wiped dampness from her eyes. As she sat up in bed, her body cried out in pain. Her breath hitched, and bit her lip to stop a fresh wave of sorrow. No more tears. At least, not for today.

She was just about to leave her room to head down to the kitchen and find something to eat, when a knock sounded on her door. "Come in," Whitney said.

The door opened, and her friend, Maria, peeked in. "You have a phone call. It's your mom."

Her mom came to the hospital to visit last night, and they'd left things on pretty good terms. What did she want now? After walking downstairs to the private room where the house phone was located, she sat and picked up the receiver. "Hello." For several seconds, silence greeted her. Then a familiar voice sounded through the line.

"Hey, baby. I wanted to see how you're doing. Molly stopped by the house this afternoon. Talked to me for a while. She told me you were released from the hospital."

"I signed the papers, Mom. My baby boy's no longer mine." Whitney's eyes burned with tears, but she refused to give into the feeling.

"I know, honey. You are so much stronger than I could ever be. I'm so proud of you. I hope one day you can be proud of me, too."

Whitney didn't know what to say. This woman was so different from the mom she'd known for the past few years. Her mom had always been flighty, but after she married Rich, things became unbearable. Now that Rich was out of their lives, could their relationship finally heal?

"When Molly was over, we talked about me going into therapy. She gave me the name of a women's shelter that counsels abused women. Helps them to stop the cycle. I'll go, Whitney. I want to be a good mom for you. I want you home, baby."

Nice words, but her trust would take time to earn. "I'm glad to hear you took Molly's advice. She only wants what's best for you. I'm staying here, at the center, for a while longer, until I know for sure home is safe."

"Okay. I understand. I miss you so much. Can I come see you tomorrow?"

Her mom actually missed her. Inside Whitney's heart, which was so battered and bruised, a small bud started to bloom. "Yes, Mom. I'd like that very much."

****

With the Firefighters' Ball less than a week away, Drew thumbed through his closet searching for a decent suit. He finally found one hiding in the back. Brushing off the dust, he examined the out-of-date suit and quickly decided he needed to go shopping.

Ann told him she was wearing a pink dress, which meant he needed a pink tie. Had he been transported back to high school? If he looked in the mirror, would a pimpled face boy with a loose afro stare back? He'd taken Sandra Johnson to the Senior Prom, and she'd left with another boy halfway through the dance—which meant Drew had gone home alone.

His lack of enthusiasm for the Firefighters' Ball was equal to what he'd felt for Senior Prom. If he couldn't go with Molly, then what was the point of attending? To make things worse, she'd dance the night away with Peter the fire dude. Well, he'd go, if only to douse any sparks between Molly and her date.

A knock sounded at the door. He tossed his old suit on the bed and went downstairs. His footsteps echoed in the empty living room. Opening the door, he was surprised to see Grace standing on his front porch.

"Hi." Grace's folded hands rested on her baby bulge. "I hope I'm not interrupting."

"No. Come on in." He held open the door. "Do you know where I can buy a suit on short notice?"

"You're cutting it close. The Ball is this Friday night." Grace entered, and her gaze scanned the room then rested on Drew. "Try the Bighorn Department Store. They sell nice suits in their men's department."

"Thanks." He led her into the kitchen. "I've

procrastinated, big time. I don't like dressing up. Makes me itchy."

Grace laughed and took a seat at the kitchen table. "You sound like Heath."

"Can I get you something to drink?"

"Ice water would be great." Grace rested her hands on the table. "I want to talk to you about the Ball."

"About me not owning a decent suit or tie?" He doubted she wanted to talk fashion. He'd seen that look on Grace's face before—concern mixed with granite determination.

"No, but I should take you shopping. I'm here because of Molly."

His blood pressure spiked. "What about Molly? Is she still having problems with Rich Logan?" If she was having trouble, she would have called him. As far as Drew knew, Rich was locked up in a jail cell.

Grace exhaled a long breath. "Drew, she's overwhelmed with everything going on. She'd never tell you but attending the training academy scares her. Then, being a DEA Agent will be big adjustment. Instead of speeders and rowdy kids, she'll chase hardened drug dealers and thugs."

He poured a glass of water and set it on the table before Grace then he took a seat. "I've told her she's better off in Liberty Ridge."

"I know your intentions are in the right place, but you're not helping." Grace took a drink of water. "You're messing with her heart."

"Messing with her heart?" Drew's own heart pounded hard and fast. "She's the one who's leaving." And when she did move away, he didn't know how he'd fill the hole in his life.

"I'm not blaming you. Well, not entirely." Grace's mouth lifted in a soft smile. "Molly is as stubborn as one of my bulls, and she will succeed in the DEA. But when you come on to her, well…the emotions stirred up make a complicated situation even tougher."

"She told you I come on to her?" He thought back to their kiss by the creek on the night of her birthday party, and his body flooded with warmth.

"Molly and I have been friends for a long time, so I read her pretty well. I know she's not innocent." Grinning, Grace wagged a finger in the air. "She probably initiates your kissing sessions more often than not. But you're pulling on her heart, which is harder to resist than a physical attraction." She took another drink. "Gosh, I'm so thirsty lately."

Drew stood and leaned a hip against the counter. "We fit together. Molly is my best friend, and she challenges me in so many ways. I've fallen in love with her." His chest squeezed at the word love. He did love her, but love wasn't enough.

"What would you give up to be together?" Grace's expression softened. "Your big house filled with lots of kids? A wife who's waiting at home with dinner on the table?"

"That's not fair, Grace. You know I've waited a long time for those things. When someone is your soul mate, you both should want the same things. Neither should compromise. Molly and I are like Mercury and Pluto." The heavy weight of impending failure pressed on his shoulders. "We couldn't be more different."

"What?" Grace scratched her head. "Never mind. No more science analogies. You think love is easy. Ask Heath how hard our love story was. We both compromised to make our marriage work. Need I remind you I was engaged to another man when I met Heath?"

"No," Drew mumbled. Sure, all relationships needed work, but he couldn't imagine trading his dream of a stable family for a wife who worked crazy hours in a dangerous job. His mom lived that life every day—never knowing if your spouse would come home at the end of their shift. As a child, he'd feared losing his dad. Still did. Honestly, part of him feared loving a woman like Molly. "You and Heath are different. You loved the ranch and were happy to give up your old life to stay with Heath."

"I'm not convincing you to give anything up for Molly. Give her your blessing and let her leave in peace." Grace stood and stretched her back. Then she walked close to give Drew a kiss on the cheek. "I care about both of you, that's all."

"I respect your opinion, but I won't let her leave without telling her how I feel. I love her, Grace." He straightened his posture, as if standing at attention. "I'm a trained, battle-tested soldier. I don't walk away from a fight."

Chapter Twenty-Three

So far, nothing had quelled the bundle of nerves growing in her core. The thought of going anywhere with styled hair and makeup left her queasy. Even a ten-mile run that morning hadn't taken off the edge. Now, Molly slid her body into the red, formal dress and caught her reflection in the mirror. She had to admit— she looked really good.

The dress fit her perfectly after a few alterations by *Mamá*. Despite her objections, Grace had dragged her to a salon that morning. Looking at her reflection in the mirror now, she marveled at her hair, which was pulled up in an elaborate twist. So many bobby pins held together the silky curls, she'd lost count. Molly stepped even farther out of her comfort zone by using foundation, eyeshadow, eyeliner, and mascara. She'd held the knock-out punch for her lips, which were stained a deep red to match her dress.

The sudden noise of the doorbell downstairs made her arm jerk, and the necklace in her hand flew onto the floor. She bent over to pick up her necklace, careful not to let any body parts slip out of her low-cut dress, and set the jewelry back on the bathroom counter. Then, she went downstairs to see Rider sitting by the front door with his tail thumping.

"Sorry, boy, that's not Drew." She opened the door to see Peter. He was dressed in a black suit and looked devilishly gorgeous.

"Wow." He grinned and gave her a wink. "I'm the luckiest man alive."

"Come on in." Molly moved back, careful not to trip over Rider or step on the hem of her dress.

Peter handed her a red rose. "This rose pales in comparison to your beauty. I don't know if it's safe for me to drive with you next to me."

Oh, please. He was laying the charm on a bit thick. But the platitudes calmed her jitters, so she decided to just go with his sweet talk and enjoy the ride. "Thanks." She held the stem of the rose, carefully avoiding the numerous sharp thorns. "I have to go back upstairs to get my shoes. Then we can go."

As he stood in her entryway, her eyes drank in the sight of him. Peter could easily pass for a model, with his styled blond hair and bright blue eyes. He was every woman's dream date but not hers. Molly's dream man would be at the ball with another woman. A fact she'd face soon.

"Make yourself comfortable." She glanced around her family room, which was filled with moving boxes. "Sorry about the mess. All this stuff is going to storage soon." No Christmas tree this year. She'd celebrate the holidays with her family before leaving for Virginia.

Peter bent down to pet Rider with a long arm. "How is it possible for a dog to have this much fur?"

Molly climbed the steps, wishing her heart wanted the handsome firefighter downstairs. Besides a slight physical attraction, she didn't feel much for Peter. He didn't make her melt into a gooey mess the way Drew could. After spending an entire night with Peter, being wined and dined, maybe she'd start to fall for him. If only to prove to herself she could feel attraction for a man other than Drew.

As they rode to the country club in Peter's black sports car, he continued to steal glances. While they sat at a red light, he reached over to hold her hand.

His large hand encased hers in a blanket of warmth. Instinctively, she pulled away.

"Have I told you yet how stoked I am about tonight?"

Only every other sentence. "Maybe once or twice." She forced a smile.

"I want us to hang out again, even though you're leaving for Quantico soon. Being a drug cop is pretty cool, by the way."

Peter's smile showed off his cute dimples. Why couldn't she muster the urge to throw herself at this guy who was clearly into her? Her throat closed around the words her brain wanted her to say—*sure, I'd love for you to take me out again.* Her heart set a barricade. Little orange cones of devotion to a man she couldn't have.

"Let's see how tonight goes." That was as much as she was willing to commit.

With Drew, Molly had gotten a taste of real desire. Not only in the kisses they'd shared but more importantly, from their time spent in conversation. She simply loved being with him. Without that kind of passion, any other relationship she'd attempt was doomed.

So, she'd made the decision to remain single and unattached for the foreseeable future. Her new job would be stressful enough without adding man troubles.

Peter put his gaze back on the road, clearly not

used to being denied. When they arrived, he took her arm and escorted her inside. The theme for this year's Firefighters' Ball was Spark & Ember. The ballroom glowed in reflected light, which gave the illusion of flames dancing on the walls. Surrounded by the elegance of the room, her dress glowed in harmony with the flickering light. As she walked through the room, the crowd parted. Tonight, she was fire. Tomorrow, she'd be left to the ashes.

A string quartet played classical music on a small stage in the corner. The room was filled with locals all dressed to impress, and the hum of multiple conversations played back up to the music.

Peter pulled out a chair at their table. "I'll get something for us to drink."

"I'll take a dirty martini, extra olives." She really needed her good friend vodka right now and its calming effects.

"Cool. Be right back."

As Peter weaved toward the bar, stopping to talk along the way, Molly scanned the room. Mr. Hillman had brought his much-younger, new wife. Holly Richter was hanging on to her date like he was the last man on earth. Molly stifled a laugh as Holly stepped on the hem of her dress and nearly flashed everyone in the room.

When Drew and Ann entered the ballroom, her smile and good humor faded. Her chest squeezed, causing her heart to pound against her ribs.

The sight of him, wearing a tailored dark blue suit, made her skin tingle. His dark, wavy hair was trimmed short. Drew's handsome face left her struggling to breathe.

Ann stood next to Drew, probably five foot ten in

heels. Tall and lean, with the stature of a model. Her pink dress was frilly and sweet. Her smile grew too broad.

When Molly returned her gaze to Drew, she saw him staring her way. She recognized the look of passion in his eyes. She'd seen it before, but highly inappropriate with his date standing next to him.

Peter returned with her martini—finally. She took a long drink. The tang of vodka mixed with the salty olives bit her tongue. "Thanks."

He sat beside her and rested his arm on the back of her chair. "I'll keep 'em coming." Peter winked. "You just say the word."

Molly had no intention of getting drunk tonight or even buzzed. With Peter on one side, looking for any advantage, and Drew on the other, messing with her heart, she couldn't be anything but on her game.

Their table filled with people Molly knew, which in a small town was no surprise. She couldn't wait to live in a city where she could move around with more anonymity. Where she didn't have to worry about being the subject of the local gossip over coffee. Working with the Feds, she'd be known for what she did in her career, not what she lacked in her personal life.

The previous comments and questions echoed in her head. Molly, you're so pretty. How can you still be single? You should lay off the kickboxing. Your aggressiveness scares away men. Why are you so focused on your career?

People made assumptions. She wouldn't waste her time and energy explaining her decisions, which were no one else's business, anyway.

Drew and Ann sat at a table catty-corner from her,

giving her a clear view. By the time dinner was served, Molly had lost her appetite. Most of the food on her plate went untouched. Luckily, Peter didn't mind cleaning her plate along with his own.

A new band started setting up. This one had electric guitars and a drum set. They looked to be livelier than the classical dinner music, which had almost put her to sleep. The lead singer grabbed the microphone and signaled the band to begin. With his shaggy beard and tattoo sleeves, he reminded her of Heath.

So far, she hadn't noticed either Heath or Grace in the ballroom. Probably because all her attention had been focused on Drew. Along with imagining what would happen if she locked his date in the utility closet. She could have done it, too, if she really wanted to. Ann was way too nice and trusting for her own good.

Molly finally spotted Grace at the back of the ballroom. "I'm going to say hi to my friend. Be back in a few," she told Peter.

"Sure." He returned to his conversation with the man sitting on his other side.

They'd been talking about fire hoses and water pressure for so long, she was afraid her eyes would cross. In her black dress, Grace could be mistaken for royalty. Her best friend stood elegantly with a tumbler of ice water in her hand. The healthy glow of pregnancy radiated off her skin.

"Molly...that dress," Grace said as she approached. "You are stunning." She took Molly's hand and spun her around.

"Ditto. Knocked up is a good look on you."

Heath stood next to his wife and wrapped his arm

around her waist. His face displayed a loving glow. Molly had to admit Heath Carter cleaned up pretty nice. "What did you bribe him with to get him into that suit?" she asked Grace.

"Don't ask." Grace brushed a hand down Heath's arm. "I give him thirty more minutes then the tie's coming off."

"I only agreed to wear this monkey suit so I'd be a worthy escort for my beautiful wife." Heath gave Grace a kiss on the cheek.

From the look in his eyes, Molly knew he wanted to do more than one chaste kiss. "Monkey suit is right," Molly teased. She stepped back, and her foot hit something behind her. As she stumbled, strong hands grabbed her waist. Her head turned and there stood Drew, still holding her. She recoiled like she'd been bitten. "You shouldn't sneak up on people."

Heath laughed. "Drew lacks self-awareness these days. He's been distracted all night. That dress is attracting him like a bull to a red cape. Watch out, man, she'll end up stabbing you."

"Shut it," Molly and Drew said in unison.

"You look lovely." Drew turned his back on Heath, gazing only at Molly.

She went soft and warm under the heat of his stare. "I should get back to my date. Catch up with you later, Grace."

"Will you save me a dance, Molly?" Heath called after her.

"Absolutely not," she replied. Footsteps sounded behind her. If that was Heath, she'd punch him in the throat.

"How about me?" Drew asked with a sexy smile on

his lips. "Will you save me a dance?"

Molly glanced over her shoulder at Ann. "I don't think so. Your date shouldn't have to share you."

"Come on. One last dance before you leave?"

Underneath the lighthearted teasing was a hint of desperation. His thumb brushed down her arm, causing her to shiver.

"Find me later," she whispered before walking away. The time had come to say goodbye.

****

Drew returned to Ann, whose napkin sat twisted on her lap. "Would you like more wine?"

Her blue eyes peered upward. "You're in love with her."

A statement of fact more than a question. His knees gave way, and he sank to his chair. "You must think I'm a jerk."

Ann placed a hand over his. "You can't make your feelings disappear. Anyone paying attention can see how hard you've fallen."

Why were his emotions so easy for others to read? "I must look like a fool."

"No," she said with a soft laugh. "You're a man in love. To be honest, I remember when I dreamt you'd look at me that way. But I see your heart's already taken."

His chest ached. "I never meant to hurt you." But he had anyway.

"I know. It's okay, Drew. You deserve to find true love."

"I doubt that will ever be possible." Drew glanced into Ann's blue eyes. They were the color of a summer sky. He wished Ann could've made him half as crazy as

Molly did. "How do I get over her?"

Her eyebrows drew together. "Why would you want to?"

Frustration rose inside him, not with Ann, but with himself. If he was at the gym instead of a ballroom, he'd pour all his anger into a punching bag. "Molly is traveling on a different road. She's leaving in two weeks to start at the DEA Training Academy." He waved his hand. "I'm staying here."

Ann stood, grabbed both his hands, and tugged him to his feet. "Come on. Let's dance."

Her pink dress glittered in the low light of the ballroom. The band switched tempos and played a slow song. Drew rested his hand on her back. He felt like he was dancing with his sister.

The lead singer's raspy voice crooned words about love and eternal devotion. Drew watched Molly, who danced in the arms of Peter. The whole scene was wrong. He should be the one holding Molly. Her body, draped in beautiful red silk, should be pressed firmly against him.

When he'd first seen her tonight, he'd been struck speechless. She'd shed her blue police uniform and transformed into an alluring siren. He craved her more than anything.

Ann sighed as they continued to slow dance. "I hope you don't think I'm being a busybody, but I'm such a romantic. True love should always win in the end, like it did for Aurora, Cinderella, and Rapunzel."

"Huh?" He screwed up his face, thoroughly perplexed.

"Every woman wants a happily ever after. Maybe it's love, maybe it's a career, maybe it's a child, or something all her own."

"I guess years in the military have left me a little out of touch." He'd never been one for fairytales, not even when he was younger. But he did remember seeing his sister dance around the house wearing a sparkling dress, always with a tiara on her head.

Ann moved out of his arms. "Go to her. Tonight might be your last chance."

With a surge of determination, he strode across the dance floor and tapped Peter on the shoulder. For the moment, he'd act like a gentleman. "Mind if I steal a dance with your lovely date?"

Peter's eyes flashed. "I'll be at the bar. One song," he said to Drew before releasing her.

Pulling Molly with him, they moved to the center of the dance floor. With her so close, a chemical chain reaction started in Drew's body. In that moment, he knew he could never live without her. She was the air he breathed. He would move heaven and earth to keep her right here in his arms.

All his lonely years, stationed in some of the most horrid places on earth, left him sure. He didn't need a woman to fit into the mold he'd created in his head. Love would map out the future. "I love you," he whispered.

Molly's head jerked up, her eyes wide and bright. "Stop messing with me."

"I'm not messing with you, Pixie." One hand rested on the small of her back and the other caressed a path down her bare arm. "I'm hopelessly in love with you."

Other dancers swirled around them, stealing glances their way.

"Let's go outside." Molly narrowed her eyes. "I need some fresh air."

"What about your date?" Drew asked as the band started a new song. "He said I only had you for one song."

"Peter doesn't own me," she quipped.

With nerves buzzing, he walked at her side toward a set of doors that opened to the patio.

The air outside was cool, and Molly wrapped her arms around herself.

Drew reached out to pull her back to him, but she stepped away.

"No more games." She raised her hand, palm facing him. "Why are you doing this...now?"

Time to pick up the sword and fight. "I love you, Molly Hernandez. You're brash, stubborn, and can beat me at any sport." He laughed as she smiled. "You're special. That's why I love you."

The muffled sounds of music and laughter floated from inside the ballroom. The evening carried a gentle breeze.

Molly turned away. "Why now? You have Ann, and I'm leaving."

"Ann's the one who told me to go after you." He put his heart on the line. No more flirty innuendoes. Just the brutal truth. "Will you give us a chance?"

Molly's response was silence. She stood frozen, like a red rose encased in ice.

As the seconds ticked by without a response, tension built inside him. He'd acted unusually rash and impulsive, and doubt seized him. Had he been wrong about Molly's feelings? Judging from her reaction, she might deliver a final blow to his heart.

****

Molly's willpower cracked under the weight of Drew's words. Could they really find a way to be together? How much would he give up? What would she do in order to keep him in her life?

With a steadying breath, she decided to test his words of devotion. Her hand trembled as she rested it on his arm. "I really care about you, more than I want to admit. You say you're in love with me, but what about your big, empty house? The one you want to fill with a family. You already know I'm not the one to do that with. How do you see us being together and both getting what we want?"

"I was so focused on a distant dream that I didn't see what was right in front of me. I want the life I can share with you." His breath misted in the December air.

If only a future together was so easy. She shivered and pushed down the nausea churning in her stomach. "You're willing to move wherever I'm assigned? Leave everything you have here—your job, the Second Step Program?"

Drew wrapped his arms around her and kissed the top of her head. "I'm willing to compromise. None of those things matter without you in my life."

With his romantic words, hope sprouted. As Molly's body warmed against his, her brain set off warning lights. "What about children?"

"We can wait, until you're ready," he murmured into her hair. "But I do want them with you. We'll make the prettiest babies."

Every muscle in her body went cold and stiff. "No, we won't."

Drew tipped her head up to meet his gaze. "You

never want to have children?"

"I can't." Hot tears burned her eyes, but she refused to let them loose. The time had come to tell him the complete truth, even if doing so could drive away Drew forever. "Two years ago, I became a cervical cancer survivor. Beating cancer meant losing any chance of having children. I woke up after surgery with a new desire to live my life to the fullest. For me, that means pursuing my career goals. Someday, I might want to adopt a child. But there's the chance I might be fulfilled with a life without children. Will you be content with just me?"

"I don't know what to say." He gazed off into the darkness.

"I understand." Yes, on a rational level, she did understand his reaction. Her fear of his rejection was the reason she kept her infertility a secret. Try explaining that to her breaking heart. "Giving up on ever seeing yourself reflected back in your child is a lot to ask. I would never spend the rest of my life with someone who didn't feel like I'm enough."

"I've always imagined a family with my children." He shoved his hands into the front pockets of his dress slacks.

Molly allowed numbness to take over, expanding to encompass her crushed heart. Inside, she was dead. She'd always known he wanted her, but he also wanted more. And she couldn't fault him. "I've had two years to come to terms with the fact I can't have children. During that time, I've decided to take advantage of my health, strength, and my commitment to make our country a better place. We have different dreams." She lifted herself up on tiptoes and kissed him softly on the lips. "Bye, Drew."

"I'm sorry, Molly." He reached for her but hesitated, and then crossed his arms.

His apology, though sincere, didn't make her feel better. Leaving him on the patio, she walked back into the ballroom. After seeing Peter down another drink at the other end of the room, she decided he was in no condition to drive her home. As she searched for Grace, the room spun. Her emotions began thawing her heart. Molly leaned against the wall for support and closed her eyes.

"I saw you leave with Drew." Grace rested a hand on her arm. "What happened?"

She was so thankful for her friend. "I don't want to talk about it right now. Are you guys ready to leave? I'd love to get out of here."

"Sure. Let me get Heath. What about Peter?"

Molly watched Peter order another drink. "I'll tell him I'm leaving with you. He won't care." She approached him and captured his attention just long enough to declare she was heading out. After a brief protest, he turned back to the group of guys assembled by the bar.

The mixture of noise in the ballroom had the effect of pounding nails into her temples. She found her purse, pushed through the crowd, and burst out the front doors. Finally, in the fresh air, she could think straight. Her Cinderella ball had turned into a disaster. Taking off her heels, she pitched them into the bushes. Her aching feet thanked her for the relief.

The deed was done. She'd finally been one-hundred percent honest with Drew. He'd been honest with her. Her eyes burned, and she swiped off rogue tears with the back of her hand. Very soon, she'd leave to start her new job with the DEA. She was ready to move on.

Chapter Twenty-Four

Drew downed the last few drops of coffee in his mug. His coffee pot was now empty. Sleep last night had been as elusive as the legendary Yeti. Every time he closed his eyes, he saw Molly. Last night, he'd surrendered during the most important battle of his life. From the look on her face, his reaction had been exactly what she had expected. He'd failed her. His head ached with the crushing admission.

He loved her but not enough to compromise. Could he give up the dream of having children after wanting fatherhood for so long? Molly's confession had snapped his resolve. He didn't see a way to align their futures.

With caffeine buzzing through his body, he made quick work of his Saturday to-do list. Then he looked around for more. Anything to keep his body busy and his mind off the memory of Molly's pain-filled eyes.

He pushed down the heartache. Nothing he could do about it now. She'd risked sharing something deeply personal, and he'd fumbled. Once he'd seen her chin rise and her lips set tight, he knew he'd lost her. Game over.

Grabbing a screwdriver, he winced in pain. A row of blisters ran along his right palm from his earlier fix-it tasks. He should put away the tools for the day. Maybe a short run would help work out some of his tension. He was bent over, tying his shoe lace, when his front door flew open, almost hitting him in the face.

"Oops. Sorry, man. I didn't expect to see you hanging out behind the door." Heath stood in the entry, a white bag in his hand.

Whatever was inside filled his entryway with the scent of cinnamon and sugar. "Why don't you just come on in and make yourself at home." Drew stood and peeked at the bag. "What do you got in there?"

"Bribery from my wife. She baked these, shoved the bag in my hands, and tossed me out of the house. Said I couldn't come back until I talked with you."

"Smells good. Let's go back to the kitchen. Why would Grace need to bribe me?"

"Not for you, dipstick. Bribery for me." Heath slapped his back. "I don't know what went down between you and Molly last night, but I do know it wasn't good. How are you holding up?"

"I'm fine," Drew said, hoping Heath wouldn't notice the strain in his voice.

Heath pulled out plates from the cabinet and unpacked two cinnamon rolls from his bag. Then, he sat at the kitchen table and reclined back in the chair. "We drove Molly home from the Ball. She was quiet, which was scarier than when she's yelling at me. What happened?"

"My idiocy, that's what happened." He slumped into a chair.

Rubbing his hand across his chin, Heath exhaled. "I know about Molly's cancer. You did the right thing by letting her go."

Anger turned his skin hot. "I did the right thing? She shared something extremely personal, and I broke her heart."

"Dude, chill." Heath took a bite of cinnamon roll and chewed. Flecks of cinnamon and sugar decorated his beard. "You want to be a dad. That's not something you should be ashamed of. Molly's infertile. She may not want to go through the emotional turmoil of adoption. Or she may feel that in her line of work, caring for a child will be too difficult."

"What's your point?" Drew held his temper. Instead of snapping, he took another bite of Grace's bakery. The roll was still warm, and the sweet taste put him in a slightly better mood.

"My point is that Molly needs a man who can accept her. Not someone who, years down the road, might resent she can't have children. You got any coffee?" Heath waved toward the empty coffee cup on the table.

Drew sighed and started brewing another pot. "Molly must hate me."

"She knew all along you wanted this big house filled with a bunch of crazy kids."

Drew waited for the pot to partially fill then poured a cup for both Heath and himself. "I love her, but will love always be enough?"

"Man, that's what I've been trying to tell you." Heath leaned forward in his seat. "You need to decide what you want before you say one more word to Ms. Hernandez."

All the caffeine Drew had ingested gave him a headache. "What's your secret? How did you and Grace find your way back to each other?"

"For that, amigo, you'll have to buy the book." Heath laughed and put his old baseball cap on his head.

"Love's not easy, but when it's right, the struggle is worthwhile."

After Heath left, Drew went outside and watched the birds flutter around his yard. He thought about Julia and her health. He thought about adoption and how difficult the process could be. He imagined his life here without Molly—leaving for work every morning without kissing her goodbye, coming home at the end of the day to her smile, and all the other moments of life he'd want to share with her but would instead be alone. He felt like a boy who had been handed a beautifully wrapped present, just to throw it back— spoiled and ungrateful for what he'd been given.

All his big plans seemed lifeless and uninhabitable. He considered what Heath said about being sure a life with just Molly would be enough. Could he endure a life without her?

****

Molly closed her suitcase and looked around her bedroom one last time. In one hour, she'd leave for eighteen weeks of Basic Agent Training. Her parents would arrive soon to take her to the airport. Then she'd be off to Quantico to start the next stage of her life.

Rider lay on his dog bed, totally unaware of the changes to his life.

Drew had offered to take him while she was away. He'd be here any minute to get him.

She'd have to face Drew Atwater one more time. After a year of working toward her goal, she was finally at the starting line. The thought of the challenges to come left her jittery with anticipation. Deep down, she knew she'd make it through to graduation. In four months, she'd be a Special Agent for the DEA. She'd then be assigned as a field agent and start her war on drugs.

The teens from the Second Step program were still on Christmas break. She'd made the rounds to visit each one and say goodbye. Yesterday, she'd cleaned out her desk at the station. Her coworkers had thrown her a little party, complete with a cake from A Bonnie Bakery. The reality of leaving proved harder than she'd expected. Her time working with the youth of the community meant so much. Saying goodbye to Whitney had been the hardest. If Molly would have stayed in Liberty Ridge, she'd done so for that special teenage girl.

Rider's bark alerted her to Drew's truck pulling into her driveway. She wiped the rogue tear off her cheek and followed Rider downstairs. Her sweet dog paced back and forth by the back door, eager to see his friend.

"Come in," Molly yelled as she entered the kitchen. She set down Rider's bed next to the bag of dog food on the floor.

The sight of Drew left her body weak. All her energy flowed out of her and toward him. He wore jeans and a yellow T-shirt, but in her mind, he was still dressed in the suit from the Firefighters' Ball. She could almost feel the warmth of his arms around her as they'd danced.

When he bent over to pet Rider, his gaze lingered on her. "Hey, there."

"Thanks for taking him while I'm gone. Caring for a dog is a lot to ask." Only talk of Rider would be allowed. Anything else would be too painful.

"My pleasure. Rider's my buddy. We'll have loads

of fun."

His smile didn't camouflage the sadness in his eyes. "All his doggie stuff is here," Molly said as she wiped off her sweaty palms on the legs of her pants. "I have a full bag of food. He likes to eat but only feed him twice a day. Hide the bag or you'll come home and find it empty. Oh, and I know you have a fenced-in back yard, but he will attempt to escape if he sees a squirrel. He loves chasing squirrels."

Drew put a hand on her shoulder and squeezed. "Don't worry about Rider. I'll take good care of him. I promise."

Inhaling deeply, she turned to get the leash. Leaving Rider behind was torture on her already battered heart.

"Do you have a ride to the airport?" Drew asked.

"My parents are taking me."

"Good." He paced back and forth in front of the kitchen sink. "I hate how we left things between us."

The one subject she hoped to avoid. "There's nothing more to say. I appreciate you taking Rider for me. I'll be very busy with Basic Agent Training, and I can't be distracted. I'm over it, Drew."

"But I'm not." His shoulders slumped. "Please understand...you had time to come to terms with the fact that you can't have children. You gave me one minute."

"Do you really think more time will change anything?" Molly straightened her posture and firmed her resolve. "Honestly, Drew, my future involves moving wherever the Federal Government decides. I'll work crazy hours in a very dangerous job. I'm not on the mommy track. Instead, I'm on the exact opposite. In the end, we are working toward opposite goals."

Drew took her hand and kissed each knuckle. "I have an offer. Take the next four months and kick butt during training. Graduate and get your first field assignment. One hundred and forty days from now, I want to meet you on the Hickory River Bridge." He looked up and connected with her gaze.

"Why?" Molly's legs were in danger of giving way. Every muscle in her body turned to rubber. Her chest tightened with shallow breaths.

"Because I want to make things right. Some time apart will give us the space we need to clarify how we feel about each other. But I'll tell you right now, Molly, I don't think I can live without you."

"Let me get this straight. You want to meet me in Liberty Ridge after my graduation?" Her strained heart pounded as fast and loud as a machine gun.

"I want you to come back home, and then we'll take the next step—whether to depart as friends or merge our lives together."

She didn't trust her own emotions. Could she put everything into BAT while worrying about a future with Drew? Any little distraction could lessen her chances of graduation. But the passion she saw in Drew's eyes made her wonder if her feelings for him would give her extra strength for the trials to come. Her gaze dropped to their joined hands, and she drew courage from their connection.

Her decision became clear. She'd risk another fall, because she loved him. "I'll meet you on the bridge. Don't be late." His wide smile thawed the last ice chip off her heart.

"I won't be late, Pixie." He kissed the top of her

head. "Now, go show those boys at Quantico that big things come in small packages. I'll be waiting."

****

Whitney sat in the nearly empty courtroom with her mom at her side. Today was Rich Logan's trial. The guy got the book thrown at him—domestic abuse, physical abuse of a minor, malicious destruction of property, and the list went on and on. Ten charges in all.

Molly was now in Virginia, but she gave her sworn testimony against Rich before she'd left. Whitney would take the stand for the prosecution, along with her mom. She still couldn't believe her mom was testifying against her husband, or she should say almost exhusband. But here they were, ready to make sure the scum bag got a nice long vacation in jail.

As Whitney and Barbara sat in the public gallery, the lawyers from both sides shuffled papers at their desks. A side door opened, and Rich was escorted inside by two police officers. He wore a suit that looked a few sizes too big, and his hands were cuffed. The sight of him left her stomach sick, but she was no longer afraid. He appeared small and helpless, not the powerful menace he'd once been.

Before he sat next to his Public Defender, he sent them a scowl.

She almost laughed. Did he realize he had no power?

The trial progressed with little drama. Before Whitney took the stand, her mom gave her hand a quick squeeze. All the nerves plaguing her before disappeared. She took the witness stand and told her story, freeing herself from years of oppression.

When her mom stepped forward, Whitney sensed hesitation. Standing up to Rich was a big step. Her mom took the witness chair and told the truth about how he'd abused her even before they were married. How he made her feel like she was worthless. As Whitney sat and listened to her mom's testimony, she couldn't stop the tears flowing down her cheeks. She was so proud of how far her mom had come.

The trial only lasted two days, and she was back in the courtroom for the verdict. Guilty on all charges. Rich Logan was sentenced to nine years in jail. Not nearly long enough in her opinion, but she would accept the judge's ruling and move on with her life. She and her mom got up to leave the courtroom.

Rich was led out. On his way, he yelled at them.

She felt her mom's hand jerk in response. "It's all right, Mom. He can't hurt us anymore."

Barbara shivered, and then turned her focus on Whitney. "Yes, baby, you're right. Let's go home."

Chapter Twenty-Five

What had Drew been thinking when he proposed such a crazy deal? Meet Molly on the Hickory River Bridge in one hundred and forty days. The February wind howled outside his house like a teacher's scolding. Since Molly left, he'd spent the past forty days driving himself crazy. Forty days seemed an eternity when separated from the woman he loved.

At first, the strength of his feelings scared him. Every morning, he woke with Molly on his mind. What was she doing? How were her training classes? Did she miss him? Grace had heard from Molly a few times, who then passed the news along to Drew.

Grace reported Molly was excelling at Quantico, which was no shock. Her success validated she was where she was meant to be.

During their time apart, he'd made some self-discoveries. Sometimes, plans were made to be ripped apart and tossed into the wind. He'd spent a long time putting together the perfect future, when all along he'd forgotten the most important piece—a woman whom he loved above all else.

This new future, the one he wanted with Molly, left him breathless with excitement. Instead of being sure of every step, now each one would be discovered along the way. Waiting another one hundred days to see Molly would rip his heart from his chest. He needed her now.

She might have decided a life with him wasn't what she wanted. After getting a taste of her adventurous career, she may not want to be tied down by a relationship. As he drove down the road to Molly's parents' house, he prayed that wasn't the case.

As he parked next to their house, he saw *Mamá* Hernandez come out the door to greet him. He opened the car door, and Rider climbed over his lap to jump out.

"*Hola*," she said first to the dog and then to Drew.

"Thanks for dog sitting on such short notice." He removed Rider's things out of the bed of his truck.

"Dog sitting is no problem." The dark-haired woman smiled. "Don't feel bad if you get home too late on Sunday to pick him up. He can stay as long as you need."

By Sunday, he'd have the answers he was traveling to Virginia for. Either he'd be coming home flying high as an airplane or ready to crash and burn. Molly held the key to his trip's success. Although, she didn't even know he was coming.

After her first month of training, she'd started getting weekends off. Drew learned from Grace that Molly planned on spending her free-time on base, studying. Well, he had other ideas. Hopefully, she wouldn't be too mad at the change.

Drew patted the small box in his coat pocket. He took a few deep breaths to relax his rolling stomach. If he didn't get this over with soon, he'd throw-up. "Is your husband home? I have a question for both of you."

Mamá Hernandez's eyes glimmered. She took him by the arm and pulled him into the house. "Oh, *mi hijo*.

I thought you'd never ask."

****

Instead of sleeping in on her Saturday off, Molly woke early to go for a run. She stuck to her course around the DEA and FBI training grounds. The air was brisk and cool. As she ran, she passed several assemblies of Marines doing their morning PT. The Marine base at Quantico was down the road from where Molly spent the last six weeks. The grounds of the Training Academy were always humming with activity, whatever the time of day or night.

She finished at the dormitory building and began her post-run stretches. The physical demands of the Training Academy left every muscle in her body sore, even the ones she hadn't known existed. As for her brain, the mental challenges were the true test of her resolve. Hours were spent in the classroom. The academic instruction was rigorous and thorough.

During the first month, she almost had no time off. She'd been too busy to be homesick. But now with her weekends free, Molly found herself missing her family and friends in Liberty Ridge. She missed Rider's furry snuggles and wet kisses. Drew was always tucked away in the back of her mind. Memories of him were like a child's stuffed bunny, giving her security and confidence to face the challenges of each day.

She still had twelve more weeks of Academy left and had no doubt she'd still be here for graduation day. Nerves fluttered when she thought ahead to the date she'd meet Drew on the Hickory River Bridge. Why couldn't they meet now and get the conversation over with? No amount of time apart would change her feelings. Drew was the only man she wanted as her life partner.

During her run that morning, she'd decided Drew shouldn't be the only one to compromise. If she loved him, she'd bend in order to make him happy, which meant being open to adoption. If, when they met again, he still wanted her.

Molly dragged her weary body back to her dorm room and grabbed a towel to take a shower. On a whim, she checked her cell phone. *Mamá* habitually checked in every morning. Most times, Molly didn't have time to respond back. But today, she'd surprise her with a call. What she wouldn't give right now for a plate of *Mamá's* tamales. She looked at her phone, and her heart jumped. On her screen was a text from Drew. Her hand shook as she pressed the screen to open his message.

—Taxi will be waiting outside the main gate at noon. Please don't be late—

What did his vague text mean? Why would he send a taxi for her? What the heck was going on? He wouldn't dare mess with her. Or would he? Maybe he'd arranged a little day trip, so she could get off the training grounds.

The time now was eight o'clock, which meant she had four hours to kill. She was so tempted to text him back but stayed her hand. With her lack of reply, she'd leave him scratching his head, too.

As she considered the possibility Drew was nearby, her energy level surged. He couldn't get onto campus because of the tight security, but he could be staying at a hotel in DC or Alexandria. What if he'd come to tell her their relationship was over? Or he found someone else? If so, she hoped a hospital would be close by, for Drew's sake.

Calm down. With her mind spinning with every possibility, she'd drive herself crazy. *How about start with a shower, get dressed, and go down for breakfast?* Maybe she could spend some time studying. She checked the time again. *Ugh. Get ready for the longest morning in the history of womankind.*

By noon, she was ready to jump out of her skin. She pulled on a hoodie, grabbed her purse, and took a walk toward the main gatehouse. Instead of a taxi waiting for her, a black luxury car idled—one identical to the hundreds of others commuting around DC and the suburbs.

A driver appeared and opened the door to the back seat.

As she looked inside, her heart raced. No Drew. "Where are you taking me?" She wasn't going anywhere until she got some answers.

"I'm driving you into DC. That's all I can say."

The driver's stony face showed no hint of expression. He stood next to the car, waiting for her to enter, like he could care less whether she decided to come with him or not. *Why not go along and see what happens?* Tossing her purse onto the back seat, she slid in. The door closed behind her. Classical music—something with lots of violin—played through the speakers. A small bucket with ice and water bottles sat to her left.

Realizing her throat was drier than Arizona in July, she twisted off the cap of a water bottle and took a drink. The cool liquid soothed her throat but didn't totally quench her thirst. She wouldn't feel comfortable again until she knew Drew's plan.

The ride into DC was comfortable enough, with

rich leather seats cushioning the bumpy roads. They drove past Reagan National Airport, over the Potomac River, and past the Jefferson Memorial. The Washington Monument stood like a tall watchman over the nation's Capital. She still had no idea where this misadventure would end.

After turning onto Maryland Ave, the U.S. Capitol Building loomed ahead, but the car never got that far. The driver stopped in front of a glass-domed building, and the door opened. Molly stepped out onto the sidewalk.

United States Botanical Garden was etched into the stone at the top of the building.

"Why am I here?" she asked the impassive driver. To his credit, he was probably used to driving around high-ranking government officials and dignitaries, instead of a fussy DEA Special Agent in training.

"Go inside." He turned on his heel, climbed into the car, and then pulled away from the curb.

She had no choice now, unless she wanted to hop on a Metro train and make her way back to Quantico. Curiosity got the better of her, and she opened the glass door of the Botanical Garden. A friendly security guard greeted her from his desk in the lobby.

"I would suggest the Orchid Room first," he said with a large, toothy smile. "That location's always a guest favorite."

"Thanks." She walked through a large doorway and into the courtyard. Brightly colored flowers, many she'd never seen before, surrounded her. Two blue-tiled pools lay on either side of the room. The water played a soothing melody. Inside the cocoon of the vegetation, her strained nerves relaxed. She sniffed the air, and an earthy and sweet scent filled her nose. Everywhere she looked burst with life. The light filtered the space with an energetic green.

The security guard had told her to go to the Orchid Room. Was he in on Drew's little game, too? She checked the map and walked through the Conservatory, toward the back, and to the right.

As soon as she stepped into the room, filled with colorful orchids, she saw him. The weight of stress and anxiety lifted, making her feel like she walked on air.

Drew stood before a collection of fuchsia and yellow flowers. A smile bloomed on his face. His hand was in the pocket of his jacket, fidgeting with whatever junk he had tucked in there. "You came," he said, after a brief hesitation. "I didn't know if you would."

Her eyes drank in the sight of him, like a desert plant greedily absorbing rain. "What's this all about? Last I heard, you wanted to meet me after my graduation on the Hickory River Bridge."

He shifted his weight, back and forth. A muscle twitched in his jaw. "The last six weeks haven't gone exactly as planned. The day you left, I realized what I needed to do."

Her heart pounded at an abnormal rate. She was sure he'd come to end things. At least, he had the guts to say the words to her face.

Drew pulled his hand out of his coat pocket. Resting on top his palm was a black box.

Is what's inside what I think it is? Between Drew's proximity and the heavy floral scent of the air, her head became light and dizzy.

After taking both her hands and kissing each one, he pressed them to his heart. "I love you like crazy,

Molly. I want a future with you. I'll follow you to the ends of the earth and support your dreams." Drew let go of her hands, dropped to one knee, and opened the jewelry box. Inside was a ring, with a deep red ruby at its center, flanked on either side by a diamond. "Please, Molly, marry me."

Her tongue stuck to the roof of her mouth. She couldn't formulate words. What he offered her was priceless. In response to her silence, Drew's smile faltered.

"I've made mistakes. I know that. I created my plans in stone and couldn't see past my own nose, but I'm finding reality is much sweeter. Molly, the only plan I have right now is winning your heart. You complete me." Still holding her hands, Drew stood.

My heart is yours. Her body responded before her mouth could. She jumped and flung her arms around his neck. Her legs wrapped around his waist.

He held her up, looping his hands under her backside.

Molly kissed him solidly on the mouth. His lips tasted so good. How had Drew put it? Even sweeter than a cookie from A Bonnie Bakery.

Other visitors in the Orchid Room gave them a wide berth, a few even broke out into applause.

Finally, she parted to catch her breath. "If I say yes, you realize what you're getting yourself into?"

He laughed. "I'm getting the pixie who stole my heart."

"Then, yes," she said in between kisses. "I love you."

"I'll be there for your graduation. Then, we'll find out the next step in our journey."

"How did I get so lucky?" Still lifted in his arms, she trailed her finger down his straight nose and gave the end a pinch.

"You are my heart." He set her on her feet, kissed the top of her head, and looked down with a mischievous grin. "I'm ready for one more adventure. We'll be in it together, because that's what love is, after all."

Epilogue

Molly wove around multiple desks until she got back to her own. The meeting she'd just led had gone well. The mission was coming together, and she was proud to have a role in putting together the action plan.

She only had a few more hours of work before she could head out and go home to Drew. While she pulled up a document on her computer, she heard her phone chime once then twice. Sighing, she tore her gaze from the screen. She was almost done with her reports for the day. When she'd left the police force to become a Special Agent, she'd thought she'd have less paperwork. *Ha, now I have even more.*

Her case involved one of the biggest illegal prescription drug operations in Houston. Every detail had to be accurately recorded. One mistake and they wouldn't get the warrants needed to put these scum in jail. When she saw the number flash on the caller ID, she quickly answered. "Hey, Drew. What's up?"

"I got a call today." His voice shook. "Can you come home now?"

"I don't know." She looked around the office. Things seemed to be quiet. Very unusual for the Houston Division Office. She'd been very fortunate to be assigned to a Texas location after graduation. Being fluent in Spanish meant she was an asset to the border state. After their wedding, she and Drew moved to

Houston. Drew found a teaching job in the Sugarland School District. Right now, he was home enjoying summer vacation. She wasn't so lucky.

"You'll need the rest of the day off, if not the week," Drew said.

She reclined in her office chair. "Just spit it out, okay? What's going on?"

Drew's laughter sounded through the phone. "The adoption agency called. They have a baby for us. We need to get to the hospital."

A tremor of excitement shivered across her skin. She felt hot and cold all at the same time. Finally, after a year on the waiting list, their adoption was happening. She'd be a mother. Her grip on the phone tightened. "Are you serious? Drew, is it true?"

"Yes." He laughed. "Let's go meet our daughter."

Tears built in Molly's eyes. A daughter. She and Drew had a daughter. "I'll talk to the Special Agent in Charge. Once I explain the situation, I'm sure he'll let me check out."

"Okay, but hurry. I'll meet you at home."

Molly hung up the phone with trembling hands. When they'd decided to contact an adoption agency, they'd done so with caution. If they'd be blessed with a baby, they'd love their child as much as each other. But if not, they'd be happy living as a family of two.

She knew nothing was final, even after the baby went home. Legal issues would be a concern for some time. Molly pushed those fears out of her mind. She and Drew had a daughter to welcome into their family.

Two hours later, they held hands in the hospital lobby. The adoption agent arrived, a tall woman with black hair and a friendly smile, and escorted them up to the maternity wing.

Molly's heart ached at the memory of Whitney and for this birth mother. She hoped their baby's mother would have as bright of future as Whitney, who'd just finished her first year at the University of Texas.

Molly stood before the glass window and looked into the nursery, and Drew squeezed her hand. Excitement and joy bubbled up. The baby lay wrapped in a pink blanket. Dark curls topped her tiny head. The baby stirred and started crying.

"Would you like to hold her?" the adoption agent asked.

All Molly could do was nod. She wanted to hold her daughter more than anything. Both she and Drew went into the nursery. She put on a hospital gown and scrubbed her hands. Once Molly sat in the rocking chair, a nurse handed her the pink bundle. The pure, sweet smell of newborn wafted up to her nose and she inhaled, savoring the scent.

Drew's gaze met hers, and her heart burst with love.

"We have some major shopping to do." Drew's hand brushed over the baby's hair. "We are very unprepared."

"I'm sure you have a list of all the baby supplies we need tucked away somewhere."

"Actually, I do." He smiled wryly. "Old habits die hard."

"What should we name her?" Molly studied the baby, who slept contently in her arms. "Adele, Mackenzie, Mia?"

Drew leaned over and kissed the baby's forehead. "She looks like love."

One day, this little one would understand how lucky she was to have Drew for a father. She watched their daughter's beautiful face and was filled with bliss. Their life together had been a rollercoaster ride. Now, this little unexpected bend was the start of a new, wonderful adventure.

If you enjoyed *After All*, you'll want to look for Book 4
of the Warriors of the Heart series.
Enjoy this sample chapter:

Winner Takes All

by

Laurie Winter

Warriors of the Heart Series, Book 4

Chapter One

A strong gust of wind ripped the sign from Colleen Gardner's festival booth and sent it soaring into the air. The park was filled with a large crowd, but unfortunately at that moment, no one was standing on the other side of her table to help.

"Shoot." She jumped to grab hold of a corner. The cursed thing had the nerve to slice her finger before the wind swept it up, out of reach. She stood on the ground, totally helpless, while the sheet of white cardstock rode an air current before starting its descent.

"You better hurry before our sign gets away." Grace sat behind the raffle booth, her baby son snug against her chest.

Colleen sprinted toward the wayward sign as it floated back to the earth before coming to rest at the base of a thick oak tree. She could barely make out the red printing spelling out—*50/50 Raffle to Benefit Veterans' Retreat*. Two more steps and the sign would be within reach, but the wind picked up again and sent it flying toward the river.

Stupid wind. Her sign wasn't the only thing being tossed around at the Founders' Day Celebration. Food vendors waged their own battle, in an attempt to keep their plates, napkins, cups, and even their tents from blowing away.

Eventually, she accepted defeat and returned to the

welcome shade of a tent. Beads of sweat slithered down her back like rain on a windowpane. Oh well. She'd return to her booth and rustle up something to create another one. She had six more hours to sell raffle tickets. No way she'd accept defeat so easily.

The sound of a banjo and fiddle duet filled the air, along with the delicious scents drifting from the BBQ pit operating in the booth next-door. A heavyset man wearing striped denim overalls lifted one of the lids, sending up a cloud of thick, sweet smelling smoke. Her hungry stomach growled.

As she waved goodbye to her sign, which flew in the air toward the bank of the river, she observed a hand reached up out of the crowd and grabbed it. She glanced at the hand, and then lingered down a very muscular arm, which connected to a solidly male body. Finally, she looked at the man's face, and her breath hitched. He was gorgeous.

When their gazes met, the unexpected intimacy nudged her memory. But she didn't remember seeing him before. Liberty Ridge was the size of a town where, for better or worse, everyone knew one another. Once she'd totally taken in his handsome face, she noticed a little girl held in his other arm.

The girl reached her pudgy hands up toward the sign, causing the man to hide it behind his back.

With a scowl on his face, he took long strides toward Colleen and handed her the sign.

"Thanks." She gratefully accepted her runaway sign. "You have ninja reflexes."

His face didn't crack a smile.

Instead, he watched her with serious, dark brown eyes. A green baseball cap covered his head and shaded his face. The blond hair curling from under it only enhanced his rugged appeal. "I'm Colleen Gardner." She attempted to break the uncomfortable silence. "Who's the little princess?" She reached over to touch the girl's hand.

The man stepped back and scowled.

The little girl started wailing. Her pink face streaked with tears. "I want balloon." She tugged on the man's shirt and pointed to the person making balloon animals.

"I said later," he whispered. "We have to find Grandma first."

"Now," the girl cried. Her hair swung wildly as she shook her head back and forth. Her small cheeks burned red.

"Harper, once we find Grandma, then we can get you a balloon." He brushed back her hair with the palm of his hand. "But if you cry, we're going home."

"I want home. I want Momma." Harper howled and arched her back.

"Would you like me to stay with her here while you find your mom?" Colleen didn't have children of her own, but she'd learned a lot from helping Grace with baby John. "I promise I'm trustworthy. I'm from Liberty Ridge. Everybody here knows me. Your daughter will be safe until you get back."

"I don't think that's a good idea," he said over the crying child and started walking away.

"I'm sorry, but I never got your name?" She followed him, unable to help herself.

He spun to face her, a scowl on his face. "I'm surprised you don't remember me, Colleen. It's been a long time, but I thought I'd made a lasting impression."

3

Venom seeped through every word. The tone of his voice forced her to retreat a step. Uneasiness replaced her pleasant mood. Searching his face, she tried placing him in her memories of Liberty Ridge. She'd grown up here until at the age of eighteen, she'd moved away to attend college. This man didn't look familiar. Could he be a veteran she'd treated in the past?

He laughed.

For a second, Colleen thought she may have misinterpreted his anger.

"Colleen Gardner...you haven't changed a bit. Let me know once you've figured it out." With his little girl clinging onto his neck, her thumb stuck in her puckered mouth, he strode away.

Strange. She slowly walked back to her booth, sign in hand.

"Great, you got it," Grace said. Baby John started fussing, and Grace rocked back and forth in an attempt to calm him.

Why did her presence compel children to cry? "The weirdest thing just happened. This guy grabbed my sign before it flew into the river. When he gave it back to me, he acted like I should know him. He was really cute. If I'd met him before, I definitely would have remembered."

"Cute, huh." Grace continued swaying with the whimpering baby.

"Very. If I see him again, I'll point him out." She scanned the crowd. "Maybe you'll recognize him."

Baby John tossed back his head and let out a scream, leaving little doubt of his current mood. He was only three months old but had a strong set of lungs

Grace picked up the diaper bag. "I need to find a

private place and feed him. Then Heath can take him home. The temp's too hot for a baby."

The temperature was too hot for her, too, but Colleen needed to work the booth. This raffle would only be a drop in the bucket toward the total she needed to open her veterans' retreat. Between the cost of land, building ADA compliant facilities, and hiring staff, the sum of money she had to raise seemed well out of reach.

Well, she wasn't giving up. Starting the retreat was the reason she'd moved back home. Through her practice, she'd seen too many veterans suffer with the consequences of their service in war zones. They deserved a safe place to come and heal. She only wished the financial aspect of the project wasn't holding her back. No telling when she'd finally open her doors. The nation's vets needed the retreat now. Every day, suicide rates continued to climb. "Go take care of the baby," she said to Grace. "I can work the booth myself. Come back when you can." Armed with a roll of masking tape, she went to work resecuring the sign to the front of her booth.

During the next hour, she sold almost four hundred dollars in fifty/fifty raffle tickets. The winner would be announced over the festival's loudspeaker at five o'clock. The people in her hometown were very supportive of what she wanted to accomplish. But most people weren't rich by any means. They did what they could to help.

A gust of wind made Colleen reach across the table and hold down her sign. Catty-corner from her own booth, flyers on an unoccupied one blew away like birds taking flight.

A young woman darted forward in an attempt to rescue a few sheets still nearby.

Colleen ran over to help wrangle the remaining flyers. "This wind is crazy." She handed the woman a small stack.

"Thanks. I should have known better than to leave these without weighing them down." She set the flyers back on her table and covered them with her laptop.

"What are you recruiting for?" Colleen read one of the flyers. "A reality TV show?"

"Yup." The young woman brushed off a few strands of brown hair stuck to her brow. "A new show called The Great American Scavenger Hunt. We're casting contestants from all over the country. You should send in an application video. The winner receives one million dollars."

Holy cannoli, that's a lot of money. "I'd never want to be on a reality show." Colleen imagined depositing a million dollars into her savings and how far the sum would go to fund her dream.

"Take the information." The woman handed Colleen a wrinkled flyer. "Look it over. You might change your mind. I'm sure you could find a way to spend one million dollars."

Duh. No one would turn away that kind of money. What demeaning things would she have to do on national TV in order to have a shot at winning it? No way. Instead of tossing away the flyer, she folded it up and slipped it inside her purse.

As she sat and sold raffle tickets, she continued to scan the crowd for her mystery man. She'd been racking her brain in an attempt to put a name to the face. Nothing. Why had he'd been so hostile toward her? Was he someone she'd known when she was much younger? Growing up, she certainly had not been a Pollyanna. Just the opposite, in fact. She'd been the school's resident mean girl.

If the mystery guy had attended school with her, he would have remembered Colleen. But if he had been that good-looking back then, she should remember him, too. Now, if she could just get another look, maybe she'd place him in her memories.

A glimpse of green baseball cap above the crowds sent her heart leaping. Was that him? She craned her neck to get a better look. Oh, there he was. His little girl toddled alongside him with a firm hold on his hand.

She noticed a woman wearing a long, colorful skirt on his far side. His mother, maybe? She was too far away for her to get a good look.

Standing to stretch her legs, she watched as they passed. They were almost out of sight when he turned his head and looked straight at her. Under the shade of his baseball cap, she recognized contempt in his eyes. Despite the heat, her skin chilled. The scents of food cooking around her, which had smelled delicious before, turned her stomach sour.

Who was this man? And why did he hate her? She had a bad feeling he meant trouble for her fresh start in Liberty Ridge.

****

Just his luck to run into the one person in Liberty Ridge whom he didn't want to see. Storm Thompson had only been back for two days. He'd hoped to avoid seeing Colleen Gardner for as long as possible. He should have known she'd be here. The perfect citizen supporting her hometown community. *Blah*—the sight of her had made him sick.

Colleen still had the look of a princess. Her blonde hair had darkened slightly over the years, but those eyes were as distinct as a fingerprint. Ice blue, the color of a glacier, and just as cold. Of course, she hadn't recognized him. Storm had changed a lot since high school. If she'd known his name, she probably wouldn't have been so kind.

"Daddy." Harper pulled on his hand. "Up."

Now, here was a true princess. He lifted his daughter into his arms and gave her a kiss. Her lips tasted like peaches. The result of a few bites of pie she'd eaten earlier. Harper was one reason he'd returned to Liberty Ridge. His mother was the other.

Rose Petal Thompson sat on a park bench, staring blankly ahead. Most people classified his mom as an aging hippie. Her long hair was braided into two thick ropes, and she wore loose, colorful clothes made of hemp. Growing up, Storm had lived with her on a small commune on the outskirts of town. Her strange behavior had been chalked up to her lifestyle, but he knew the truth. Rose Petal had Schizoaffective disorder. As she aged, her condition grew worse.

"How do you feel, Mom? You ready to go?" He tapped on Rose's shoulder. "Mom, did you hear me? Are you ready to leave?"

"No, let's stay a little longer." Her voice was high and reedy. "The baby's having fun."

"Okay." Storm scanned the large crowd, which grew and became louder by the second. "How about we sit in the shade, and I'll get you some shaved ice? The weather's hotter than Hades out here."

They found a quiet spot, away from the noise of the

crowds.

"Leave the baby with me," Rose said after she got seated. "You can't carry her and the cups of shaved ice at the same time."

He shook his head. "Harper's coming with me. You sit here and relax." After spending the past two days with his mom, he'd come to the conclusion she didn't have the attention span to safely watch an active toddler.

She wagged a finger. "Storm, I raised you, don't forget. I promise I won't let Harper out of my sight."

Yes, she'd raised him. Which was why he was so concerned. If not for the other members of the commune where he'd grown up, he might not have survived past childhood. He'd learned from an early age his mother was not someone to be counted on. If he needed something, he found a way to take care of things himself. His upbringing had made him very self-reliant, as well as being the source of many of the problems he carried into adulthood.

"Harper's staying with me. I won't argue with you." He adjusted the weight of the little girl in his arms, who became heavier as the day progressed. "I'll be right back. Don't leave this bench."

"Nana," Harper cried and reached out.

Storm continued walking, ignoring both his daughter's and his mother's shouts of protest.

Valerie had trusted him with the care of their daughter for the week. No way would he take the chance of losing Harper in the crowd. Normally, he saw his daughter every other weekend. Not nearly enough time. Now that he'd moved back to Liberty Ridge, he'd see her even less.

Litter blew across his path. Other people would blame the mess on the strong wind, but he found the weather no excuse to dump garbage on the ground. He reached down to pick up a few sheets of paper, doing his part to keep the planet clean, when the writing on one caught his eye.

Send in your application video for a chance to win one million dollars!

He read a bit farther. A production company from LA was sending out a casting call for a new reality TV show called The Great American Scavenger Hunt. The winner would receive one million dollars. That amount of money was incomprehensible. One million dollars would definitely breathe life into his dreams.

But he never wanted to be on a reality show. Even so, he stuffed the ad into his back pocket instead of the recycle bin. After a short walk, he approached a very long line for shaved ice. Of course it was long. The temperature had to be in the mid-nineties.

"Down." Harper wiggled in his arms.

Up, down, up, down—the playlist of his day. "Stand next me," he instructed the two year old as he set down her small feet onto the grass.

"No way," a man's deep voice sounded. "Storm Thompson. I don't believe it."

Storm turned to see a familiar face. Rocky had gained weight since the last time he'd seen his friend on graduation day. The same day Storm had packed a small bag and left town. "Rocky Diaz," he said with a laugh. "I should have known you'd grow up to be an accountant."

The men embraced in a quick hug.

"How did you know I was an accountant?" Rocky

cocked an eyebrow.

"Dude, you're wearing socks with sandals." Storm's only friend in high school had been a math genius. The nerdy attire only confirmed his assumption.

"What brings you back to town?" Rocky pushed his wire-rim glasses up his nose. "Must be twelve years since I saw you last. You've changed so much I almost didn't recognize you. Actually, the sound of your voice was what jogged my memory."

"I'm here for my mom. Her friend from the commune called a few weeks ago and said they asked her to leave. Her behavior became too disruptive."

Rocky nodded. "Sorry to hear that. So, you back for good?"

He'd been the only person Storm had trusted with the truth about his mother's illness. "Maybe." He grabbed hold of Harper's hand to keep her from following the clown walking past. "I hope to convince my mom to continue seeing her Psychiatrist. Of course, she's resisting. I'm also looking at buying a piece of local farmland to start an organic farm."

"Plenty of available farmland around here." Rocky glanced down at the small girl attached to Storm's side. "And who is this little one?"

"My daughter, Harper." As he introduced his daughter, pride radiated off Storm. After all the crap he'd been dealt in his life, Harper was the one bright star. Being her father was the only thing he cared about getting right.

"She's a cutie. About my own daughter's age. Anyways, let me know if I can help with a loan to buy land. I'm an accountant, as you've already figured out, and can help put together a business plan for the bank."

"Thanks. I'm not sure you can work enough magic to get a bank to approve me for a loan. My work history is not solid." To say the least. Storm had worked for the past five years as an organic farm consultant. He'd traveled around Northern California, from farm to farm, and was usually paid in cash. Besides a small savings and the joy of doing what he loved, he had little to show for his work.

"Let's find a time to sit together and discuss the matter," Rocky said as they made their way to the front of the line. "You see anyone else from high school here? There're a lot of us still hanging around town."

As Storm ordered three shaved ices, Colleen's pretty face came to mind. The ringleader of his tormentors. Where was she now? He'd love to drop this cherry ice all over her expensive haircut. "No." The memory of her 'Judas kiss' at their graduation party left him physically sick. That night had been his last in Liberty Ridge, and the last time he'd seen Colleen Gardner. "No one here I care to see. You know how they treated me…treated us."

"People change, you know." Rocky raised his hand and pointed around at the crowd. "Some of my good friends are people I never would have talked to in high school."

Rocky had grown up in a normal family, with a mom and dad who weren't crazy. Rocky was capable of forgiveness. Storm was not.

A word about the author...

Laurie Winter is a true warrior of the heart. Inspired by her dreams, she creates authentic characters who overcome the odds and find true love.

She keeps her life balanced with regular yoga practice and running. When not pounding the pavement or the keyboard, she's enjoying time with her family, who are scattered in Wisconsin and Michigan. Laurie has three kids and one fantastic husband, all of whom inspire her to chase her dreams.

http://lauriewinter.com

~*~

Other Titles by Laurie Winter

Home Field
True Horizon